Eternal Starling

ANGELA CORBETT

PENDRELL PUBLISHING

LIBRARY OF CONGRESS IN PUBLICATION DATA IS AVAILABLE

ISBN 978-0-9827297-6-2
E-BOOK AVAILABLE
FIRST EDITION
10 9 8 7 6 5 4 3 2 1

THIS BOOK IS TYPESET IN PALATINO
COVER DESIGN BY ALMA TAIT
COVER PHOTOGRAPHY ©2011 SWEET EXPRESSIONS PHOTOGRAPHY

PENDRELL PUBLISHING
CULVER CITY CALIFORNIA
WWW.PENDRELLPUBLISHING.COM
INFO@PENDRELLPUBLISHING.COM

For Dan and Ashley

My constants

$\mathcal{L}$ove is the emblem of eternity
It confounds all notion of time,
effaces all memory of a beginning,
all fear of an end.

~$\mathcal{M}$adame de Staël

Prologue

London, England

I let my fear carry me and I ran. I didn't dare look behind me, too scared of who might be following. Lights flickered as I passed them, one thought pounding in my head: he had let me leave. Sadness and anger warred in my chest. Maybe it was love, maybe it was guilt, but he told me I had to go. I couldn't stay knowing what he was part of, but despite everything, I wouldn't deny I still loved him. The pain would diminish and though I wouldn't remember it, our bond would always exist.

I sprinted through the uneven stone streets as my dress wound its way between my legs, threatening to trip me with every step. The narrow alleyways were hot and crowded. I pushed men and women out of my way and hoped they didn't meet the people I was running from.

I ran from the illusion I was living and blinked away the tears clouding my vision. I ran to the one place I knew I would be safe. I opened the door and entered the stone house; the room was illuminated by candlelight. The heavy door shut behind me with a thud and a lock fell into place. I collapsed on the floor. It was over.

I wouldn't have to run anymore. Someone knelt next to me and took my hand. My body reacted to the touch and I looked up. This time, I made the right choice.

Chapter 1

When there's a real possibility you might not live another day, you go through a range of emotions. I had already hit fear, then panic. I was currently dwelling on anger, which was leading me straight to blame and Luke Woods was the target of my wrath. It's not like I even cared about him that much when we were dating, and I liked him even less when I walked into the history room during Senior Prom and found him getting to know cheerleader Crystal Benson in a way he'd never gotten to know me.

He blamed my "irrational morals" for his cheating. I called him an arrogant pig with a brain the size of a pea. He said I looked like a marshmallow and it escalated to a full-on war from there. At one point, a rumor circulated that my classic Mustang was seen leaving the high school parking lot after the oil was drained from the engine in Luke's Dodge Ram. Rumors are crazy like that.

I dealt with the gossip from the other kids at school until high school graduation then moved to Gunnison, Colorado, three months before the beginning of my freshman year of college.

"Stupid, rotten, snake-of-a-boy," I mumbled to myself as I stomped through wild grass, bushes, and if the itching on my leg was any indication, probably some poison ivy. "That dumb jerk! I'm lost in the middle of the freaking Rocky Mountains and it's *all* his fault!" I'd been talking to myself for a while now and tried to remember if shouting at no one was a sign of a panic attack—I already knew it was a sign of insanity.

In my current, frazzled state of mind, I rationalized that if Loser Luke hadn't cheated on me, I wouldn't have left the safety of my parents' Montana home, wouldn't have decided to go hiking in the unfamiliar mountains of Black Canyon, and wouldn't be lost. In an impressive feat of deflected responsibility, I convinced myself Luke was at least somewhat accountable for my impending death. Blaming him made the thought of dying much easier to handle. If I'd had a pen on me, I would have written a note implicating him so that when the rescue crews found my frozen body, they'd know who to arrest.

Okay, so it was partially my fault. I had a perfectly good hiking bag at home equipped with a blanket and GPS, but I hadn't grabbed it when I left because I wasn't planning on a long hike. I had been searching for a way down the mountain for three hours and spent the whole time mentally, and sometimes physically, smacking myself in the head for leaving the house unprepared.

Wind ruffled through the trees while I continued walking, paying close attention to my surroundings in case I needed to backtrack. As I came to a clearing, the quiet of the mountain made it easy to hear the sharp sounds of twigs snapping. Great. A wild animal. I shook my head. As if being lost wasn't enough of a problem, now I'd probably be eaten by a bear.

Running seemed like a good way to make myself look like dinner, so instead, I took a deep breath and tried not to panic as the noises grew louder. Whatever it was, it was big—and it was getting closer. I began backing slowly away from the direction of the rustling noise, wondering what animal was about to appear and use my arms as an appetizer.

So you can imagine my surprise when a *guy* stepped out of the trees. He looked a little older than me and was at least six feet tall. His dark brown hair accented bronze skin, and his white T-shirt did nothing to hide the hard lines of his chest, broad shoulders, or his massive biceps. His eyes were a bright shade of green that seemed to change from one part of his irises to another. I licked my lips without realizing I'd done it and had the fleeting thought that if he wanted to have me for dinner, I'd help him light the charcoal.

He smiled at me and I couldn't look away. Somewhere in the recesses of my mind, something flickered; those eyes and that smile, something about him was so— familiar. I'm not certain how long I stared, but it must have been a few minutes because I kept seeing his flawless lips move before his deep voice finally registered. "Are you okay?"

I nodded, more times than necessary, and still staring, I wiped my hand across my chin to check for drool.

"I think I scared you when I came out of the trees," he said.

I watched him with wary eyes while he put his backpack on the ground and unzipped it. He took a water bottle out and as he handed it to me, I saw a black ring on his index finger. I probably wouldn't have noticed it, except the face of the ring was as big as a quarter and it seemed to be some sort of polished stone. I took the bottle and assessed him as I unscrewed the lid. He didn't look scary, and unless he was lost too, he probably had a compass and could get me back to my car.

I took a drink and answered, "Scared?" I made a *psssh* noise. "No, I was just . . . startled. You could have been . . . a bear . . . or something." I mumbled the last part, realizing I probably sounded insane.

He raised his eyebrows like he was questioning how lucid I actually was. "You should have your reflexes checked, most people run when they think they're about to come face-to-face with a bear."

"I'm not most people," I said, "and running is not what the 'How to Survive the Colorado Mountains' brochure tells you to do." I had grabbed the brochure while I was in line at the grocery store a few days ago. Unfortunately, the brochure didn't cover exceptionally hot guys who seemed to appear out of nowhere.

"What does your brochure say to do when you come across a girl who thought she was about to have an encounter with a wild animal?" His eyes were sparkling in a way that was almost as playful as his voice.

I didn't know whether to flirt or glare. "Who's to say I'm not having one right now?"

He smiled, his eyes lighting up again. "I'm Alex." He stepped forward like he was about to shake my hand, but stopped and pulled back.

I watched him for a few beats and said, "I'm Evangeline. Thanks for the water by the way." I tossed the bottle back to him.

He caught it and put it in his pack. "So have you hiked before, Evie, or is this your first time?" He shortened my name, which most people did, but usually not until they got to know me better.

I folded my arms across my chest in a defiant gesture. "I started hiking when I was a kid. I bet I know more about the mountains than most of the people who hike up here."

"That's interesting." He pushed his eyebrows

together and ran his tongue over the inside of his cheek as he assessed me. "So, if you were, say, ten feet from a cliff face with a two-hundred foot drop-off . . . that would be on purpose?"

I didn't give him the chance to see the worry register on my face and answered, "Is it ten feet away? I thought it was five." *Crap*, where *was* I?

The corners of his mouth twitched like he was trying to suppress a smile and failing. The attraction I'd had when I first saw him was quickly being undermined by his sarcasm. He was the definition of eye-candy—I just needed to get him to stop opening his mouth.

"And if I told you that you'd been walking in circles for the last three hours, would that also be on purpose?" he asked.

I scowled, but at the same time wondered how he knew that. "If someone knew I'd been walking in circles for three hours, I would say they're a stalker and probably more dangerous than the bear I was waiting for."

He laughed. "The ground around this area has been trampled; it looks like a circus came through here."

Hmm. He was perceptive, I'd give him that.

"For someone who knows more about this mountain than ninety-five percent of the people who hike it, you seem pretty lost," he said.

"There's a difference between being lost and exploring," I mumbled, not caring if I froze to death as long as it meant I didn't have to ask *this* guy for help. "I'll find my way back to the trail eventually."

"Huh," he said. "When you do that, do you plan to roll down the cliff, or slide?"

"I'd rather slide, but rolling would get me to my car faster." I was not about to give in.

"Or to the hospital," he said. The concern lacing his tone seemed odd. Alex had just met me. Why would he care if I went careening off a cliff?

"It wouldn't be the first time," I said.

Emotion flashed across his face, but before I could analyze it, he caught me staring and turned away. "Well," he said. "I'm hiking down the mountain. Since we're already together, and one of us is lost, maybe the lost party should follow the person who actually *knows* where they're going, back to the parking lot."

Apparently, like every other hot guy on the planet, Alex had caught a particularly potent strain of arrogance. I gave him my best impression of a beauty queen smile. "Sure, Alex, if you want to follow me, I wouldn't mind. I understand how confusing these mountains can be."

"I'm the one with the compass, Evie, so I should probably lead."

I pushed my eyebrows together. "How do you know I don't have a compass?"

He paused. "Would you have wandered in circles for hours if you did?"

I stared, not wanting to admit he had a good argument. "I usually hike alone you know." For some reason, I thought pointing that out would redeem me for getting lost.

"Then it's a good thing I found you. Maybe in the future you should reconsider your policy for doing things alone. Are you ready to go?"

I put my head up, shoulders back, and walked forward instead of answering. I purposely avoided looking at Alex's face, but out of the corner of my eye I noticed his mouth curve into a smug smile as I passed him. As much as I hated to admit it, I was glad I'd run into him. I really didn't know if I could have gotten off the mountain without his help.

I decided since Alex was keeping me company while we hiked, I should try to be nice. "So when you aren't pretending to be a bear, Alex, what do you do?"

He hesitated like the question had caught him off-guard. "I help an organization, kind of volunteer work," he replied. "What about you?"

"I just graduated from high school. I start school at Western State College in three months."

"Do you know what your major is going to be?"

I nodded. "Psychology." He glanced back at me as we kept walking. "Do you go to college?" I asked

"I did. I already graduated."

Already graduated? I thought he was older than me, but not bachelor's degree old. "Oh, you look younger than that," I said, trying to sound offhand.

"I'm twenty-one."

I was confused. "So you graduated early?"

"I was in an accelerated program." He said it in a nonchalant way, like he was trying to impress me with his intelligence by not making a big deal out of it. The attitude bugged me.

"That's nice," I said, trying to be polite. "So, you only volunteer places? You don't have a job?"

He lifted his shoulder slightly. "I don't really need one."

I narrowed my eyes. "What do you mean you don't need one? Don't tell me you're one of those trust-fund babies," I teased.

"Well," he said, "obviously the baby part isn't accurate."

"Oh." It was as much of a response as I could come up with. As aggravating as he was, Alex was still the most stunning guy I'd ever seen. We definitely had chemistry and for a millisecond, I'd hoped something might happen between the two of us. His financial revelation made that thought obsolete; I knew there was no way I would have a chance with him. Guys like Alex dated ridiculous six-foot tall super models with a waist the circumference of a DVD.

We walked along in silence for a while until Alex changed the subject.

"Why do you always hike alone? Where's your boyfriend?"

That was subtle, I scoffed to myself. "I'm not dating anyone. What about you? Couldn't your girlfriend come with you this week, or is she one of those girls who won't get dirt on their six-inch stilettos?" I asked, still picturing the Angelina Jolie look-alike he was surely dating. I had stood next to Angelina at Madame Tussaud's Wax Museum and I was pretty sure I was twice her size.

He gave a soft laugh and I thought I heard him mumble something about being feisty before saying, "I'm not seeing anyone at the moment either."

"Well, it won't take you long to find someone, trust me." I stopped short, realizing what I'd said. I hadn't intended the sentence to make it out of my head and escape my mouth.

Alex stopped, turned, and locked eyes with me. He slowly moved forward until he was standing less than a foot away. "Do you know someone who might be interested?" His eyes grew dark and he was suddenly intimidating in a way that had nothing to do with fear.

I could feel my face turning various shades of crimson. I tried to cover for myself by turning away from him and said, "I know a lot of girls who would be interested." *Like every girl who has ever set eyes on you.*

He walked around me until he could once again

see my scarlet cheeks. His dark gaze roamed over me as he searched my expression. "Are you one of them?"

That was direct. Why in the world would he want to know that? He could literally have any girl he wanted, and probably had. This conversation was getting way too serious, way too fast for my comfort level. I felt my blushing face had already betrayed me, but I wasn't going to embarrass myself further by saying it out loud. Before I had to come up with a response, I noticed the Black Canyon parking lot and breathed a sigh of relief. "We're here! Thanks for keeping me company, Alex."

He frowned. He seemed bothered that I hadn't answered his question, but he didn't say anything.

"Where did you park?" I asked.

He nodded toward a bright blue Audi TTS convertible on the other side of the parking lot. Of course it was an Audi. It surprised me that it wasn't a Lamborghini.

"What about you?" he asked.

I pointed to a dark purple 1966 GT Mustang, two white stripes running along the bottom of the doors, and a matching white vinyl top with white leather seats. Some people like the scent of cookies and cakes baking; I love the smell of a classic V8 muscle car. A group of guys were standing around the car, ogling it.

"Is the fan club yours?" he asked in a tone that seemed almost irritated.

I lifted a shoulder. "It comes with the car."

I pulled my keys from my pocket and Alex followed me to my Mustang.

"Hey," I said to the group of guys. There were six of them and I noticed they were all wearing long-sleeved dark grey fleece jackets like they were on some sort of team. They looked at me, the car, and back at me again, in shock.

"Nice car," a tall guy with auburn hair said.

"Thanks."

"Is the engine a 289?"

I fought the urge to roll my eyes. I loved when guys tried to test me, like I was driving a car I knew nothing about. "Most 1966 Mustang engines are."

"Standard?" he asked.

I was sure he'd already looked in the window and could tell what kind of transmission it had. "It's an automatic."

The auburn-haired guy watched while I unlocked the car door. "Did your dad or boyfriend let you borrow it?" he asked. The other boys snickered waiting for my answer.

I glared. I hated when people assumed the only way I could have a classic muscle car was if a man in my life had let me use it. I was done being nice. "I built it, but you probably don't understand something that complicated. I'm sure you have a difficult time figuring out the toothpaste cap." The rest of the boys started laughing.

The auburn-haired guy smiled, but the look of defeat I was hoping for didn't register on his face. "I'd like to see you sometime," he said. The invitation was so abrupt that I almost laughed.

I could see Alex standing a car length back. His face was tight like he was upset. There was no way he could actually be jealous—was there? I just met him! The guy noticed where my gaze was directed and saw Alex, then seemed to appraise him. Alex returned the look with a hard, confident glare.

I turned back to the guy. "Sorry, I don't date idiots."

Instead of answering, the guy took a paper out of his pocket. Another boy with long, mousy blonde hair handed him a pen and I watched as he wrote. When he finished, he folded the note. "My number, and a question," he said, handing the paper to me.

I took the note and scowled at him in return, but he had shifted his focal point and fixed his eyes sharply on Alex. Alex ignored him.

The guy turned back to me. "Let me know if you change your mind," he said.

I watched them walk away and ripped the paper up without looking at it. I put the remaining scraps in my pocket.

I glanced up and saw Alex approaching. When he reached me, he leaned his back against the Mustang crossing his legs in front of him. "*They* certainly seemed interested in you," he said.

I rolled my eyes. "Whatever. You're a guy, Alex. You know they were only talking to me because they were hoping for the chance to drive my car. Believe me; I've had plenty of experience in this area. If guys could ask my car out instead of me, they would."

Alex gave me a long stare. "The fact that I'm a guy is exactly how I know that your car has little to do with their interest."

I blinked, slightly stunned. What in the world did he mean by that?

He interrupted my thought by asking, "You restored this?" He seemed impressed as his eyes traveled from the front to the back of my car.

"Not all of it. Some of the work was done by a body shop, but I did as much as I could. My dad helped." The restoration project was one of the few things my dad and I had ever bonded over.

Alex ran his hand over the white vinyl top. "You're definitely not the average girl."

I gave him a bold smile. "I pride myself on it."

He was thoughtful for a second. "Is there anything else I should know about you?"

I realized this might be my opportunity to get to

know him better. I decided to take a chance. "Come with me next weekend and find out."

He didn't hesitate as he answered, "Okay."

Chapter 2

I pulled into the driveway of the house I shared with my best friend, Jasmine, and got out of the car. Jasmine and I had grown up together. Even though she was a year older than me, we had always been close. We knew we wanted to go to the same college, so we picked Western State and Jasmine got here a year before me.

When I opened the back door of the house, I was greeted by the slightly burned smell of microwave popcorn. Jasmine and her boyfriend, Zach, were watching a movie when I walked into the living room. They were cuddling on the couch and her skin, the color of melted chocolate, was the perfect complement to Zach's tan arms. Jasmine's brown hair fell in curls to her shoulders and sweetly framed her heart-shaped face.

Jasmine and Zach met while playing volleyball almost a year ago and they've been dating ever since. He's funny, nice, and treats Jasmine like a queen. The truth is I'm a little jealous. My experience with men put the majority of them in the Loser Luke category. I figured the Awesome Zach group was on the verge of extinction.

"Hey," I said. "What are you two doing here?" Jasmine spent most of her time at Zach's apartment, so it was always a surprise to find them hanging out at our place.

"Hey," Zach said. He grabbed some popcorn from the bag in his lap and threw a kernel in the air, trying to catch it in his mouth.

Jasmine blew a huge pink bubble with the gum she was chewing. She had a bubble gum habit the way other people have drug habits. When the bubble popped she answered my question. "One of Zach's roommates was having a party so we decided to come back here where it was quiet. How was your hike?"

"Good. Weird." I put my keys on a side table and went into the bathroom to get some anti-itch cream and cotton balls for the rash on my leg. "I got lost and wandered around for a while. Then I met a guy who helped me get off the mountain." I sat down on the couch and began rubbing cream on the red splotches near my knee.

I saw Jas bolt up from Zach's lap where she'd been lounging and the bubble she was blowing exploded all over her face. The questions came at me like machine gun fire. "Who is he? What's he like? I want details!" Jasmine said, pulling gum from her cheeks and chin. She was ever-vigilant about the state of my love life.

I lifted my head, my brow raised. "Hello? Did you hear me?" I asked. "I said I got lost and wandered around for three hours. I could've died!"

Jasmine gave me a disbelieving look. "Obviously, you're not dead. Did you get hurt?"

I wrinkled my nose and relented, "Aside from the poison ivy, no."

Jasmine smiled. "See, you're fine. Now, who is he, what's he like, and give me all the details about how you met?"

I sighed as the cream started to take away some of the irritation. "That's the weird part," I answered, leaning back into the couch cushion. "He showed up in a random clearing while I was trying to figure out how to get back to my car."

"What's his name?" Jasmine asked.

"Alex." At the mention of Alex's name, Zach ran his hand through his light brown hair and turned up the volume on the TV. I was pretty sure the men in my life ranked right up there with shoes on Zach's list of interests.

"Was he nice?"

"In a cynical way," I said.

"What did he look like?"

I relayed my first impressions of Alex to Jasmine. Zach continued watching the movie and eating popcorn as I detailed Alex's Adonis-like qualities—and the ego that went along with them.

"Are you going to see him again?" Jasmine was so excited I thought she might start bouncing on the couch.

"Yeah, next weekend. I dared him to come with me for an adventure. Speaking of that, Zach, can I borrow your four-wheeler, trailer, and Jeep?" I asked.

"Sure," he answered absently, still watching the movie. After a couple of seconds, my question must have sunk in because he turned and glanced at me. "Wait. Has this guy ever ridden a quad?"

"I don't know. I didn't tell him what we're doing."

"Huh," Zach paused, thinking. Finally he said, "You can use it, but you have to promise you'll make your boyfriend drive *your* quad in case he crashes it,"

I threw a cotton ball at him. "He's not my boyfriend! I just met him. But I'll make sure he rides my Honda and I'll ride your Suzuki."

Zach laughed—the cotton ball didn't even make

it to the couch. "Okay, you can pick everything up on Friday."

"Thanks," I said, walking toward the stairs. "I'll see you guys in the morning."

"You *have* to tell me everything that happens next weekend," Jasmine said.

I started climbing the stairs to my room. "If anything happens, you'll be the first to know." I was still thinking about Alex while I cleaned out my pockets. I found the scraps of paper from the note the guy in the parking lot had given me and dropped them on my dresser before I stripped my clothes off, eager to take a shower. As I reached for my robe, I glanced over my shoulder in the mirror and noticed that the lily-shaped birthmark between my shoulder blades seemed darker than normal. Usually it was pale pink and barely visible, but today it had more pigment—like the color of bare hands bitten by winter frost. I thought it was strange, but shrugged it off as some sort of skin reaction from my hike. I grabbed a towel and headed for the shower.

I'd gotten a part-time summer job in the Western State College communications office. The job mostly consisted of filing, sending emails, and playing on the computer until someone needed my help—so it wasn't difficult. After I finished work on Wednesday, I called Alex to give him the details about our excursion. We agreed to meet in the parking lot of the sporting goods store at eight o'clock Saturday morning.

I pulled into the parking lot at seven-forty-five listening to *Wicked* the musical, singing along with it when I could hit the notes. I didn't see Alex's Audi anywhere, so I ran across the street to a coffee shop for a caramel latte. I hated mornings, but it gave me an excuse to drink sugar and cream-filled coffee with only a little bit of guilt.

When I came out of the coffee shop, I saw Alex standing by the trailer assessing the two four-wheelers. He was dressed in jeans and a light blue T-shirt, a backpack slung over his shoulder. I stood there for a minute staring at him and wondering what in the world I was thinking. Alex was perfect, and I'm ordinary. I'm not ashamed of my curves—though I have yet to find a guy who feels the same way. I'm 5'9" and don't know how much I weigh. I think scales were invented by the devil and only doctors and masochists own them. I judge my weight by my clothes size, which fluctuates between twelve and fourteen depending on how much hiking I've done and how many cookies I've had. Alex turned and saw me staring. I shook off my feelings of inadequacy and waved at him as I crossed the street.

"I didn't know if you'd show up," I teased.

He arched an eyebrow. "Considering how your last solo adventure went, I thought I should probably be here."

I didn't find his commentary about getting lost last week amusing and considered leaving him in the parking lot. Okay, I really wouldn't have, but it was nice to at least think the threat. "I do most things alone and I usually manage fine," I said, taking a sip of coffee. "Do you want anything?" I gestured to the coffee shop.

His gaze never wavered from me. "I think I have everything I need." His tone was filled with innuendo and there was a glint in his eye.

I gave him a smile that probably looked as awkward as it felt. I silently wondered if Western State offered a class in flirting—I could use all the help I could get.

"Okaaay. Let's go."

I opened the door to the Jeep and hopped in. Alex climbed in the passenger side and threw his backpack on the seat behind him. He put his water bottle in one of the cup holders. We pulled out of the parking lot, the *Wicked* soundtrack still playing in the background. Alex choked back a laugh.

"Muscle cars and Broadway musicals?" he said, motioning to the radio. "You just keep getting more fascinating."

I glanced at him. "It's good to be interested in a lot of things."

"I know. You intrigue me." I felt blood rush to my cheeks and could see him looking at me out of the corner of my eye. I was glad my long hair gave me a screen between the two of us. I was relieved when he decided not to pursue the issue. Instead, he grabbed my coffee out of the cup holder and took a sip.

"Help yourself," I said, not believing he'd taken a drink of my coffee without even asking.

He scrunched up his face. "What is this?"

"A caramel latte with whipped cream and extra caramel."

"You could get diabetes from that. You can't even taste the coffee!"

I shrugged. "I like my coffee enhanced," I said. "Since it's my drink, I don't really care what you think."

He studied the cup for a minute before putting it back in the cup holder and smiling at me from across the seat. "I think I'll call you sugar. It fits."

I scowled a little. "Or you could call me Evie, since that's my name."

He shook his head. "Nope. Sugar is cute, like you." Great. Now I was cute. Babies, puppies, and kittens are cute. Cute was *not* how I wanted Alex describing me.

"I've been called a lot of names, but I don't think cute has ever been one of them."

The corner of his mouth hitched. "Then I'm your first—" he paused deliberately, "to call you cute I mean." My face flushed instantly. Alex's grin shifted from mischievous to amused as he grabbed his water bottle. "So are you going to tell me what we're doing today?"

Still embarrassed about his insinuation and my blushing, I decided to respond with sarcasm. "Oh, did you miss the trailer?" I asked, feigning sincerity. "Because I thought it was pretty obvious."

He took a swig of water. "All I know is that we're towing two four-wheelers. I assume we'll be riding them at some point, but I don't know when, or where we're going."

"We're driving to the mountains where we'll park the Jeep, unload the Honda and Suzuki, and follow a trail."

He didn't seem opposed to the idea, but he wasn't as excited as most of the guys I usually went riding with. For a minute, he almost seemed anxious, but the look passed and the mocking smile I was acquainted with reappeared.

"I hope you don't usually go four-wheeling alone," he said. "I can only imagine the disasters you'd get yourself into."

I glared at him. "I'm not a kid, Alex. I don't need a babysitter."

His response was lightning fast. "Don't you?" he asked. The light tone had vanished from his voice.

I shifted in my seat, surprised at the sudden attitude change. "Wow. You're off to a good start this morning. I hope you brought your trusty compass, because I might leave you in the mountains."

"There's no doubt in my mind," he said, his lips

curved almost like he was taunting me, "that I would make it back to the car before you did."

"Only because you'd turn around before you got halfway up the trail," I shot back.

"I guess we'll see who's right."

"Yeah. I guess we will."

Annoyance from our argument lingered and the SUV was silent for about five minutes until Alex turned to me, the look of amusement back on his face. "Let's bet on it."

"Bet on what?" I asked, trying not to growl.

"I bet that today you'll get in some sort of mess and need my help to get out of it," he said with unwavering sureness.

"You're on," I said, determination ringing in my voice. "What are the terms?"

He gave me a slow stare from across the seat. "If I win, you come out with *me* next Saturday—no questions asked."

That seemed simple enough. Truth be told, I wouldn't turn down the chance to spend more time with him. Even though he had a talent for frustrating me, being with Alex made my heart race in a way I wasn't used to.

"Okay," I agreed, thinking for a moment about what I would want when I won. "And if I win—"

He snorted. "That's unlikely."

I continued as if I hadn't been interrupted, "You have to honestly answer any question I ask." I figured that would be a good way to get to know him better.

He pursed his lips for the slightest second, making me wonder if that was a promise he didn't want to make. But his mouth slid into a smile as he said, "Sounds fair; and since I have no doubt you'll lose the bet, I'll start planning our date for next weekend."

His body was turned toward me, completely open and conveying the same confidence as his tone of voice. "Has anyone ever told you that you have a *huge* ego?" I asked.

He smiled as he took another drink of water. "It's been mentioned before."

We drove to an area above Blue Mesa Reservoir that Zach told me had a lot of good riding trails. We pulled into a camping spot and unloaded the four-wheelers. Each time I caught Alex watching me, my stomach jumped. I'd never reacted to a guy this way, though my hormones had never encountered someone like Alex either.

I grabbed the helmets from the back seat and gave Alex one. "Have you ever been on a quad?" I asked.

"A few times," he answered.

"So you know how the Honda works?"

He looked at me from under his brow and scoffed. "I think I'll manage."

I laughed to myself. I didn't tell him how touchy the clutch was. Since he seemed to think he knew *every-thing*, I thought I'd let him figure that one out for himself.

We both put our helmets on and started the four-wheelers. I turned my head, making sure Alex was ready to go, and eased off my clutch. To my surprise, he followed me without hesitation. Most people who ride my Honda have a problem getting used to the clutch even when they know how sensitive it is. Alex didn't know and rode the four-wheeler like he'd been on it a hundred times. I was impressed and decided he must have more riding experience than he'd implied earlier.

As we wound our way through the mountain trail, a light breeze danced on my arms and I noticed the trees and foliage coming out of dormancy from winter. The higher elevations still had snow, but we weren't going far enough up the mountain to worry about it.

We stayed on the trail, trying not to disturb the surrounding area. Every so often I glanced back to check on Alex. He kept pace with me, touchy clutch and all. After about two hours on the trail, the trees opened up into a beautiful lake. The runoff was higher than I anticipated. Zach had explained we would be able to drive around the lake to get to the other side, but the lake was brimming out over the shore and into the surrounding trees. I stopped at the edge of the water trying to decide what to do.

Alex pulled up behind me and got off the four-wheeler so he could talk to me. "What's going on?" he asked over the sound of the engines.

I really wanted to get across the lake. Zach had told me the view on the other side was spectacular and overlooked several waterfalls. The lake was only about three hundred feet across and didn't seem *too* deep . . . I made a decision.

"We're going across," I yelled back.

Alex shook his head.

"Don't be a pansy," I yelled again, "just follow me, you'll be fine."

I took a minute to search for the best route. Taking my hand off the clutch, I eased into the water, trying to stick as close to what should be the shore as possible. I was concentrating on driving and trying not to get wet, the Suzuki creating waves as I slowly moved through the water.

I was about halfway across the lake when I saw steam rising from the hot engine as it reacted to the icy lake water. I had seriously underestimated the depth of the lake. I tried to reverse and make it back to the other side, but as I did, the engine sputtered twice, then died. I noticed the silence once my engine cut out and realized Alex's four-wheeler must have died before mine. I turned around to look for him . . . and there he was, sitting on the Honda, still back at the shore. His helmet was off and he was leaning on the handlebars, laughing.

I was angry at myself, and at Alex for being a jerk, but humiliation was by far my dominant emotion. I was literally stuck in the middle of a lake.

"I guess this means you're spending next Saturday with me," Alex yelled.

There was nothing I wanted more than to prove him wrong, but I couldn't do anything about it now. "I don't know how you think you're going to help me from all the way over there."

"I'm going to pull you out," he said.

"You and your invisible rope?" I yelled back.

I could see his smile even from my vinyl and foam seat. He pointed at the water. "Look down, Evie."

I shifted my eyes. A ribbon of white an inch thick trailed after me on the surface of the water. One end was attached to the back of my four-wheeler, the other end attached to the front of his.

"Where did you get *that*?" I asked.

"I've learned to be prepared when I'm around you."

I gave an indignant huff even though he couldn't hear me. "So now you're a Boy Scout?" My sarcasm was in response to Alex being right and the fact that I once again needed his help.

"Not exactly," he said, "but I do know quite a bit about knots."

I watched him pull the rope and make sure the knot was secure. "And what do you mean you've learned to be prepared around me?" I asked. "You've only known me for a week." I was irritated that he was pigeonholing me even though we'd spent less than six hours together.

"Trust me," he said, "I've been around you long

enough."

Alex started the Honda. As he slowly backed up, the rope became taut. I didn't have a lot of faith in his plan working. He had to pull both the four-wheeler and me. I was contemplating snide comments I would make about his towing strategy when the Suzuki started to move. Crap. Why was he always right?

I felt like an idiot. When he got me back to the shore, he was still laughing. "What do you do when you get in these predicaments and there's no one around to save you?" he asked.

"I save myself," I answered. "If you hadn't been here, I would have pushed the four-wheeler back to shore."

"Snakes and leeches don't bother you?"

"When I don't have a choice, I adapt."

I got off the Suzuki to check and see if I'd done any permanent damage. Zach was nuts to want me driving his four-wheeler instead of Alex. I made several attempts to start the engine, but it wouldn't turn over.

"Do you know what's wrong with it, or do you want me to take a look?" Alex asked, smirking.

"The air filter is wet and there's water in the exhaust. It needs to dry out," I answered.

Alex raised an eyebrow, a smile playing across his lips. "Have you done this before?"

"Not recently," I answered, pulling the starter to get the water out of the exhaust. The filter wasn't as wet as I thought it would be and the heat from the engine would dry it once we were riding again. But, I decided it wouldn't be a bad idea to let it air dry for a few minutes.

I put the filter on top of the Suzuki seat and sat down in a patch of grass. I pulled my knees up to my chest and wrapped my arms around them; the sunlight felt like a warm embrace. The lake rippled with the movement of unseen animals and the distinct fragrance of grass, flowers, and pine permeated the air. Alex followed, sitting down parallel to me a few feet away. He leaned back on his forearms and stretched his long legs out in front of him.

I turned my head, narrowing my eyes at him. "You brought a rope," I accused.

He lifted his shoulder in a half shrug. "I thought I might need it."

"Really? A rope? Don't you think that's going a little overboard?"

He met my eyes without a hint of apology. "Given the circumstances, it's a good thing I had it with me." I stared at him, wondering how conceited he really was. "I wasn't sure the rope would be long enough. I thought you'd realize how deep the water was getting a lot sooner."

"If only we all had your gift of perception," I scoffed.

"Yeah," he agreed, "that would be pretty helpful."

I rolled my eyes before grabbing a handful of grass and threw it at him. He grinned and brushed the green blades off his chest. "So you're going to assault me with plants for the rest of the afternoon?" he asked.

"No. Only until the filter dries. It shouldn't take long."

He nodded. "I enjoy the company," he said. "Thanks to your adventures in four-wheeler boating, I'll get to enjoy it again next week."

He'd been so adamant about the bet that I was curious what he had planned. "Are you going to tell me what we're doing next Saturday?" I pressed.

"No," he answered with a sly smile.

"No hints at all?" I asked.

He pondered, then teased, "By the time it's over,

you'll probably be in love with me."

My mouth fell open. "That's an impressive goal, Alex." I had *never* been in love with anyone.

"Wanna make another bet about it?" he asked.

I narrowed my eyes. "I met you a week ago. I don't even know if I'll still like you next Saturday, let alone be in love with you in a week."

"You're right," he agreed, the corners of his mouth twitching. "It will probably happen before then."

My mouth gaped in complete disbelief. I knew he had to be joking, but somehow, the way he said it—made me think he wasn't kidding, not at all.

"If you believe this little event you're planning will make me crazy about you, it must be something you've tried. So, how many girls have you used this trick of yours on?"

He smiled, leaning his shoulder and chest in next to me. Only inches from my face, he whispered, "You'll be the first." His breath on my cheek made me tremble. I met his gaze, unsure about what was going to happen next.

I could barely find my voice to speak. When a noise did come out, it was quiet and a little shaky. "That's . . . flattering," I took a staggered breath, still locked onto his bright, green eyes.

He started to reach toward me like he wanted to touch me, but stopped before he made contact. Instead, he moved his head so his mouth was close enough to my ear that I could feel his breath. "You don't deserve any-thing less," he said with a sincere voice.

I wanted the moment to last forever, my heart raced and my breath was uneven. I was completely focused on the image in my mind of his mouth coming together with my own in the spotlight of the sun. The thought of his perfect lips and chiseled body made it difficult to concentrate on anything else.

"Can I ask you a question?" His voice was soft and deep. I knew he was about to kiss me, and I knew it would be fantastic. I had never been so sure of anything in my life.

I gulped. "Uh huh." It was practically a squeak and I was preparing myself for what would surely be the best kiss of my eighteen years.

"Is the air filter dry?" he asked with that dumb mocking grin. "It's getting hot out here."

His question registered in my mind and I realized kissing me was the last thing he wanted to do. I was humiliated and furious. I stood in a huff; the moment was ruined and I was pissed off. Stupid guy, stupid smile, stupid non-kiss.

"I hope so." The anger saturated my voice and I didn't try to disguise it.

I avoided looking at Alex as I walked briskly to the Suzuki and grabbed the air filter. It wasn't dry, but I prayed it would start and I could get out of the private lake setting that should have been a lot more romantic than it turned out to be.

Who was I kidding? I'd gotten stuck in the middle of a lake and had to be pulled to shore by my own personal tugboat. Alex probably didn't think I could function in general, let alone successfully kiss him. I shoved the air filter in position. Alex was up now and standing a few feet away, watching me. I glanced at him and his expression was pained. After three attempts to start it, the Suzuki roared to life. I grabbed my helmet without saying a word. Alex walked to the Honda and put on his helmet as I turned the Suzuki around. As soon as I heard Alex's four-wheeler start, I took off without looking back.

I arrived at camp and felt a little guilty for driving full speed to get away from Alex and not really caring whether he was behind me or not. He caught up to me though and pulled onto the trailer while I was loading the Suzuki. He helped me tie down the Honda without a word. When we were finished, we both got in the Jeep.

We drove in silence and I couldn't help but think about what a mess our date had been. Why had he acted like he wanted to kiss me if he didn't? The embarrassment seemed unbearable and I just wanted the day to be over with. So much for having a relationship with Alex.

The sky was bright blue and feathered with wisps of clouds as we drove into town. I needed to know where to drop Alex off so I could get him out of my life. I broke the silence and asked, "Is your car at the sporting goods store?"

"Yep."

I pulled into the parking lot and saw his blue Audi sitting in a spot on the north side of the lot. I stopped the Jeep next to his car and watched as he shifted to grab his backpack from the back seat. I was relieved we wouldn't have to spend any more time together.

Alex opened the door. He was about to get out when he turned around, his intense eyes searching mine. He paused, leaning toward me again, inches from my face. This time though, I wasn't expecting anything. In a low voice he said, "Since you lost the bet, I'll see you Saturday." He was out of the car before I realized it, my neck still tingling from the spot where his breath had hit it.

Chapter 3

"That's it?" Jasmine asked, her eyebrows skimming her hairline. "After everything that happened, the only thing he said to you the whole way home was, 'I'll see you Saturday'?"

Jasmine was grilling me about the disaster date. I was concentrating on the pan I was scrubbing in the sink and Jasmine was sitting at the kitchen table chewing her gum and blowing bubbles.

"No, he also said, 'Since you lost the bet, I'll see you Saturday." I rinsed the pan and wiped my hands on a dishcloth. I sat down across from Jasmine and started eating some candy from the dish on the table. "I can't believe what a jerk he is. Wait, yes I can. I have a habit of dating idiots."

"Has he called you about the date yet?" she asked.

"Not yet. I'm hoping he doesn't. I don't want to see him." As I unwrapped a pink Starburst, I heard a knock on the door. "Is Zach coming over?" I asked.

"I don't think so." Jas got up to answer the door. After a minute, she came around the corner holding a pink-tinted vase half her size. It was overflowing with pink orchids, each one sparkling like it had been sprinkled with glitter. I gasped when I saw them—pink orchids were my favorite.

Jasmine was even more excited than I was. "Read the card! Read the card!"

"I have to find it first, help me look for it!"

We searched through the orchids as daintily as we could, trying not to disturb the flawless arrangement. I saw a black card between two flowers and pulled it out. I sliced the envelope open. Inside was a piece of black cardstock with silver writing. The handwriting was neat with sharp angles. I read the note out loud:

Evie,

Since you don't strike me as the type of girl who goes back on her word, I assume you're planning to hold up your end of the bet. Be ready at 6:30 Saturday night. I'm sending someone to pick you up.

—Alex

I stood by the kitchen counter, glaring at the flowers and seething at Alex's arrogance.

"What are you going to do?" Jasmine asked.

I tapped the card against the counter. "I'm going on the stupid date and I'm going to let him know exactly what I think of him!"

Jas tilted her head and narrowed her eyes. "Do you really think that's a good idea?"

I gave her a confident nod. "He's challenging me. I'm not backing down."

By Saturday I was still angry, but I was also nervous.

I wasn't sure which emotion would win out when I finally saw Alex face-to-face. Jasmine made sure she and Zach were at the house. She didn't want to miss the confrontation in case Alex decided to pick me up instead of 'sending someone.'

I was ready by six, my long chestnut hair flowing in large curls down my back and framing my face. I wore a black lacy wrap-around shirt and dark-wash jeans. My perfume was light, the scent a mixture of tropical flowers. I put on makeup, concentrating on my favorite part of my face: my eyes. When I was finished I sat around talking to Jasmine and Zach until, at precisely six-thirty, the doorbell rang. I got up, grabbed my purse from the couch, and answered the door. I couldn't believe my eyes. Standing in front of my house was an actual horse, and behind it, a carriage. The carriage was enclosed so I couldn't tell if Alex was inside or not. Jasmine and Zach were watching through the window, their mouths hanging open at the sight of my ride.

"I'm looking for Evangeline," said the man at the door. He was dressed in a jet black suit, crisp white shirt, and black satin tie.

"That's me," I responded, dumbfounded.

"Mr. Night has instructed me to take you to your destination."

I was still trying to wrap my head around the transportation parked in my driveway when I realized the man had called Alex 'Mr. Night.' At least now I knew his last name—something I probably should have found out before agreeing to go out with him on a mysterious date. I managed to gather my thoughts enough to say, "Great. Any idea where my destination might be?"

The man chuckled. "Mr. Night said you would ask that question. He said to tell you to enjoy the surprise."

"Of course he did." I turned to Jas and Zach and

rolled my eyes. "I'll see you later," I said as I walked out the door.

"Good luck," Jas said.

"Try not to kill him," Zach offered.

The man opened the carriage door for me. I sat down and looked out the window. As we clip-clopped away, I could still see Zach and Jas watching me from the house.

I rode in the carriage for about twenty minutes. I wasn't sure how long it took to get somewhere by horse. I had to admit, this was the most elaborate date anyone had ever planned for me. When we stopped, the driver opened my door.

"We have arrived," he said.

"Thank you." I stepped out of the carriage onto a cobblestone driveway that would be better suited to a street in Europe than the mountains of Gunnison. I looked around, noting the house had been built on a secluded mountainside. The house was stunning; a red brick home flanked by large turrets that reminded me of the towers from childhood fairytales that maidens were always trapped in—not necessarily a comforting thought considering no one knew where I was tonight. I could see lights on in the house, illuminating a gorgeous curving wood staircase. The wood alone was probably worth a small fortune. I took the time to wonder if this was some sort of reception hall, or if Alex could really afford a house like this. I was jolted away from my awe by the voice of the carriage driver.

"Mr. Night asked me to give you this." He handed me a note, then climbed back onto the carriage seat and took the reins. I could hear the horse's hooves on the pavement as I opened the black envelope. Another black card with silver writing was inside.

Follow the path on your left. –Alex

At least there was no snarky comment this time. I looked to my left and saw the path illuminated by landscape lights and followed it. The path wound around the outside of the house through a canopy of trees. Sweet floral scents and the smell of freshly turned soil surrounded me as I walked. I wasn't on the trail for long when I noticed something shimmering ahead of me. The path became less obvious and soon I was on grass, trying to get a clear picture of the lights I kept seeing. As I came around a corner, the trees blocking my view were gone and I gasped. I saw at least a hundred black and white candles set up strategically throughout the massive yard. The glimmer I had seen was coming from the trees. They were glistening with what appeared to be thousands of crystals hanging from the branches.

I was taking it all in when I saw a figure step out of the shadows. Alex looked more mouthwatering than ever dressed in a grey suit with a sea-green colored shirt that magnified his bright eyes, and a silver tie. It almost made me forget I was supposed to be mad at him.

"What do you think?" he asked, a pleased smile on his face.

I wasn't sure whether he was asking about the yard or his clothes. The answer was the same either way. "I've never seen anything like it." I turned to look behind me. "Do you leave those up year-round?" I asked, thinking the scene reminded me of an elaborate Christmas display.

He laughed. "Of course not, those are for you."

My chin dropped. "Why?" I asked. "I mean, I can't believe anyone would go to all this trouble for me."

He inclined his head and answered, "You deserve it."

I was too stunned to speak.

Alex broke the silence. "I thought it might be nice to do something a little . . . less exciting, than your usual activities. Are you hungry? Our dinner is ready." He gestured to a round table sitting on the patio. The table was covered in black linen and set with real glasses and silverware—something I noticed since my glasses at home were all plastic and my silverware usually comes from fast food restaurants. I walked toward the table and Alex followed me. As I got closer, I saw more candles, the flames sparkling like fireworks. Stems of pink orchids were scattered around the candles reminding me of the beautiful flowers at my house.

"The orchids," I said. "How did you know they're my favorite?"

His lips curved into a slow smile as he held my gaze. "You don't seem like the roses type."

I sat down, trying to reign in the vertigo I was feeling. Almost immediately, a waiter came out of the softly-lit home carrying two plates of salad. The salad had creamy ribbons of raspberry dressing covering delicate leaves of spinach; walnuts and feta cheese were sprinkled over the top of the salad like confetti. The bright salad dressing and green leaves provided a stark contrast to the white square plate the salad was served on. It looked like something that should be in an art museum instead of on a dinner plate. The waiter took a pitcher off the table and filled our glasses with fresh squeezed lemonade—my favorite. I slid my silverware off the black linen napkin on the table, put the napkin on my lap, and picked up my fork. Alex must have noticed how intently I was looking at my food.

"It won't bite you," he said.

I glared at him for a second. "It looks so elegant. I don't want to ruin it by eating."

"Well, I could have them bring out another plate

with a messier salad," he teased.

I moved my head to the side. "I think I'll be fine, thanks." I scanned the yard, then turned back to my salad, picking up my fork. I glanced up after a few bites and Alex was watching me.

"What are you thinking about?" he asked.

"You really pulled out all the stops tonight," I said.

He contemplated something for a moment. "Details are important," he said. "They let people know you care about them."

"So all *this*," I gestured to the candles, crystals, and food, "means you care about me?" I didn't believe that for a second, not after what had happened at the lake.

He looked at me like he thought I was joking. When he realized I wasn't, he said, "In the past couple of weeks I've saved you from what you thought was a wild animal, stopped you from flinging yourself off the side of a cliff, been your personal mountain guide, and pulled you out of a lake. After all that, I still asked you out. I thought my feelings for you were pretty obvious."

With Alex's ego back in full-force, I found the anger I had forgotten when I walked into his backyard and saw the fancy date he'd planned. "You know, I came here to tell you off." Alex cocked an eyebrow as he leaned back in his chair and gestured with his hand like I should go ahead, which made me even madder. I didn't need permission to tell him what a jerk he was. "How could your feelings have been obvious?" I asked, my voice rising. "You make comments that imply you're interested in me, but your actions are the complete opposite! You won't even touch me."

He didn't flinch, tell me I was crazy, or accuse me of being hormonal. Instead, he looked straight at me. "I'm sorry I upset you. I didn't mean to."

I waited for him to continue. He didn't. "That's it?"

I asked. "You're not going to explain yourself?"

He closed his eyes, rubbing his forehead with the tips of his fingers. "I wouldn't know where to begin." He took a deep breath. "I'm sorry, Evie. I didn't mean to make you mad. I want to spend more time with you and see what happens between us."

I watched him for a minute, assessing his anxious expression. He seemed sincere and I could tell he really was sorry. Finally, I nodded. "Okay. We can try it. But you need to stop acting like such a pretentious idiot or this isn't going to work at all."

Alex gave a soft laugh as he picked up his fork. "I'll try to stop pushing your buttons."

I smiled and took a sip of lemonade. "If we're going to have some sort of relationship, I need to know you better," I said. "Tell me about your family."

"There's not much to say. My parents died a long time ago. I was an only child. Since my parents were gone, I was basically raised in a boarding school. It's one of the reasons I graduated from college so early. I spent most of my time studying and college was pretty easy to get through."

I felt horrible for thinking he'd been self-righteous when I first met him and he told me he'd been in an accelerated degree program.

"My family was well-off. When my parents died, I inherited all of their assets and invested the money I received."

I was dumbfounded at his casual manner talking about his family and what must have been a horrible tragedy. I had the urge to reach over and squeeze his arm in a gesture of comfort, but for some reason, I didn't feel like I should. "I'm so sorry," I said. "I can't imagine what that must have been like."

He shrugged. "It's okay. Everything happens for

a reason." He looked down at his ring, which took on an ethereal glow in the candlelight. His eyes seemed to focus, like he was remembering another place and time.

"Did you get the ring from your parents?" I asked quietly.

He didn't answer for a moment, but eventually said, "In a way, I suppose. The ring was a gift."

I waited for him to elaborate, but he didn't. I knew it was probably difficult talking about the death of his family, so I let the discussion rest.

During the lull in conversation, the waiter brought out the main course: new potatoes roasted in olive oil and herbs, lightly breaded chicken, carrots, and rolls. The food looked great and we continued eating.

Between bites, Alex said, "Tell me about your family. Do you have siblings?"

"No siblings, just me and my parents," I answered, choosing a roll from the basket on the table.

"Do they live near here?"

"No, they live in a small town in Montana called White Sulphur Springs."

"How did they handle you moving to Colorado for school?"

I picked up my knife, spreading salty butter on my bread while I answered, "It was hard for my mom. I moved as soon as I graduated from high school. My mom was expecting to have three more months with me. It wasn't easy, but I needed to get away and experience new things."

He nodded his head in understanding. "Do you think they'll visit often?"

I swallowed my food so I could talk. "I'm sure they'll come down once or twice a year. They try to give me space, but my mom calls and emails a lot. My dad sends me maintenance reminders for my car and my mom mails me her special chocolate chip cookies."

"I'm going to have to meet your mom," Alex said. "I don't think I've ever had someone send me homemade cookies."

"I'll let her know. She'll start cooking tonight and you'll have more cookies than you could ever wish for."

He smiled like he was imagining his own mom making him cookies. "That would be nice," he said.

A few more minutes passed as we ate.

"Do you think you'll like college?" Alex asked, picking up his glass and taking a drink.

I nodded. "I'm excited to meet new people and I love to learn, so despite it being a lot of work, I can't wait for school to start."

"That's great," he said. "College was one of the best experiences I ever had."

"What did you study?"

"I was a history major, but took a lot of different classes."

"What did you want to do with a history major?" I asked. I didn't know anyone who chose that major unless they planned on being a teacher or getting their Ph.D.

"I liked history the most. I knew having a career wouldn't be as vital for me as it is for most people. I wanted to learn about a topic I enjoyed. Now I use my time and resources helping causes I believe in."

I finished eating and slid toward the back of my chair.

"The volunteer work you do," I said, "what exactly is it?"

His body tensed slightly. "I help people get out of bad situations."

Something about his response triggered that feeling of familiarity in my mind. I closed my eyes, trying to get rid of the odd sensation.

"What's wrong?" Alex asked, concerned.

I tried to laugh it off. "You'll think I'm crazy, but ever since I met you I've felt like I know you from somewhere."

Alex held my gaze for a long time. He ran his tongue over his lips and replied, "I feel the same way about you. We must have one of those connections." He smiled, quickly changing the subject, "Do you want to go inside?"

I smiled back, glad he didn't think I was insane. "I'd love to."

I followed him through a massive set of mahogany French doors. We walked through a room with walls filled from floor to ceiling with books, the furniture antique.

I walked next to him as we went down a hall and into a massive room that seemed to be an art gallery. There were more paintings on the walls of the room than I had seen in some museums, and many seemed familiar. Alex stood back and watched as I strolled around the room, noticing the names next to the paintings: Philippe Mercier, William Hogarth, Benjamin West. I came to one painting that caught my eye. The clouds and bright pinks and blues of the sunset were reflected in the lake surrounded by hills with mountains in the background. The artist's name was Richard Wilson and something about the painting made me think I'd seen the place, though I couldn't remember where it was. I let my eyes wander as I tried to place it and was immediately sidetracked when I noticed a painting I would have recognized anywhere. The canvas was a copy of Vincent van Gogh's *Starry Night*, my favorite painting. It was a fantastic reproduction; the brush strokes and parchment it was painted on looked so authentic.

I became aware that Alex was standing next to me. "This is beautiful," I said, engrossed in the colors and chaos-like beauty of the swirling stars. "It's my favorite painting."

He didn't answer for a couple of seconds. "It's one of my favorites also."

"It looks so real!" I reached up, mesmerized. I traced the brush strokes in the air with my fingertips.

Alex's laugh brought me out of my trance. "It is real, Evie."

I gasped and jumped back, not even wanting my air fingerprints to be near the painting if Alex was telling the truth. "You *cannot* be serious," I said, completely stunned.

"My parents loved the arts and started this collection. I continued the tradition after they died. I acquired *Starry Night* several years ago."

"I thought the original was on display at the Museum of Modern Art in New York," I said, the disbelief still clear in my tone.

"I loan my family's artwork to museums for extended periods of time. I borrowed this one back for tonight." His implication was lost on me. If I'd been thinking clearly, I would have been more intrigued with why he would bring this particular painting, *my* favorite painting, back home when he did.

Instead, I stared, astonished. I absolutely couldn't believe it and started looking more closely at the rest of the artwork in the room. Some I recognized, a Monet for sure, another that looked like a Picasso. For all I knew, he had the Mona Lisa stashed on a wall around the corner.

Amazed, I asked, "And the rest of these? They're all the original pieces as well?"

He smiled again, seeming to enjoy shocking me. "Yes, they are."

How did this happen? In Gunnison, Colorado, some of the most famous artwork in the world was hanging on the wall of one of the most beautiful homes I'd ever seen. I wondered what I would discover on the rest of the tour. Maybe the Venus De Milo was in the foyer.

"Will you come with me?" Alex asked, his eyes glittering. "I want to show you one more thing."

"Sure," I agreed, wondering what else there could possibly be to see.

I followed him through the foyer and up the wide winding staircase with railings of mahogany like the French doors. When we reached the top, we were standing in front of two enormous doors. He glanced at me, opening the doors slowly and stepping out of the way. For the tenth time that night, my jaw dropped. The floors were the same redwood I had seen in the art room below. A breeze flowed from windows that ran every eight feet along the perimeter of the room. The entire top floor was an enormous ballroom. I remembered my mouth was still open and closed it.

"You must like dancing," I said.

He laughed and walked over to a technical array of stereo equipment. After about thirty seconds, I heard music start to play. It was "Moon River" by Andy Williams, one of my favorite classic songs. Either Alex was a spy, or he guessed really well—then again, maybe we both liked the same things.

He locked eyes with me as he walked back to where I was standing. My heart was beating so fast I didn't know how long I could stand on my own. Alex's dark hair rippled as the breeze blew through the windows. His eyes flickered like flames and an unfamiliar determination lingered on his face. He stopped when he was about two feet in front of me, pausing for what seemed like an eternity. "Will you dance with me?" he asked, extending his hand out toward me.

We'd never touched, but just being this close to one

another felt like an electrical current flowing between us. I gave him a huge smile and nodded. Slowly, feeling the current get stronger, I reached toward him and rested my hand in his. As soon as we touched, I noticed a warmth rush into my back right where my lily-shaped birthmark was, but I was too busy concentrating on Alex to dwell on the heat. The connection between our hands was intense, like I was being pulled into him, and a part of me I didn't know existed was suddenly present.

And then, without warning, I felt like I was falling into a dream. I watched as a girl not much older than me brushed chestnut colored ringlets off her face with a gloved hand. She was beautiful in a long scarlet ball gown with a deep lacy neck, and skirt that opened slightly in the front, showing a ruffled petticoat underneath. A male figure stood about ten feet in front of her. They were outside, shrouded by darkness and trees. Though I could see the girl clearly, the male figure was too far away to make out any details—but I could hear him.

"This is your choice?" he asked, contempt obvious in his tone.

The girl nodded in response, the slight movement emitting a palpable sadness.

"Why him?" he asked. *"Why now?"*

"I can't help what I feel," the girl said. *"I'm in love with him."*

"No," he said through his teeth. He paused, then stalked to a tree and punched his fist against the trunk. *"You're in love with what he wants you to see, not who he is."* He exhaled in disbelief and shook his head. *"I've done everything I can up to this point, and now you tell me you're in love with him? Stabbing me in the heart would be no less painful."*

The girl moved toward him, her eyes downcast. "I'm sorry," she said, coming up behind him and putting a hand on his shoulder. "I didn't mean to hurt you."

He tilted his head toward the spot her hand was resting and abruptly reached around her and grabbed her by the waist, pulling her with him into the darkness. She gasped in surprise as he leaned down and kissed her, hard at first, like he was trying to prove a point, then becoming gentler until he pulled back from her lips and rested his head against her forehead. In a husky voice, he asked, "Do you still think you love him?"

She didn't move.

"Do you?"

She didn't look at him as she gave an almost imperceptible nod.

He dropped her from his embrace and stepped away, turning his back toward her. Minutes ticked by and the muscles in his shoulders tensed. He shifted his head to the side, his profile barely visible, and said, "He will disappoint you." He stood for a few seconds more, before he started walking away from her.

She ran her fingers lightly over her lips and looked up, eyes wide as she watched him leave. "Wait!" she yelled. "Where are you going?"

He stopped and pivoted on his heel, his legs apart and arms crossed over his chest. His face was shrouded by his shoulder length hair as he stared at her. Then he answered her question, "To prove which of us truly loves you more."

As the dream faded and I came back into consciousness, I stumbled away from Alex.

"Are you all right?" Worry lines formed at Alex's eyes. I nodded my head, still trying to understand what I'd seen and if it was even real. "What happened?" he asked. "I took your hand and you closed your eyes, then you almost fell down."

I shook my head, trying to clear it. "I don't know." I was about to tell him I'd had some sort of waking dream, but thought better of it. There was no reason to make Alex think I was going crazy. If I'd been acting strange during the dream, Alex didn't seem to notice. "It was nothing," I answered, trying to convince both Alex and myself. "I was just dizzy all of a sudden."

Alex pressed his lips together, trying to decide if I was really okay.

"Honestly! I'm fine," I tried to sound reassuring. "And you owe me a dance."

Alex cracked a smile and walked back over to the stereo equipment. "Moon River" started to play again. The vision—if that's what it was—happened right after I touched Alex. I wondered if it would happen again. As Alex came closer, I reached toward him, gently taking his hand. Nothing. I smiled in relief and tried to assure myself that what I'd seen had been my imagination. I had no other explanation for it.

Alex put his right hand on the small of my back and held his other hand out for me to take. I put my left hand on his shoulder, trying desperately to remember something, anything, from my high school ballroom dancing class. But when he guided me into the middle of the room, my feet glided over the dance floor like I'd been waltzing professionally for years. I breathed in the cedar scent of Alex's cologne and could still feel the current everywhere our bodies touched.

The song changed and Alex pulled away, his expression tight like he was having a mental argument with himself. After a moment, he moved back toward me, this time pulling me in so close that we were embracing. I wrapped my arms around his neck resting my head on his broad chest and sighed. Alex wrapped his arms more tightly around me.

As we danced, I couldn't help but wonder what was happening to me. In a matter of hours, my feelings for Alex had shifted from controlled dislike to romantic interest. I'm usually a very rational person. I'm not spontaneous and I always over-analyze every decision I make. But I couldn't deny how comfortable I felt in Alex's arms—happy, absolutely content. Almost like I was supposed to be there.

We stood holding each other for what felt like only a few minutes, but the changing songs alerted me that it was probably longer than that. The heat on my back hadn't dissipated and I was lost in the euphoria of the moment: a touch, a dance, more intimate than any kiss I'd ever had. Too soon, before I was ready to stop, Alex whispered in my ear.

"Evie, it's late. I should probably get you home."

I sighed again, only this time in resignation. "What if I don't want to leave?"

Alex's mouth slid into a smile. "I don't want you to leave either," he said, "but I don't want to mess this up."

I couldn't really argue with that, I knew moving too fast could ruin a relationship. I took a moment to realize I had just thought about us in a relationship. Did Alex think we were in a relationship too?

Alex held my hand, the electricity even stronger now. I walked next to him as we glided down the beautiful stairway. He guided me into the kitchen, complete with top of the line stainless steel appliances and black marble countertops. He opened a cabinet and grabbed a set of keys. We walked out the back door through the maze of trees dangling with crystals, still shimmering, this time from the light of the moon and stars instead of candles.

Alex's familiar Audi was parked outside the massive garage. He held the door open for me as I got in.

Alex moved to the driver's side and started the car. Getting home didn't take nearly as long as getting to Alex's house in the carriage—which was disappointing after what had turned out to be such a great night. I had never met a person I wanted to talk to this much. I wanted to know everything about him from his favorite foods to his most embarrassing moments. I would have gladly stayed up with him, talking all night and into the next day.

We pulled up to my house. Alex turned the engine off and got out of the car. I already had my door open and was halfway out of the seat when I saw Alex standing in front of me.

"Evie," Alex said, disapproval on his face.

I stood up, confused at his expression. "Yeah?"

"You didn't let me open your door for you."

I started to laugh. "Is acting helpless some sort of requirement for being around you?"

"It's not being helpless," he said. "It's chivalry."

I smiled as sweetly as I could. "I can open my own doors."

"It's not a question of whether you can open your door. It's a matter of being a gentleman."

I gave him an assessing gaze. "You know, history major, there was this whole idea in the 1960s called the women's movement. You should look into that."

Alex frowned like I should know better. "It has nothing to do with your independence, and everything to do with how well I treat you and how special I want you to know you are to me."

I considered that, realizing I wasn't going to win this argument, at least not tonight. "I guess I can see your point."

A hint of victory flashed through his smile. "So, you'll let me open your doors from now on?"

My eyebrows puckered. "If I remember, fine."

"I won't let you forget."

"But," I added, "only if I can get the door for you sometimes too."

Alex seemed caught off-guard, and laughed. "Sounds good."

I grabbed my purse, ready to go in the house. Alex took my hand unexpectedly and it was like a lightning bolt shot through me again and my birthmark flared with heat. He walked me to the porch, taking my keys from me. As I waited for Alex to unlock the door, I saw a shadow move in the front yard. It ran from a tree to the side of my house near some bushes. Maybe it was a trick of the light, but it startled me. Alex noticed. "What's wrong?"

I leaned to look around him. "I thought I saw a shadow by the side of the house. It disappeared into the bushes."

I stepped away and tried to move past him to investigate what I'd seen, but Alex, who had opened the door, pushed my shoulders back until I was standing in the house. "Stay here," he ordered, shutting the screen door.

I watched Alex walk quietly down the front steps and onto the lawn. I opened the door slowly and followed him. He was combing through the sweet-scented rose bushes and square-trimmed boxwood shrubs that separated my house from the neighbor's when I came up behind him. "Find anything?" I asked.

Alex tensed and turned around. "I know I told you to stay inside."

"I don't like being told what to do," I said. "You should probably learn that about me."

"I've known it for a while. But I keep hoping one of these times you'll listen." He moved more boxwood branches and turned back to me. "I'm not sure what you saw, but it seems to be gone now. I'll check the backyard before I leave."

I shrugged. "It was probably just a stray dog." Alex's eyes continued to dart around the yard and I could tell he was still concerned. "Or maybe it was some kind of monster," I joked, trying to lighten the mood.

Alex stared at me. "I'm sure you're right." He seemed lost in thought and took my hand. "Let's get you inside."

Chapter 4

The next week, I was sitting at the table trying to think of a clever Facebook status update when I heard a knock at the door. I got up to answer it and saw Alex on the other side holding a red petunia he'd picked from the flower garden in my yard.

"Hey." He smiled as he walked into the house and handed me the flower.

"Hey, yourself," I said. "I wasn't expecting you."

He turned his attention to some photos of me and Jasmine hanging on the wall. "I could go outside and call first if you want."

I laughed. "That's okay. Do you want to sit?" I asked, motioning to the couches.

Alex walked past the love seat and settled into the couch. I was about to sit next to him when the phone rang. I had a feeling I knew who it was. I'd replied to an email from my mom earlier and mentioned a guy I'd been seeing. I was sure she was calling for details.

"That was quick," I muttered as I got up. I wondered how long my mom had been waiting at the computer for my email response.

A crease formed between Alex's eyebrows. "What was quick?"

"Nothing," I answered. I was dreading having to deflect Mom's questions while Alex was with me.

I kept my eyes on Alex as I picked up the phone. "Hello?"

"Evie?" The voice on the other end wasn't my mom, it was Jasmine. I breathed a sigh of relief.

"Hey, Jas! What's going on?"

"Zach and I are going to the pizzeria for dinner tonight. Do you want to come? You could call Alex and meet us there."

"Actually, Alex just got here. Let me see if we have plans."

I put my hand over the receiver. "Do you want to go to dinner with Jas and Zach tonight?" I asked.

Alex perked up, interested. "Sure."

I got back on the phone. "That sounds great. When do you want to go?"

"We could meet there in about thirty minutes?"

"Thirty minutes?" I glanced at Alex. He nodded. "That works for us."

"Yay!" Jas said, "A double date; I'm so excited! See you soon!"

After I put the phone back on the hook, I sat down next to Alex. He reached for my hand and I smiled. I was glad our relationship had progressed enough that he felt comfortable touching me.

"It will be nice to spend some time with your friends," Alex said. He had met Jasmine and Zach a couple of days ago when he stopped by the house to take me out for coffee. Zach had seemed surprised at how nice Alex was, and Jasmine couldn't keep her chin off the floor. As soon as Alex left, Jas went on for a full hour about how hot he was. Zach hadn't been thrilled.

"Yeah, it will," I agreed. "I haven't been out with them in awhile."

"Where are we eating?" Alex asked.

"The pizzeria. Have you been there? It's pretty good."

Alex laughed. "Pizza is always good when you're in college."

It seemed like he wasn't a pizza fan . . . which could be a problem for the future of our relationship. "Do you want to go somewhere else? I could call them back."

"No, the pizzeria is fine." He seemed to have something on his mind. Finally he turned to me and asked, "Were you expecting Jasmine to call?"

I wrinkled my brow at the question. "No, why?"

"When you got up to answer the phone, it sounded like you were expecting to hear from someone."

"Oh, right," I said, remembering. "I thought it was my mom. I sent her an email right before you came over and thought she was calling about it."

That piqued his interest. "What did you write that would make her call so quickly?"

Huh. This was going to be uncomfortable. "Nothing," I said. "I mean, I just answered some questions."

He watched me as he moved his thumb back and forth over the top of my hand. "What kind of questions?" he asked innocently.

I lifted a shoulder. "You know," I hedged. "Stuff about work, dating, friends, Jasmine, reminders about my car." I was hoping I'd slipped in the dating part covertly enough that Alex wouldn't notice it. I was wrong.

"Hmmm . . . and what did you tell her about dating?" he asked, trying to hold back a smile.

I looked down at my hand in his. "I told her I met a guy hiking in the mountains and we were hanging out a lot."

He frowned. "That's it?"

"Yeah, pretty much."

He furrowed his brow. "That doesn't seem like a topic that would provoke an immediate phone call from a parent."

"You don't know my mom," I assured him.

"You didn't tell her anything else?" he pushed, curiosity evident in his tone.

I was embarrassed, but thought I'd get it out of the way. "Um . . . well . . . I might have mentioned that I like you." I tried to race through the last part hoping he wouldn't be able to decipher it. I glanced up quickly to see his reaction. At first, he was smiling as he thought about what I'd said. But after a few seconds, his expression changed as he pushed his eyebrows together, perplexed. Great, I'd scared him off already.

"What's wrong?" I asked. "Was I not supposed to say that?"

"No, that's not it," he licked his lips and turned to me. "I thought we were past just liking each other."

I pulled my shoulders back, sitting up straighter. "Oh!" I said, the surprise registering in my voice. "Well, I wasn't sure. We haven't really talked about it."

He considered that, holding my gaze. "Maybe we should."

After a few awkward seconds that involved a lot of stomach fluttering, I broke my eyes from his and did a thorough inspection of my cuticles instead of responding. I wasn't sure how to start a relationship conversation, or what to say. He noticed, and raised his hand to my chin gently lifting my head until we were looking at each other again. "My feelings for you are strong, Evie. How do you feel about me?" he asked.

I bit my lip and considered. Since my last relationship ended with Luke's seized truck engine, I didn't think I was too great at intense relationship discussions. Because I was a novice at this, I had to really think about what to say. Alex took my hesitation as a bad omen. "It's okay if you don't feel the same way about me that I feel about you," he assured me, though his expression was somber.

"No, that's not it. The way I feel about you is . . . incomprehensible." Alex's face gave away his confusion. "What I mean is that I've never felt like this about anyone. My feelings for you are also very . . . strong."

Alex grinned—almost gloated—at my admission.

"So where does that leave us?" I asked.

He thought about it. "Next time you talk to your mom, I think it would be wise to tell her about your boyfriend." His smile radiated and I couldn't help but smile myself.

"Okay, but be prepared, she'll probably want to start emailing you. You'll also get the chocolate chip cookies as often as I do."

Alex laughed. "I can't wait."

I was glad to have that conversation out of the way, and proud of myself for getting through a relationship issue without resorting to any sort of vandalism. I noticed the time. "We should go. We're supposed to meet Jas and Zach in ten minutes."

I grabbed my keys and walked out the door. "I'll drive," Alex said. "My car is blocking the driveway."

"Okay. I'll drive next time," I said, as Alex opened the car door for me and I got in.

"We'll see," he murmured as he shut the door. I was sure he hadn't meant for me to hear him.

"What is, 'we'll see' supposed to mean?" I asked when he got in the driver's seat.

"Nothing," he said with big, innocent eyes.

I looked at him as I buckled my seatbelt. "Since

when do you have a problem with my driving?" I asked, a little irked.

Alex exhaled as he started the car and backed out of the driveway. "It's not so much your driving—though that's scary too. I have a problem with your car."

My mouth gaped. "What are you talking about? Most guys would murder to have a girlfriend with a car like mine." I was so annoyed I didn't even recognize that I'd called myself his girlfriend for the first time.

"That's exactly my point," he said. "You get more attention than you realize when you're in your car."

I gave him the most incredulous look I could muster. "Are you honestly jealous of a *car*?" I was completely baffled. I'd never had to deal with a guy who didn't like my Mustang.

"I'm . . . uncomfortable with how many people notice you when you're in your car," he qualified.

"Well," I huffed, "you'll have to get over it. I love driving my car."

He gave me a calculating look. "Fine, we'll compromise," he said. "You can drive your Mustang when you go out, but I get to drive when we're together."

"That's stupid," I said flatly.

"Very mature."

"Oh yeah, and you're the poster child for maturity, being jealous over some metal and paint."

A muscle worked in Alex's jaw like he was trying to hold back what he really wanted to say.

"And what did you mean when you said my driving is scary?" He had started it, so we might as well get all the car issues out of the way.

"Evie," he turned to face me, "you drive like a bat out of hell."

I inhaled sharply. "No I don't!" I couldn't believe I had to defend my driving abilities.

Alex took a deep breath. "Do you even realize there's a speed bump on your street? There's a bright yellow sign that says 'bump' and huge white arrows on the street pointing to it. I don't think you've ever noticed. You hit it like you're Evil Knievel trying to clear twenty cars every time. The sign might as well say 'ramp'."

I glowered at him. "So what? I like to drive fast; no one's getting hurt by it."

"Not yet," he said, the disapproval clear in his tone.

"Who do you think you are? My dad?"

He looked at me with a slight frown that said he thought I was overreacting. "I'd just like to keep you alive for a while."

I rolled my eyes. "We split the driving, fifty-fifty," I offered.

He considered that and his eyes brightened. "All right," he said, "but since your Mustang doesn't have air conditioning, we drive my car if it's over seventy degrees. And since Mustangs are rear-wheel drive, we take my car if there's any chance of rain or snow."

"Do we need to write down the rules?" I asked snidely.

Alex grinned. "I can type them up for you."

By that time, we were pulling into the pizzeria parking lot. I really couldn't argue with him about the air conditioning and rear-wheel drive since he was right. "Fine, we have a compromise."

Alex was smug, like he'd won another victory. His attitude bothered me, but I wasn't going to let it ruin our night. I started to open the car door, but Alex was right there holding it open for me. He just smiled as I got out and glared at him. He shut the door, setting the alarm and taking my hand. As soon as I felt his touch I calmed down, at least mentally; the rest of my body became a lot more restless.

Jas and Zach were waiting for us in the lobby of the restaurant.

"Hey guys!" Jas's face lit up when she saw us.

"Hi Jas. Hi Zach," I said.

"Hello," Alex's deep voice was seductive even to me. I couldn't imagine the effect it was having on Jasmine.

Zach exchanged a head-nod with Alex and Jasmine smiled shyly. "Hi Alex. I'm glad you guys could come with us tonight." Jas was being overly cordial and chewing her bubble gum like she was in a race. I hadn't seen her so antsy since we were almost caught toilet papering the yard of our high school math teacher.

"Me too," Alex said.

The hostess took some menus from her stand and we followed her to a table in the corner of the pizzeria. The smell of garlic, bread, and cheese permeated the air as we scanned the menus and placed our order. Zach immediately asked the server for a Pepsi; it was the only thing he ever drank and he was fanatical about it. Even though he wasn't at our house much, we always kept a twenty-four pack of Pepsi chilling in the fridge for him.

While we waited for our food, Zach asked Alex all the general getting-to-know-you questions that I'd asked him when we first met. Alex reciprocated with questions for Jasmine and Zach.

The server brought our food and we talked as we ate. Alex asked Jasmine and Zach how they met. That conversation eventually led to Jasmine's observations about my dating life.

"You're definitely an improvement," Jas said to Alex. His expression was curious, inviting her to go on. "Evie doesn't have the best luck with guys," she explained.

"Hey!" I said, trying to defend myself. "They haven't all been bad."

"Oh, really? Let's see," she raised her eyes as she thought. "There was the guy obsessed with jerky. Remember the theme card he made you for Valentine's Day? When you opened it, it mooed." She shuddered as she thought about it. "Or the one who asked you to prom with the stipulation that he be allowed to drive you there in your own car." Jas leaned forward on the table looking straight at me, "And let's not forget the holy grail of asshats: Luke," she said, turning her attention back to Alex. "I could tell you stories about that idiot for hours. One of my favorites was when he told her he didn't have time to deal with her feelings so she should think through her emotions and journal it, then get back to him when she wasn't so pissy."

A muscle under Alex's eye pulsed as he smiled in a way that said he wasn't at all amused. "Guys like that don't deserve someone like Evie. In fact," he paused, as if considering whether or not to continue, "if I'd been there, I would have dumped a glass of lemonade on his head."

My mouth fell open a little. I looked at Jasmine to see her wearing the same shocked expression as me. After a few seconds, Jasmine regained her composure. "Actually, that's exactly what Evie did," Jasmine said. "Only she was drinking Sprite at the time." Jasmine assessed Alex warily. "How did you know that?"

Alex's mouth slid into a sly smile. "Lucky guess," he said, picking up his glass and taking a drink. When he finished, he put the glass on the table and continued his explanation, "Throwing your drink on a guy isn't a new concept. Girls do it all the time in movies and TV shows."

Still stunned, I flicked my eyes back and forth between Jasmine and Alex. Jasmine clearly wasn't convinced. Alex leaned on the table and laughed, "Or maybe I'm psychic," he said, waving his fingers to lighten the mood.

Zach snorted. "If so, I need your help with my Fantasy Football team roster."

Alex put his fingertips to his temples like he was divining the answer. "Can't go wrong with Drew Brees," Alex said. He grabbed the check the waiter had left and went up to the counter to pay for our food. Zach started to follow him but Alex told him not to worry about it, he was buying everyone's dinner.

As soon as Alex was out of earshot, Zach said, "I like him, Evie." He nodded to indicate Alex had passed some sort of man test. "He's a good guy." Zach leaned back in his chair. "I've never heard that story. Did you really dump Sprite on Luke's head?"

"Of course she did! He deserved every drop," Jasmine answered for me, waving Zach off. She put her elbows on the table, directing her attention back to me like Zach wasn't even there. "Don't you think it's weird Alex mentioned that?" she asked.

I shrugged, still trying to make sense of it myself.

Jas kept talking, "I mean, it's strange he'd say something so close to what actually happened."

Before I could answer, Alex was back. "Are you ready to go?"

"Sure." I got up from the table. Jas and Zach followed me. Alex held my hand and we walked in silence to the parking lot.

"Thanks, for going to dinner with us," I said to Jas and Zach. "I had a lot of fun."

"Yeah, we'll have to do it again soon," Alex suggested.

"That sounds great," Jas answered as she opened the door to Zach's Grand Cherokee.

"I'm adding Brees to my team as soon as I get home," Zach said. He waved and hopped into the driver's seat.

Alex once again opened my door for me, and I got in the Audi. Alex made his way to the driver's side, started the car, and we drove in silence for a few minutes until I couldn't keep quiet any longer. "It was lemonade, not Sprite."

Alex slid a glance toward me, his expression giving nothing away. "What are you talking about?"

"I dumped lemonade on Luke's head, not Sprite. Jasmine was wrong. But you weren't."

Alex gave a short laugh. "Really?" he asked, paying more attention than usual to his blinker as he pushed it down. "That's a funny coincidence."

I widened my eyes. "A coincidence? That's your explanation?"

As we rolled to a stoplight, he draped his hand over the steering wheel and pegged me with a hard stare. "What else could it be, Evie?"

I put my hands out in front of me, palms up. "You tell me."

Alex shifted his eyes away from mine. "Maybe you told me about it and forgot."

I knew I hadn't. Unless I was mocking him with Jasmine, Luke wasn't a subject I cared to talk about. "I have an excellent memory. And I never told you that story."

Alex snorted. "It's not like you remember every second of every conversation we've ever had."

I lifted my shoulders, looking at him in challenge. He watched me and gave a humorless laugh. "Memory is a complicated thing. You'd be surprised at the things you forget."

"Try me," I dared.

Alex clenched his jaw and seemed to be thinking, but didn't say anything. We pulled into the driveway of my house. Alex opened the car door for me—again.

We walked up to the front door and, like always, he held out his hand for my keys. Alex opened the door and flipped the living room light on. I stepped into the house; he followed me, still silent. He sat on the couch as I went to the phone to check the voicemail. I put my purse down, my back toward Alex, and played the messages. There was a call from my mom, of course—she must have gotten my email—and another from someone looking for Jasmine. I wrote the message on a pad of paper next to the phone and hit the erase button.

I stood in front of the phone, wondering if Alex would continue our conversation. I took a deep breath, then turned around and gasped. Alex was inches from me, waiting. I hadn't even heard him walk over. I should have at least felt that he was behind me. I was generally so good about knowing when someone was in my personal space.

I looked into his eyes—they seemed to be on fire, not with anger, but something else. Suddenly our lemonade / memory discussion seemed a lot less important. Alex grabbed me around my waist, slowly guiding me until my back was pressed against the living room wall. He placed his hands palms down on the wall next to both of my shoulders. Even if I had wanted to move, and I didn't, it would have been impossible. I could smell his rustic cedar scent as he shifted his head toward mine and moved his right hand to the back of my neck. As he leaned into me, he whispered something that sounded like, "Let's see if you remember this." Before I knew it, his lips, the lips I had dreamed about every day since we sat together at the mountain lake, were on mine, pressing hard against my mouth, merging with his. The kiss was aggressive, but still gentle, his lips soft and warm, and my back tingled with a familiar heat that was quickly getting a lot hotter.

He pulled me closer and our mouths opened. My heart pounded, blood racing through my veins, the electricity was frightening. The way our mouths moved in perfect harmony was like we were made for each other.

I was breathless and the desire was so strong, I wanted every part of him as fast as I could have it. Alex was still kissing me as he dipped me down and laid me gently on the floor. He knelt next to me, one leg wrapped around both of mine. One hand cradled my head, the other one started tracing the lines of my neck, his touch like a current. He continued kissing me as he moved from gently brushing my neck to my collarbone. I didn't know how much longer I would be able to take this. Then, I felt him move off of me and lay down next to me.

"What?" I asked, lifting my head up to look at him. "What's wrong?" My voice was staggered, the breaths shallow.

"We can't do this." Alex's breath was coming more swiftly than mine. He tried to move away from me, but I grabbed his arm and pulled him back so he was still lying next to me on the floor.

"Why not?" I asked, searching eyes that had melted to a dark green.

He sighed and he looked . . . conflicted.

"I want to keep kissing you," I assured him.

"You're not the only one," he said, frustrated.

I studied his expression for a moment and decided to take charge. I sat up and moved my legs around him until I was straddling his hard stomach. I leaned down close to his face and whispered, "Then what are we waiting for?" I met his lips with my own and kissed him, my hands clutching at the shirt covering his chest. The kiss became more intense. He held his arms tightly around my back, his hands moving and my shirt scrunching up. My back seemed to be on fire, but my whole body felt that way. The stroke of his fingers on a part of my skin no man had ever touched sent shivers from my head to my toes.

I couldn't help but think about where I wanted this to go. I started running both of my hands through his hair, tugging at the roots as I kissed him even harder. He quickly grabbed my hands, moving them to my side.

Before I knew it, I was on my back, my arms pinned down by his. I closed my eyes, waiting for him to start kissing me again, but instead, I felt his hands slide slowly off mine. I heard the floor creak as he scooted toward the wall next to me and leaned his head back against it. He appeared defeated, but determined.

I sat up, smoothing my hair and rearranging my clothes. "What's wrong? Did I do something I shouldn't have?"

He ran his hands through his hair. "No, I did," he said. "I let that get out of control."

I was confused. "We were making-out. I thought getting out of control was kind of the point."

He gave a tired smile. "In most circumstances, it probably is."

"What's different about this circumstance?"

His expression made me feel naïve for some reason. "It's not the right time, Evie."

I wrinkled my brow. "Not the right time for kissing?"

He snorted. "Not just kissing, though we shouldn't be doing that either, but I couldn't help myself anymore." He scrubbed a hand over his face. "We need to take things slowly."

My voice rose in aggravation, "We were kissing!" I took a deep breath and continued in a calmer tone, "Just kissing."

He stared at me in disbelief. "You *know* where that

was heading."

I looked away. At some point, I knew I would consider having sex with Alex, but I didn't want to confuse the relationship by moving too fast. I wished Alex would give me some credit; I wasn't completely void of self-control. But maybe it was Alex who would have lost control? The thought made me strangely euphoric.

Alex spoke again, his voice was soft and the words seemed difficult for him to say. "What I mean is that there's a lot going on right now. I don't think we should take that step yet."

I scowled at him. "What could possibly be going on that has anything to do with this?"

"More than you realize."

I gritted my teeth. "I don't think we should be going that far yet either. But you're making such a big deal out of kissing, I wonder if you'll ever want anything more with me."

Alex looked at me like I'd lost my mind. "Don't be ridiculous. I am *absolutely* sure I want this as much, no more, than you do. You have no idea. . ." He mumbled something under his breath that I couldn't hear and gazed at the blank white wall across the room. He shifted his eyes back to me. "I promise; I want to be with you more than anything—but not yet."

At least we were making some progress. "If not now, when?" I asked.

"I'm not sure. But I hope it will be sooner than later."

I frowned. "That makes two of us. So, now kissing is off-limits?"

"No. We—*I*—just need to be more careful."

He moved closer and reached for me, wrapping his arms around my shoulders and pulling me into his chest. He gave a happy sigh as he pressed his lips to my neck whispering in my ear, "You have no idea how long I've waited for that kiss."

Chapter 5

It didn't take long for Alex and me to realize that we needed to keep ourselves busy or we'd end up on the living room floor again. Over the next week, we watched every movie playing at the theater, washed both of our cars, baked cookies, and even toilet papered Jasmine's bedroom. By Saturday, we'd exhausted our activity database. Instead, we decided to drive downtown and get ice cream—in Alex's Audi, of course. We pulled into the parking lot of the ice cream parlor and Alex opened the car door for me. The action, courteous or not, made me feel helpless and I didn't like it.

"Thanks," I mumbled as he closed the door.

He smiled as he placed a hand on my lower back, guiding me to the front of the shop. "You're welcome," he said, adding, "even if you don't mean it."

I reiterated my opinion, which he already knew. "I appreciate the gesture, not the meaning behind it."

"The meaning is a matter of interpretation," he said as he opened the ice cream shop door for me too.

After several tastings, we placed our order. I got

mint chocolate chip in a waffle cone and Alex decided on dark chocolate in a bowl. I stepped to the cash register to pay for the treat, but Alex cut me off, handing the guy at the register fifty bucks and telling him to keep the change. I squeezed my lips and pulled my eyebrows together in a scowl; once again, Alex wasn't letting me pull my own weight. In my mind, his trust fund wasn't an excuse for him to pay for everything we did together. As we walked out of the store, I turned to him. "You realize the tip you gave that guy was enough to buy fifteen ice cream cones?

He shrugged. "He was doing a good job. Plus, I doubt many people tip them."

I licked my ice cream and arched an eyebrow. "Not like that I'm sure." We were approaching Alex's Audi, but I didn't feel like going back to my house. "Do you want to eat at the park?" I asked.

"Sure," he said, reaching for my hand. It still sent tingles through my body and heat over my lily birthmark every time he touched me. I hoped the feeling would never go away.

We walked in silence until we came to a secluded park bench surrounded by trees and flowers. Across the street, I could see ducks swimming around a small pond, feathers shimmering in the moonlight. I thought we were alone until I noticed a man walking around the perimeter of the pond. From our vantage point on the bench, I could see the man, but we were hidden from him by the trees. He was tall, maybe as tall as Alex, with wavy blonde hair. As he stepped under a park light, I saw that he had a strange red mark that resembled a spider web circling his arm. The web seemed to wrap up his bicep and down his forearm almost like the pattern of a candy cane. I snickered, thinking the guy would seriously regret that tattoo when Spiderman wasn't popular anymore.

Alex noticed my laugh and followed my gaze. He glimpsed the man briefly, a mix of anger and panic crossing his face as he gripped my hand. Alex's eyes darted around the park. He immediately grabbed my arm and we were moving. I stumbled, unprepared for the sudden location change, and dropped my ice cream.

"Hey! What are you doing?" I asked. He had ruined the serene moment and made me drop my dessert.

"Shhh!" The noise he made was harsh. "Follow me and don't say a word," he whispered, shooting me a stern look. Alex pulled me behind him and we were almost sprinting. I looked back and couldn't believe how far we'd already run. The pond was out of sight. We wound our way through a grove of trees on the outskirts of the park where the leaves obscured our presence. We stopped for a moment while Alex's eyes flashed back and forth.

We were only there seconds when Alex grabbed my arm again, directing me down a darkened alleyway. It seemed the street would have been a safer choice. Whatever Alex thought he saw, it would be better to be in a place we could get help if we needed it instead of winding through broken alleys of cracked asphalt, the moon providing the only available light.

But, in record time, we reached Alex's Audi. He grasped the handle and almost pushed me into the passenger seat. Within seconds, he was next to me, turning the key in the ignition.

"What's going on?" I asked, out of breath and a bit panicked. "What happened back there?"

Alex stayed silent.

"Alex, *tell* me why you dragged me three blocks and are now doing eighty miles an hour down a road you should be going forty on. Jeez! And you say *I* drive like a bat out of hell."

His usual cocky smile and relaxed demeanor had been replaced with tight lips and a serious expression. "I saw something," he said, "that's all."

"Saw what?"

He took a breath. "There was a man walking by the pond. I thought I recognized him."

"So you reacted like a maniac?" I asked. "Most people say hello when they see someone they know; they don't run away." I couldn't understand what would prompt a response like that.

Alex's temples pulsed. He was holding the steering wheel with such force that I was sure the shape of his fingers would be embedded into the wheel when he released his grip. This was definitely a side of Alex I hadn't seen before. This side was enraged. Once we were out of Gunnison and driving through the canyon, Alex calmed down and said, "Some acquaintances are not the kind you ever want to see again."

Now that he was talking, I was going to get some answers. "Who was he? Why did you run? I felt like you were the Secret Service or something!"

Minutes ticked by without a response. I was starting to wonder if he would answer me at all when he said, "He's not a good person. I didn't want him to see me, or you—and I especially didn't want him to see me *with* you."

I thought about it for a second. "Well, maybe he's changed," I suggested.

Alex's face was strained and his voice hard when he spoke. "He. Has. Not."

"How do you know?" I asked. "When was the last time you saw him?"

"I just know. I need you to trust me on this." There was a warning in his tone that made me shiver and the concern in his eyes became more pronounced with each glance in my direction. "He is extremely dangerous," Alex said.

Alex's reaction and the feeling that I had something to do with his concern was disturbing, to say the least. We sat in silence again, Alex looking at me every few seconds like he was checking to see if I still existed.

Finally, I broke the silence. "So what now, Alex? We can't drive all night."

I was sure he'd been thinking the same thing, but I was completely unprepared for his response. "How do you feel about moving?" he asked.

I searched his face for the familiar smile indicating he was joking. My chin dropped to the floor when I realized he was serious. "Are you crazy?" I asked in disbelief. "I have work, friends, a lease! And that's not even addressing the level of hysteria my parents would hit if I were suddenly gone."

"Those are all things that can be taken care of." He said it like he made people disappear every day.

"Taken care of?" My voice was getting louder. "No. No *way*, Alex. This is your problem, not mine. There's no chance I'm *moving* because you saw someone who resembled a person you might know who may or may not be dangerous. That is the *dumbest* thing I've ever heard."

"No, Evie. Dumb is not listening when you're told you need to be careful."

Though he hadn't said it directly, he had questioned my intelligence, infuriating me even more. "Take me home, NOW."

Alex tensed and I could see the veins pound in his neck. "Why do you have to be so damn stubborn and independent?"

I folded my arms across my chest. "Why do you have to be so damn arrogant and controlling?"

Alex gave a hint of a sigh. "I *can't* take you home. Not until I figure out what to do."

"Figure it out when you get back to your house. Despite what you think, I don't have anything to do with this."

He turned, his eyes blazing. He took a deep breath and opened his mouth to speak, but stopped himself. After a couple of seconds he said, "You have more to do with this than you realize, Evangeline." I wanted to argue with him, but didn't know how many times I could explain that whatever was happening didn't involve me. "The fact that he might have seen me and might have also seen you in the park with me—that is incentive enough to be concerned," Alex warned.

I wanted to know what this guy had done and why Alex was so worried and adamant that I had something to do with his reaction, but I knew I wouldn't get those answers. I turned away, watching the trees drift by outside the window. I had no way to get Alex to pull over and stop. I contemplated opening the door and rolling out of the car. I'd seen it done in movies, but imagined it would hurt a lot more in real life. After about ten minutes, the car slowed and Alex pulled near the side of the road making a wide u-turn. He started driving back the way we had come. Once I knew we were going back to Gunnison, relief flooded through me.

"I will take you home," Alex said, his voice reserved, cautious. "I need to find out what's going on, figure out why he's here. I can't do that from another state or country."

I stared, astonished. Another country? He was really taking the appearance of this guy seriously. I didn't say a word. I was just glad to be going back to my house.

"There are conditions, however," he added, looking at me severely.

Why did he always think he could tell me what to do? Sometimes he made me feel like a kid and that made me mad. "What in the hell would those be?" I was still angry but Alex ignored my tone.

"First of all, I need to stay at your house every day and night until I have more information." I lifted my eyebrows, surprised. He had been so careful not to do anything that could be considered morally dubious in the past. "It's for safety purposes," he said, reading my expression. "I'll sleep on your bedroom floor."

The request didn't seem bad so I nodded my head in acquiescence. "Is that it?" I asked.

"Hardly," he said. "Until I figure this out, I don't want you to leave the house or talk to anyone you've never met."

That was completely unacceptable. There was no way I was being held prisoner because of Alex's lunatic assumptions. "Absolutely not," I said, shaking my head back and forth at his stupid demand.

"It's not a request," Alex said. "I'm giving you a choice. You can do what I ask until I find out what's going on, or you can leave tonight, right now, and go far away where you can start over. Honestly, the second choice is by far safer and preferable, but since you seem to be more stubborn about this than you have *ever* been about anything, I'm willing to compromise and see what I can learn first."

I was furious. This was not a choice, it was prison. I knew Alex was concerned for my well-being, but still didn't understand why he felt the situation was so perilous.

"The decision is yours," Alex said.

I clenched my fists as rage boiled under the surface of my skin. "You haven't given me a choice," I said, seething. "You told me I can be a prisoner in my house, or become a missing person, drop everything, and start over somewhere else."

Alex looked at me with hard eyes. "If you don't listen to me, you won't *just* be a missing person." The implications of his statement sent another shiver up my spine as he turned his Audi into my driveway and maneuvered it into the backyard where it couldn't be seen from the street.

"Stay here," he said, locking the car doors. He was gone in a flash and back before I had time to really think through his missing person statement.

"It doesn't look like anything here has been disturbed," he said, opening my door. "Let's go inside."

"You know," I said, as I got out of the car, "I think there's at least an eighty percent chance you're out of your mind."

He slid his eyes to me with a reproving look. "Let's hope you don't get proof that I'm not," he said, taking my keys and unlocking the deadbolt. I was still mad as I stomped into the kitchen. Alex went around the house double checking the door and window locks, and closing all the blinds and curtains like a dutiful security guard.

I clean when I'm angry and the dishes in the sink seemed like a good place to take out my aggression. I turned on the hot water, poured some dish soap in the sink, and watched a mountain of bubbles explode over the dirty dishes. As steam started rising, I pushed open the curtains and unlatched the lock on the window that Alex had closed so I could get some air circulating—and also to piss Alex off.

I grabbed a washcloth and started to scrub, lost in thought. Despite knowing each other for weeks, Alex still seemed to be laboring under the incorrect assumption that I'm one of those girls who does what she's told. Ordering me around and telling me that I can't leave the house is *not* okay. The fact that he left so many questions unanswered was frustrating too. I also couldn't figure out why he was constantly pulling the superior act; like he knows more about everything in the world than I do. Men with egos are trouble. I sighed and rinsed a pan, then got another and scrubbed harder. He was hot. That was my problem. He was really, really hot. And the fact that he liked me made me more willing to let things slide. I needed to stop doing that.

The breeze outside fluttered through the window, moving the curtains I'd pushed back. I looked up toward the garage. In the fleeting second I glanced out the window, I saw a dark figure dart through the yard. I started to shrug it off thinking it was probably just a college kid playing a prank, but the figure didn't move like a normal person, in fact, it seemed to glide. I leaned forward, closer to the screen to try and get a better look and figure out if something was really there, or if my eyes were playing tricks on me.

My face was inches from the screen, but I couldn't see the figure. The shadow had run from the north side of the yard by the garage, to the south side by the backdoor. I felt prickles tingling up my arms. Considering Alex's earlier reaction, I knew I should call for him, but he was anxious enough for the both of us and I didn't want to alert him if I didn't have to. My eyes refocused, scanning the backyard, but I saw nothing.

I took a deep breath, deciding my overactive imagination was terrorizing me, and started to back away from the window. As I did, inches from me, separated only by a flimsy window screen, two eyes appeared. They were almost silver, but whiter, shimmering and sinister. I didn't want to look away. The eyes were terrifyingly bright and drew me in while I stood in horror. I couldn't differentiate between the shining platinum irises and the whites of the eyes. Surrounding the eyes, I could see the dark shape of a head: a person.

The figure and I watched each other until finally, the scream that had been building in my throat released, shattering the silence of the house. The platinum eyes flickered and instantly grew dim, like the figure was backing away. But as it did, my scream still piercing the air, there was enough light radiating from the eyes for me to see a cunning, horrific smile flash across the figure's face before it vanished.

The whole incident happened so fast. In the time it took for my scream to escape my mouth, and the eyes to vanish, not more than ten seconds had passed. Alex was immediately by my side, arms around me, his eyes searching my face trying to discern what had happened.

The breeze flirted through the window again and Alex bristled at the feel of the air, the realization streaming across his face. Alex dropped me from his embrace, reaching furiously for the window, slamming it shut, and locking it. He grabbed the curtains and jerked them closed. "Why was the window open?" he asked accusingly, his eyes darting around the room and back to the window.

It took me several seconds to compose myself enough to speak. "I was doing dishes and it was hot. I opened the window to get a breeze through the house," I stammered, unable to get the memory of those shining eyes out of my mind.

Alex blew out a heavy breath in an effort to stay calm. "Tell me what happened?"

I wasn't sure where to start and was beginning to question my own sanity. "I . . . I saw . . . something."

"What did you see?" he was more apprehensive than I had ever seen him.

"I was washing dishes and saw a black figure run

across the yard. I thought maybe all the stranger talk was making me see things, so I got closer to the screen to try and get a better look." I took a deep breath, trying to shake the image of the eyes from my mind.

Alex coaxed me on. "What happened after that?"

"Two bright eyes appeared in front of the window screen. The figure kept watching me and when I screamed, the figure backed away. I saw it smile, then it was gone."

The calmness was out of Alex's voice now and rage returned. "Dammit, Evie! Why did you have to open the window? They must have connected me with you at the park and now they've seen you and know where you live."

My body kept rippling with shivers, even as I felt the sweat running down my forehead. I stood motionless next to the stove. I knew I had made a mistake. I should have taken Alex more seriously when he told me about the danger we were in, but I never would have thought opening a window could be so perilous.

Alex saw me trembling, saw the horror in my face and pulled me into him, wrapping his arms around me like a vice. "I'm sorry, I am *so* sorry. It's my fault they're here."

"Who are they, Alex?" I asked, comforted by his embrace. "What are they?"

He was holding me so tight I could barely breathe and I felt his warm breath skating across my hair. He didn't say anything at first, but eventually answered, "Remember when I told you about volunteering for an organization?" I nodded against his shoulder. "And that I help people get out of bad situations?" I nodded again. "These are the men and women I help people escape from."

I moved back from his embrace and searched his

eyes. Someone was looking for him and because of him, they were now looking for me. "What do they want?" I asked.

He reached out and tucked a strand of hair behind my ear, his fingers lingering on my cheek. "They don't like my job," he said. "I've compromised you. Now I need to figure out what to do about it."

I wanted a better explanation than that. "Shouldn't I know what's going on so I can protect myself?"

"You don't have to protect yourself," he soothed, "that's what I'm here for."

I was still shaken up and Alex insisted on putting me to bed. I didn't have high hopes of being able to sleep—the threat of nightmares was enough to keep me awake for days—but Alex sat next to me, stroking my hair, helping me relax. Even as I resisted it, I fell asleep.

I don't remember what I dreamed, or if I dreamed at all. When I woke up, Alex was in the same position he had been in when I fell asleep. I could smell something wafting up from the kitchen. For a moment, I forgot about the events of the previous night and asked, "What's that smell?"

"Bacon, eggs, and pancakes. Your favorites."

I sat up and rubbed my eyes as I stretched my arms in the air. I got out of bed and Alex followed me downstairs. He gave me a plate of food and sat across from me, not getting a plate of his own. He smiled, but it didn't reach his eyes. There was something in his expression that made my stomach tense.

"Aren't you going to eat?" I asked.

"I already did."

Strange, I hadn't noticed a plate in the sink as I walked through the kitchen. "How was your night? Did you get any sleep?"

"No," he answered evenly.

I watched him, unable to read his expression. His face was hard and he seemed troubled by his thoughts. I started eating my eggs until Alex spoke abruptly.

"Evie, we can't see each other anymore."

My heart felt like it stopped beating and my face fell. "What are you talking about?" I demanded.

He remained stoic, but underneath his hard mask, I could see he was hurting. "Last night made me realize I've put you at risk. I need to find out how to fix this and to do that, I have to leave for a while."

I rolled my eyes. Yes, the shadowy figure had been a shock and I'd been so scared I'd almost peed my pants, but Alex was overreacting. The more I thought about it, the more convinced I was that it was some college kid pulling a prank.

He narrowed his eyes. "There are things about me you don't know."

I shrugged and picked up a piece of bacon. "We haven't been dating that long. I'm sure there's a lot we don't know about each other."

Alex shook his head like I didn't understand. "These are things of consequence. Things that could change your life."

I took a bite of the pancakes Alex had made and they were fantastic. "These pancakes could change my life. Does that mean they're going to break up with me too?" I asked, trying to joke and lighten the mood.

Alex smiled faintly and glanced at me. "This is critical, Evie. They know where you are."

I threw my hands in the air. "Who knows, Alex? You haven't answered any of my questions!" I decided

I was done being nice and was plain mad. Alex actually seemed serious about breaking up with me over a stupid open window and some joker with glowing contacts.

"And it's better you don't know, safer," he said, crossing his arms over his chest and nodding to himself. "They must have tracked us. I never should have put you in that situation, but I didn't think the bond between us would be established so fast—or that they would be looking for it," he mumbled rapidly, talking more to himself than me. He collected his thoughts and turned back to me. "I have to talk to some people about this. I won't be gone, but you won't see me."

I stared at him trying to figure out what he meant, but my thoughts were interrupted by the realization that Alex had already made this decision without me and wasn't changing his mind. "If the things that happened last night were as scary as you say, isn't that more incentive for you to stay?" I asked. "To help keep the bad guys away from me?"

"Usually, yes," he answered. "But right now, my being here is the reason you're *not* safe," he said, his mouth set in a hard line.

My anger was the only thing holding back my tears. "I've never felt like this about anyone, Alex. You're egotistical, frustrating, and I wish you'd tell me what's going on, but I still care about you. A lot." I dropped my eyes and listened for Alex's response, but the hum of the refrigerator was the only sound in the room. When I got the courage to look up, Alex's expression reflected sadness, but the resolve that had been there at the beginning of the conversation was still present. "Why are you doing this?" I asked as numbness started to spread over me.

Alex walked up and put his hand on my neck caressing it, his fingers rubbing methodically, as if he were trying to rub away his memory. He started to open his mouth to deflect my question, but I grabbed his hand and locked eyes with him. "No. Give me one honest answer, you owe me that. Why are you really leaving?"

He searched my expression and as he did, the hard planes of his face seemed to soften slightly with relief. I wondered if he'd decided to actually tell me the truth. He brushed his hand across my brow, pushing my hair back, and kissed me lightly on the forehead as he said, "Because you're beautiful." Slowly, he trailed his fingers down my face and as his lips followed, he brushed a kiss over both of my cheeks. "Because you make me stop caring about consequences." He moved back enough to look into my eyes as he leaned in. "Because the way I feel makes me more dangerous to you than anything in the universe right now." He wrapped me in his arms and pressed his lips to mine in a passionate kiss, his mouth moving expertly with my own. As the kiss became lighter, I recognized it for what it was—a kiss goodbye. He broke from our embrace and held my gaze. "There are people who don't want us to be together."

I searched his eyes and managed to breathe out a ragged, "Why?"

He moved his lips to my ear, his breath hot on my neck as he whispered, "Because, Evie, I'm your soul mate."

He turned and walked through the kitchen entryway. The front door clicked shut and he was gone.

At first, I was hurt and confused. I sat on the floor of my bedroom going over the conversation in my mind again and again. Dangerous. Someone tracking him. Things between us moved too fast. The one time I asked for an honest answer, he told me a plethora of things that seemed more like reasons he shouldn't leave, and ended it with the kicker that he was leaving because he was my soul mate. Who uses that as a break up line? It made no sense. I needed clarification, some sort of closure, but I wouldn't get that now. I picked at the specks of carpet on the floor and wondered if I'd lost the person I was supposed to spend my life with. And with that, the anger started to build, because I still didn't know the exact reason he was gone.

I spent the next few weeks getting ready for school to start, working, hanging out with Jasmine, and trying to forget about Alex. I gathered everything he'd ever given me: the dried orchids, the notes from our dinner, a CD mix with the songs we'd danced to that night in his ballroom. I had every intention of throwing them out, but when I got to the garbage can, I couldn't do it. Instead, I put them in a storage box in the back of my closet where I wouldn't have to see them anymore. I tried to do the same thing with my feelings and memories, hoping those things wouldn't haunt me later.

As much as I hated to admit it, Alex had been right about one thing. Since he left, there had been no more shadows in my yard, or figures terrorizing me outside my windows. The malevolent figure from the night in the kitchen had made me feel helpless. Now, I was more aware of my surroundings and I avoided looking into the darkness for fear of what I might see. I hated that one experience caused me to be so paranoid. I used to enjoy my time alone, but now I was frightened by it.

I got my fall semester class schedule and picked up

my books at the campus bookstore. I was relieved that school would start soon. Classes would be a welcome distraction; something to keep my mind off the events of the summer—off Alex. Throwing myself into homework was exactly what I needed.

Jasmine asked if I wanted to go shopping for school supplies. I needed some notebooks and pens so we went to a store near our house.

On the way to the store, Jas asked, "How are you feeling?"

I sighed. Jas asked me this at least once a day. She knew my feelings for Alex had been different than any other guy I'd dated, and she was worried about me. The problem was that I never really knew how to answer the question. "No one broke up with me today, so things are looking up."

I meant it as a joke but her lips thinned and her cheeks pulled back in a concerned expression. I laughed. "I was kidding, Jas! Really, I'm fine."

"If you were fine, the house wouldn't be so clean. An industrial sander couldn't have gotten that many layers of grime off the kitchen floor."

I lifted my shoulders. "You know I clean when I'm angry. It's how I work through things. I'm feeling much better." Jasmine didn't know about the figure outside the kitchen window, the danger Alex had been so concerned about, or the man in the park. I thought the fewer people who knew about those incidents, the better. I'd told her and Zach that Alex had broken up with me and left without any explanation. They'd been as baffled as I was.

Jas's eyes slid over me, pausing on my face as she assessed me. When she decided I'd rather scrub the toilet than drown myself in it, she asked, "Do you think he'll ever try to get back together with you?"

My face fell. "He said he needed to figure some

things out, but that I wouldn't see him. Maybe he'll be back eventually, but I don't know what I'd do if he did show up again."

Jas's expression echoed mine, only where mine contained sadness and confusion, hers was full of pity, which made me feel worse. We pulled into the parking lot and walked inside. We both found the supplies we needed, but Jas saw the clothes section and got side-tracked. Given how upset I already was, I wasn't interested in going through the angst of trying on clothes too. I found a chair by the dressing room and waited. From my seat, I could see through the racks of clothes to one of the main aisles. I watched people walk by and every few minutes, Jas would come out of the dressing room and ask for my opinion.

There was a mother with a sneaky toddler who kept grabbing things off shelves and putting them in the shopping cart. The mom didn't seem to notice. The thought of her getting to the check-out counter and finding the extra items in her basket almost made me smile. Some younger girls, probably in junior high, were standing around a display of tank tops and shorts, discussing what colors would look best on each girl and coordinating what outfits they would wear on the first day back to school.

I glanced toward the back of the store and noticed a man dressed in jeans and a red T-shirt. He was tall and lean. His dark brown hair fell below his ears in a way that was messy-on-purpose. It seemed like he was looking right at me. My suspicions were confirmed when he realized I was staring back at him and he immediately shifted his eyes to the bra display at his right and grabbed a few off the rack. Something was familiar about the guy, but I wasn't sure what. He made me uneasy.

I got up and knocked on Jas's dressing room door.

"How much longer do you think you'll be?" I asked.

At that moment she came out of the room. "I'm done!" she smiled. "Let's go. Wanna get dinner somewhere?"

"Sure." We walked out of the dressing area. I turned toward the bra section, but the man was gone. I scanned the rest of the store, but couldn't see him anywhere.

Jas read the tabloid magazines on display while we waited in the check-out line. I was concentrating on the image of the man in my mind and trying to figure out what I recognized about him. It was clear the man wasn't in the bra section on purpose, so what was he doing there? And why was he watching me?

I glanced around the store as I thought, but stopped abruptly when I saw the man again. He was standing next to a jewelry display, about fifteen feet away, watching me with a steady gaze. As I wrenched my eyes from his, I noticed the thing that had made my memory flicker: a red web mark wrapped around his arm and bicep. Only this time, I was close enough to see that the mark wasn't a tattoo, it was some sort of scar. This wasn't the same guy I'd seen walking around the pond at the park. The chances of two men having the same scar on their arm in the same spot seemed slim. Maybe Alex had been right after all. My heart fluttered in panic. I turned to tell Jasmine we needed to leave, but in the short time I had glanced away, the man was gone again. My eyes darted around the store, but he was nowhere in sight.

As a shiver shook through me, I rubbed my arms wishing Alex was around so I could tell him about the person who had been watching me. But Alex had abandoned me. I felt mad, frustrated, and the sadness that rippled through me was equivalent to mourning. I took a deep breath trying to calm down. I had made it through eighteen years before Alex came into my life; I could make it through the next eighty without him too.

We got to the checkout line and paid for everything. I helped Jas carry her bags to the car. As we drove to the restaurant, I couldn't stop thinking about the man in the store watching me. I wondered how long it had been going on.

And why.

Chapter 6

It was my first day of school at Western State and so far, the day had gone as expected. I wasn't as nervous about starting college as some of the other students. I'd been working on campus for the last three months and it had helped me learn where all the buildings were. I'd even met some of my professors over the summer. I already had homework in two classes and I still had one more class to go.

I wandered into the College Center, scanning the dining area for Jasmine. We had agreed to meet for lunch during our break in classes, but I didn't see her anywhere. As I scanned the crowded building, my eye caught on one guy. For some inexplicable reason, he was sitting alone at a table, reading. His hair, the color of golden sand in the sunlight, fell in waves across his head. His jaw was square and the cords of muscles in his arms were showcased by the brown T-shirt he wore. I don't know how long I watched him but when he looked up, our eyes locked and it felt like I had known him forever.

Embarrassed, I quickly tried to look away, but I couldn't turn my gaze. His mouth twitched like he was

amused and he tilted his head. After continuing our staring contest for a few more seconds, he slowly got up
from his seat, never taking his eyes from mine. People
automatically parted for him as he walked through the
crowd and came toward me like he was being pulled by
a wire that was attached between my chest and his. Without stopping in front of me like most people would when
meeting someone for the first time, he moved closer and
closer until his body was inches from mine. He put his
hand on the side of my face and I shuddered involun-
tarily; he smiled at my reaction. He traced my cheekbone
with the tips of his fingers brushing them lightly down
the side of my neck. I could feel my heart beating harder with each movement and a warmth started to spread
over my back—a warmth that I hadn't felt since Alex had
touched me. I would have been furious at his intrusion
on my space—if I could move.

Then it happened again—I was falling into another
dream. This time, the girl with the chestnut ringlets was
pacing around a large room in a low-cut dark blue dress
that flowed in waves from her tightly corseted waist.
Cream colored lace accented the neckline, and elbow-
length sleeves. She was talking to someone I couldn't see.
Her voice was hoarse and tears dripped from her cheeks.

"I don't understand." The sound of her quiet sobs
echoed off the walls.

*A male voice came from the other side of the room.
"There are options."*

*She vehemently shook her head. "If I leave, they'll
find me."*

"No," he answered, "they won't."

*She looked at the rug on the floor through blurry
eyes. "How do you know?"*

*"Because," the voice said with resolve, "I'll make
sure of it."*

She clutched a handkerchief in her hand and lifted it to her face. "I think leaving you might be worse than staying."

"It will be difficult," the voice agreed in a resigned tone, "but only until you forget."

His words brought a fresh stream of tears to her eyes. When she could speak again she whispered, "And what about you? Will you forget?"

"No," he answered immediately. "Never."

And with that, the dream faded.

I blinked, trying to shake the vision from my mind and in the process, realized the boy's arm was now wrapped around my waist, his greyish-blue eyes still firmly locked on mine. His hand slipped around the back of my neck as he pulled me closer and kissed me, our lips locked in a graceful dance. I don't know when I finally remembered to breathe, or if I did. It felt like the kiss only lasted seconds. As his lips slowly stopped moving, I wanted to grab him, force him to stay there, our lips melting into one another, his cinnamon taste blending with mine. There was an intense urgency to his actions and the kiss was more powerful than any kiss I'd ever had, including the kisses with Alex. He backed a few inches away from me, his hand still on my neck, his eyes swimming in mine and I felt like I could drown there.

"You have the most beautiful sapphire eyes," he said. I felt faint and completely overcome. He gave me a slow smile. "I'm Emil Stone."

My breath was coming in short bursts. I couldn't concentrate, let alone form a sentence. He seemed entertained by my reaction. Finally, I was able to pull my gaze away for a moment and stammer, "Evie. Evie Starling."

"Is this your first year at Western State, Evie?" he asked, saying my name in a husky voice that made me shiver even though it was eighty-five degrees outside.

"Yes. Started. Freshman."

Graciously, he didn't point out that I couldn't put a sentence together. "Well," he said, "I have a favor to ask." He watched me, probably trying to ascertain how exactly he was affecting me. Maybe if he figured it out, he could let me know. "Do you think you could show me around campus? I just transferred here from a college out east."

I wasn't certain why *he* would be interested in having *me* show him around campus. It was obvious he could have the entire cheerleading squad guide him if he wanted. I was thankful for the last few months that I'd spent wandering around the college getting to know the buildings.

"Sure." My breath was becoming a little more normal.

He smiled again. "When are your classes today?"

That was a good question. Since my brain was on strike, I absent-mindedly pulled out my class schedule to check it. "I'm done at two-thirty."

"That sounds perfect," he purred. "I'll meet you by the pool tables at three."

I nodded okay and watched Emil walk back to his table to grab his book and backpack. He turned to look at me once more with an expression that made me feel like he was kissing me from across the room. His mouth slid into an amused smile as he walked out the door.

Now that he was leaving, the shock became more concentrated as I tried to figure out *what* had just happened. I'd had another dream from touching a guy and the heat on my back was making an appearance again. Why did this keep happening? And aside from the crazy dream-vision and birthmark heater, what kind of guy kisses a stranger? Every instinct I had was telling me I should have slapped him across the face. I didn't even *know* him! I was furious with myself, but no matter how hard I tried, I couldn't find the anger, even worse—I wished he would do it again.

I became aware of the whispers from other people who had witnessed the incident and realized someone was standing next to me. Jasmine. She had walked into the building at the same time I kissed, *then* met Emil. Jasmine saw the whole thing happen, along with most of the Western State student body, and was as stunned as me. Guys like Emil don't kiss girls like me, not like that, not in public, not ever.

"Holy crap!" Jasmine's eyes were huge. "Do you *know* him?" If her mouth dropped any further her gum would fall out.

I slowly moved my head from side to side.

"What did he say to you?"

"Eyes. He said I had beautiful eyes," I sputtered and swallowed so I could speak. "He asked me to show him around campus."

Jasmine blew a bubble, shaking her head in shock. "That's the single most amazing thing I've ever seen," she said. "Zach will never believe it."

I glanced down and checked my clothes. Jasmine noticed as I smoothed my hand over my stomach. "What are you doing?" she asked.

"Making sure my shirt is still on. For a minute, I thought he kissed my clothes off."

In the dizzying aftershock of my introduction to Emil, Jasmine and I grabbed some lunch. As I was sitting down to eat, I thought I recognized an angry face in the crowd behind a group of students, watching me, as if he had been there and seen the whole thing. I moved to try and get a better look, but in the time it took me to shift my position, the guy who looked like Alex was gone.

My next class was Adult Development. It seemed to go by slower than any class I'd ever been in. The professor was going over typical first-day stuff—syllabus, what was expected, how not to fail the class—but my mind was only on Emil and the amazing kiss. Not to mention the inexplicable force I felt when I thought of him, almost like we were being pushed together. The way he kissed me made it clear he had a lot of experience in that department. I frowned, wondering if kissing random girls around campus was something he did often.

Finally, class was over. My professor yelled out the reading assignment, but I was already out of the room. I would look at the syllabus and figure it out later. I walked quickly across campus, arriving at the College Center with fifteen minutes to spare. I thought I'd have to wait for Emil to arrive, but as I turned the corner, I saw him bent over a pool table. His body formed a perfect line with the cue he was holding and I noticed a black and silver ring on the fourth finger of his right hand. The sight of his flawless form knocked the wind out of me and I hoped for a repeat performance of the kiss.

When I regained my composure, I walked up to Emil. "Hey," I said, flashing the most enchanting and flirty smile I could come up with.

"Hi, sexy," he grinned. I was taken aback. No guy had ever called *me* sexy before. I looked behind me to see if I was hiding some smaller, hotter girl. I wasn't, and turned back to him, trying to conceal the confusion on my face. "How was your class?" he asked.

"Um . . . good. Are you ready for a tour?" I asked, still suspicious of his "sexy" comment.

"I would follow you to the ends of the earth." His

expression darkened for a millisecond, though I probably wouldn't have noticed if I hadn't been watching him so closely.

I gave a nervous laugh. "I don't think we'll have to go that far."

We left the building, winding through campus following the sidewalks. Western State is a small college that only spans a few blocks instead of miles like larger universities. I asked for Emil's schedule and pointed out buildings he would have classes in, and other buildings, like the library, that he would need to be familiar with.

As we came around a corner, Emil noticed the gardens.

"What's this?" he asked.

"It's the Western State botanical gardens."

He veered toward a patch of thick, dark green grass surrounded by shrubs and bright pink and white flowers. He looked over his shoulder at me and sat down. I followed, sitting beside him. In the silence, I could hear the splashing water of the creek that ran through the gardens.

"This is nice," Emil said, looking around at the trees and flowers, a rare place of solitude and privacy.

"It's one of my favorite places," I agreed. I didn't tell him I had been here a lot lately, trying to figure things out and deal with my feelings for Alex.

He grinned. "Maybe we should come here again sometime. We could do homework, or . . . something," he said with a suggestive tone.

I inhaled a rattled breath. "Anytime," I answered, hoping I wasn't blushing as much as it felt like I was. I quickly tried to change the subject. "Did you visit Western State before you transferred?"

"No," he answered. "Moving here was kind of an impromptu decision."

"Oh," I said, wanting to know more but not wanting to pry.

He seemed to understand and explained, "A friend of mine needed help."

"So you came to help a friend and decided to stay?" I was impressed by Emil. I didn't know many people who would leave their whole life behind and change everything to help someone out.

"Yeah," he answered without further explanation. Emil didn't seem like the type of guy to give more information than he needed to, which just intrigued me further. I already wanted to unravel the mystery of Emil and I had only known him a few hours.

We sat for awhile, listening to the creek. My mind was running through a million questions. I wanted to ask him about the kiss, why me, why in the middle of the College Center on the busiest day of the year, but I didn't feel like it was the right time.

"Are you living on campus?" I asked.

"No, I rent a house," he said. "How about you, do you live in the dorms?"

"No, but the people who live there say it's chaos around the clock."

Emil grinned like he was fully aware of the debauchery and hijinks that come with living in a dorm. "Where do you live?"

"I live with my best friend, Jasmine. We rent a house in a neighborhood near here."

"Do you like living with someone?" he asked.

"Yeah, she's great. You should come over sometime," I said. For a split-second, I questioned whether it was smart to invite someone I barely knew to my house. Then again, we had already kissed, and his abs were clouding my common sense. "I know Jasmine would love to meet you," I told him as I thought about her reaction earlier today during lunch.

"Okay, what are you doing tonight?" he asked.

I inclined my head, pleasantly surprised. Emil wasn't wasting any time. I took a second to shake the shock of his forwardness off my face, and almost laughed. The kiss at lunch had been brazen; asking to see me tonight was nothing compared to that.

"I don't have any plans," I said, pulling a piece of paper and pen from my backpack. "Let me give you my address and number."

I wrote down directions to my house, and handed the paper to him. We got up from the concert the creek was providing and walked back to the sidewalk. As we approached the registrar building, Emil stopped.

"I have to talk to someone about my schedule," he said.

"Okay, what time do you want to come over?" I asked.

"It's four-thirty now, so how about six?"

"That sounds great," I said, smiling.

"Great," he echoed back to me as he turned to go into the building. I started to walk away when I heard him call my name. I turned, and he locked eyes with me again. "I can't wait to see you tonight, Evie." He opened the door and was gone.

I left to find my car in the parking lot, but not before calling Jas and telling her to be home tonight if she wanted to meet the mystery-kisser. I was lost in thought as I weaved through cars. Emil definitely had my interest. He was smoking hot *and* had already kissed me.

As I got closer to my Mustang, I realized someone

was leaning against the trunk, waiting for me. My chest constricted and images of dark figures and red web scars popped into my head. I rummaged through my bag for my mace, but kept walking, determined to meet who-ever was there and not be afraid.

I moved forward until from a distance, I recognized the person. Alex. I stopped short, completely unprepared to see him. I really didn't think I'd ever see him again. I *knew* it had been Alex in the College Center earlier. What was he doing on campus watching me? I slowly started walking toward him again. His face came into focus and he was furious. I grabbed my keys from my backpack and took a deep breath as I closed in on the car. His arms were folded across his chest, his legs shoulder-width apart, and he was mad. I stood across from him on the other side of the trunk so the car separated us. We locked eyes. It felt like we were in the Wild West, getting ready to duel. I decided to shoot first.

"You are the *last* person I ever expected to see again," I said coldly. The anger I had built up since the end of our relationship was threatening to explode.

Fury radiated back at me from the hard lines of his face. "Is it your goal to make-out with every guy on campus?"

I stared at him, livid. *He* had left *me*. He had no right to question my actions. "Don't you dare judge me," I said, my eyes narrow and my voice low. "It's *none* of your business who I kiss. What are you doing here?"

He ignored my question and asked me another instead. "Do you even *know* him, Evie?"

My eyes flashed. "I do now," I smirked. "Why are you here?" I asked again, my voice terse.

His hands were balled into fists and he was look-ing at me with hard eyes. "I said I would be watching."

I laughed without humor. "I haven't seen you until

today. If you're jealous, I'll remind you, *you* broke up with me, then disappeared."

"You haven't seen me, but that doesn't mean I haven't been around. After witnessing your little episode in the College Center, I decided it was time to remind you that I said I wasn't leaving."

I bit my lip and looked at the ground, then I took a deep breath. "You did leave, Alex. Regardless of what you say, I haven't seen you for weeks. You gave me some stupid soul mate story—by far the most creative way a guy has ever broken up with me, so congrats on that—and then you left."

I could practically see Alex's blood pressure rising. I could tell he was fighting hard to stay calm. "It was *not* some stupid story, Evie."

I rolled my eyes and put my hands on my hips. "Yeah, because my *soul mate*, who's supposed to love me more than anything in the world, would tell me I'm in danger and then leave me without any explanation or ballpark date of when he'd be back. Makes sense," I said without hiding my sarcasm. I could tell he was planning to launch his defense, so I raised my hand and cut him off, "I don't want your excuses. I'm over it. As for this little confrontation, let me remind you, what I do and who I do it with is none of your business anymore."

Alex watched me with a measured stare. "What if he's dangerous?"

I smiled wickedly. "Then I'll die happy."

"No. You won't." There was authority in his voice. "You need to stop seeing him."

The conversation was going nowhere and I decided to put an end to it. I walked up to my car door and opened it. I wanted to get out of there and planned to back over him if he didn't move. But, as I was about to get in the car I felt a sudden urge to let Alex know exactly what I thought, exactly what I wasn't able to tell him those weeks after he left.

Whipping my head around, I marched back toward him, power and resolve in my stride. I got within a foot of him and slid my mouth into a sexy smile. "Oh," I said, licking my lips, "I plan to see a lot more of him than I already have." Alex froze, stunned. "But I don't want to see you ever again. Don't talk to me, don't look at me, don't even *think* about me. You had your chance. We are done." Alex was motionless as I spun back around, got in the car and took off without even looking in my rearview mirror to see where he was. I hadn't felt a bump when I backed up, so I assumed I hadn't hit him.

I was furious with Alex the whole ride home, and kept replaying our conversation in my head. He had serious nerve talking to me like that and acting as if he knew Emil. Alex had no right to try and derail my chances with a new guy. Why is it that guys never realize how much they want a girl until she shows interest in someone else? Alex's reaction just made me more determined. I was going to be with Emil.

Chapter 7

I got to the house and went inside to do a speed-clean before Emil came over. I knew Jas would be home soon too. I vacuumed and wiped down the dining room table and kitchen and bathroom countertops. I was picking up odds and ends in the living room when Jasmine came through the door.

Her eyes flashed around the room, expecting to see someone. "Is he here yet?"

"Not yet," I said, straightening the magazines on the coffee table. "He had some errands to do."

She leaned on the table, her eyes glittering. "What did you two do today?"

"I showed him around campus, then we sat in the botanical gardens for a while and talked."

"So, do you like him?" Jasmine asked, tapping her fingers against the table in anticipation.

"Yeah," I answered, my mouth curving slowly as I thought about our introduction in the College Center. "I like him."

"I told Zach about the kiss. He couldn't believe it and said the guy either had a lot of guts, or was really stupid," she said. "What did he say to you about *the* kiss?"

I brushed some dust of the fireplace mantle. "We didn't talk about it."

She stopped, motionless as a statue until she yelled, "What?" her mouth gaped open. "A guy you've never met, kissed you, *really* kissed you, in front of most of the school, and you didn't even bring it up when you had some time alone with him?"

I shrugged. "It didn't feel right. I'll ask him about it eventually."

She made a "hmmph" sound and frowned.

I changed the subject. "Guess who was standing by my car today when I left to come home?"

Jas grabbed an apple from the bowl on the table and took a bite. "Who?"

"Alex."

Jas inhaled so rapidly, I thought she might choke. The surprise quickly turned to anger. "What was *he* doing there?" she demanded.

"He saw Emil kiss me today. He said something about me needing to be more careful and Emil being dangerous." I rolled my eyes. "I think he was jealous or something."

"Why was he even on campus?" she asked. "He graduated a year ago! From another college!"

"I don't know. He was acting really weird. I told him to leave me alone because who I kiss is none of his business."

Jas smiled. "Good, he needed to hear that. He's lucky I wasn't there. He wouldn't have survived."

I laughed. "That's what makes you such a great friend," I said, giving her a quick hug.

The doorbell rang and I looked at the clock. Emil was right on time. I went to the living room and opened the door. He was holding some chocolates and a bouquet of roses, the color a cross between lavender and grey. He handed the flowers to me. "These are for you," he said. "And the chocolates are for your roommate."

I looked down at the gifts, surprised. Most guys wouldn't think to bring anything. "Thanks!" I said. "You didn't have to do this." I gestured to the flowers and chocolates.

"It's the least I could do," he answered.

"Come on in." I put the chocolates on the table and grabbed a vase from the mantle. As I arranged the uniquely colored, beautiful flowers, I couldn't help but remember Alex saying I didn't seem like the roses type. Alex was wrong about a lot of things. I could be the roses type if the right guy was bringing them to me.

Jas came bounding around the corner. I was surprised she'd been able to restrain herself for as long as she had. "Emil, this is my best friend, Jasmine. Jasmine, this is Emil."

Emil nodded at her. "It's nice to meet you, Jasmine."

"You too," Jas said, her eyes tracking from his head to his toes. With an evil little glint in her eyes, she continued. "I saw you earlier today in the College Center." I narrowed my eyes. What was she doing?

"Did you?" he grinned knowingly. "Once Evie walked in, I didn't notice anyone else."

"Well, I think it's pretty safe to say *everyone* saw the two of you."

He bit back a smile. "Yeah, we weren't very inconspicuous, were we?"

"Are you kidding?" Jas said, "I'm sure the video of that kiss is already on YouTube."

My face must not have registered the level of humiliation I felt, either that, or Emil and Jas didn't care.

"So, not to pry," Jas started.

I interrupted her, "Jas, give him a break, you just met him."

She frowned. "So did you," she said pointedly.

Emil gave me a reassuring smile. "It's all right. She's being a good friend."

Jas grinned in triumph, determined to be more of a friend than I wanted her to be, and asked, "Why did you kiss a total stranger in front of everyone at Western State?"

His lips slid into a comfortable smile that seemed to put Jas at ease. "To be honest, there was no way I could have stopped myself from kissing Evie, even if I tried—which I didn't." His eyes penetrated mine like they had earlier today when I saw him in the College Center. I felt like I might fall over.

"Huh," Jas said. "So, what's on the agenda for tomorrow? Are you going to propose?"

I gasped. "Jasmine!" Her best friend status was in serious peril.

Emil's eyes sparkled. "I thought I'd save that for next week. Do you think she'll say yes?"

What the hell was happening? "Okay, the two of you can stop planning my future." I said. They both turned toward me like they'd forgotten I was there. I'd had enough of guys proclaiming their feelings for me too soon. I didn't need that from Emil too. "Are you guys hungry?" I asked. "Do you want to get dinner?"

"I could eat," Emil said.

Jas jumped up. "I'll call Zach and see if he wants to meet us somewhere."

We decided to eat at an Italian place in town and Emil offered to drive. I stopped short when I saw his car in the driveway, my eyes taking in the sleek lines of German engineering. It was a black 545xi BMW with black tinted windows and silver rims. I moved slowly to open the door, my fingers lingering lightly over the paint that seemed to change from pitch black to glittering onyx mixed with deep sapphire. The interior was grey and black with grey wood paneling. If Satan drove a car, I was sure this would be the one he picked. Emil's BMW looked like pure evil. As I buckled my seat belt, I couldn't help thinking that as we drove through Gunnison, people would either think we were famous, or drug dealers.

The restaurant was only five minutes away. When we got there, Zach was waiting outside for us, enjoying the cool mountain air. We approached him and Jas skipped ahead of us into Zach's arms where he kissed her. I smiled, and noticed Emil was smiling too.

"Hey," Zach nodded toward us.

"Hi, Zach," I said. "This is Emil, a friend of mine. Emil, this is Jas's boyfriend, Zach."

"This is the guy from earlier?" Zach asked Jas. Jasmine nodded as she held back a giggle.

"I've got to tell you, man. You've got balls," Zach said. I glared hard, hoping the arrows in my eyes would hit him.

Emil grinned. "Thanks. Girls like Evie don't come along every day. I thought a grand gesture was in order," he said as we turned to walk into the restaurant.

The hostess seated us in a corner booth and we were quiet while we decided what to eat. When the server came to the table, Zach asked for a Pepsi immediately. Jasmine teased Zach about his body being sixty percent Pepsi instead of water. Jas ordered a meatball sandwich and Zach asked for spaghetti. Emil picked fettuccine alfredo with chicken and I ordered gnocchi, my favorite dish. When the server left, we started talking again.

"How were your classes today?" Zach asked Emil and me.

"Good," Emil and I both responded at the same

time. Jas and Zach shot each other a glance and smiled.

"How about you guys?" I asked Zach and Jasmine.

"My chemistry class is gonna suck," Zach said, "but other than that, everything's good so far."

"My classes should be pretty easy this semester," Jas said, taking a drink of her soda.

Zach turned his attention back to Emil. "Is this your first year at Western State?"

Emil grabbed a breadstick from the plate the server had brought. "Yeah, I just transferred. I like how small the college is, and the weather couldn't be better. I love having the mountains so close too."

"Do you like hiking?" Jas asked, peeking at me.

"I love it," Emil said.

"Evie loves to hike," Jas informed him. "You should go with her. She finds all the best places." I felt like my friends were dating Emil, not me. I had barely said a word.

Emil turned to me. "Really? We should go sometime."

I smiled. "That would be fun, I usually go on weekends, but haven't been for a while." The thought of why I hadn't been—the fear that had stopped me from doing things alone—caused a shiver to cascade through me. Emil noticed and put his arm around me, not understanding why I shuddered. The mountains would be great if I had someone to go with me, plus it would be nice to spend more time with Emil.

The server came out with our food and while we ate, Emil asked Jas and Zach what they were studying. Jas's major changed almost monthly, but today, she told Emil it was nursing. Zach said he was pre-med.

"Do you know your major yet, Emil?" Zach asked.

"Political science," Emil answered. "I'm going to law school after I graduate."

Zach nodded in approval. "Wow, what year are you in?"

"I'm a senior," Emil said.

I whipped my head to the side to look at him, completely baffled. He was nicer or crazier than I thought. What person in their right mind transfers to a different college for their senior year?

Jas was thinking the same thing. "You transferred your senior year?" she asked, shocked. "I would never be able to do that! Didn't you lose a ton of credits?"

"It wasn't bad," Emil said. "Western State was willing to work with me and most of my credits transferred."

So, he was graduating, and probably leaving to go to law school somewhere far away. I sighed and decided it was fun while it lasted. I sulked inwardly over his impending departure until a thought popped into my head. I had been spending far too much time marinating over the events of the summer and Alex. Why shouldn't I take some time to enjoy myself?

I liked Emil, but I hardly knew him, plus he was leaving within a year. He was the ideal candidate for a rebound relationship. He was gorgeous, and for some reason, he already liked me. Most importantly, when I was with Emil, my mind was much less apt to wander to memories about the summer. Emil was perfect for my plan to get over Alex.

We talked more while we ate. When dinner was over, we walked to our cars.

Jas pulled me to the side. "I'm staying at Zach's, so if it's okay with you, I'm going to ride with him," she whispered.

"Yeah, that's fine," I said, turning to Emil. He and Zach were laughing about something. "Emil, Jas is staying at Zach's tonight, could you give me a ride back to the house?"

Emil nodded, his lips curving. "No problem."

"Thanks," I smiled back. "Have a good night guys, I'll see you tomorrow."

"You too," Zach said.

"It was nice to meet the man behind the kiss," Jas winked as she opened her car door.

I waved and walked to Emil's car. He unlocked the doors and the alarm chirped. We both climbed inside.

"Does Jasmine stay at Zach's a lot?" he asked on the way back to my house.

"Yeah, they've been together for a year. They show up at the house randomly. I never know if they'll be there when I get home."

He nodded his head and seemed lost in thought for a moment before he said, "Thanks for inviting me over. Your friends are nice." He sounded sincere.

"Sorry about all the questions," I winced. "They're a bit over-protective."

"I get it," he said. "They're your friends and want to make sure the person you're spending time with is a good guy."

I looked at him in disbelief. Most guys wouldn't be that understanding. "Wow, is there anything you do wrong?" I asked.

He gave a short laugh. "I've been known to be presumptuous."

I knew he was talking about the kiss earlier. "Sometimes that's not a bad thing."

We pulled up to a stoplight and Emil shifted his head toward me. "I hope I didn't offend you when I kissed you."

I blinked. If that kiss was offensive, he could insult me all he wants. The light turned green. "No, not at all. I was just surprised. It's not every day a stranger . . . kisses you. Usually girls have to work a lot harder to get that kind of public display of affection. You do realize that now *everyone* thinks we're dating?" I said.

One of Emil's eyebrows shot up and the corners of his mouth twitched into a sly grin. "I definitely think we should . . . *date.*"

"Oh!" I said, startled and trying to regain my composure—again.

"Are you okay with that?" Emil asked.

"Sure. I mean, it's great!" I answered, still trying to wrap my head around the fact that ten hours ago, I had never met Emil, and now we were dating. Given my views on relationships, this was moving *really* fast. Plus, I still couldn't figure out why we had such a strong connection to each other.

Emil noticed my expression. "What are you thinking about?" he asked, breaking me from my thoughts.

"Nothing," I lied.

He could tell. "You can be honest with me. What is it?"

How was I supposed to say this? I had to know though, even if this was only a rebound relationship, I had to have this question answered. "Well, I was . . . wondering." His eyes searched my face waiting for a question. "Why me?" I asked. "Of all the girls you could have kissed, why did you choose me?"

He laughed and grinned. "You'll think I'm crazy," he said.

Clearly, he didn't know I'd recently dated a lunatic. "Try me."

He took a deep breath. "When I saw you standing in the College Center today, I felt . . . pulled to you." He looked at me to see how I was handling his idea of metaphysics. "Once our eyes met, I had to be near you. Everyone else in the building disappeared. All I saw was you."

I reminded myself to breathe.

He pulled into my driveway, parking the car. He turned toward me, looking deep into my eyes again and I couldn't move. "I wanted to kiss you more than I've wanted anything in a very long time." He smiled slowly. "I wasn't disappointed."

I was still for a moment as Emil cut the engine. "I felt something similar for you. I saw you and couldn't look away."

He reached over and wrapped his fingers through mine. "You have no idea how happy I am to hear that," he admitted.

I squeezed our intertwined hands and smiled. "So, we're dating."

He nodded. "We should probably get to know each other a little better."

"Yeah," I agreed. "That would be good."

"Do you like playing pool?" he asked.

I wrinkled my nose. "I like it. I'm not very good at it," I confessed, "but I enjoy playing."

"By the time we're done, you'll be an expert," he said. "We can play whenever we have a break between classes."

I didn't think about how much I was going to embarrass myself. The thought of spending more time with him and watching him lean over the pool table was too hard to pass up. "That sounds good."

He grinned, his teeth bright white in the darkness. We got out of the car and Emil walked me to my front porch.

"Thanks for spending the day with me," I said. "I needed that."

He held my gaze as he brushed a piece of hair blowing in the breeze away from my face. "I'm so glad I found you, Evie." He leaned down, illuminated in the porch light, and sweetly kissed me. This kiss didn't have the same edge that had been there earlier today, it was gentle, but still exciting, and the feeling of warmth on my back flared. "It's late, I should go," he said, though his hand lingering on my cheek made it clear he didn't want to leave.

I nodded, taking my keys from my purse. He waited for me to open the door and smiled as he walked away. I watched Emil's bright white headlights as he pulled out of the driveway. When he was gone, I locked the door, leaning my back against it. Looking up at the ceiling, I smiled, wondering what I had gotten myself into, and excited about what was ahead.

Chapter 8

The next morning, I drove to school think-ing about the previous day and night with Emil. I pulled into the parking lot and grabbed my bag. I was locking my car when I heard a cat-call whistle from across the parking lot. I turned at the sound and saw Emil approaching me. He walked up and put his arms around my waist. "Hey sexy, I missed you."

I smiled and couldn't stop thinking that I could definitely get used to this. "Hey yourself," I said.

He turned toward my car, his gaze appreciative. "N-i-i-i-ce," he said. "Is that a '66 GT Mustang?"

I raised my eyebrows, he knew his classic cars. "Yeah, I restored it." I said, forgetting that he hadn't seen my car—since I just met him yesterday.

He was impressed. "You'll have to give me a ride in it," he said. "How do you still have a license? I bet this car is a cop magnet."

"I had to get a radar detector," I grinned. "My dad was so proud of my first ticket, he framed it."

Emil laughed. "I think I'd like your dad." We start-ed walking.

"When do your classes start?" I asked.

"At ten. How about you?"

"Ten," I answered.

"When do you finish today?"

"I have a break for lunch at one. I'm done at three."

"I finish at two-thirty," he said. "Do you want to meet me after your three o'clock class and get started on those pool lessons?"

I grinned, remembering how he'd looked playing yesterday. "Absolutely."

Emil walked me to the building I had class in, then left for his own class. It was difficult to concentrate on school stuff when I wanted to be with Emil, but finally my classes were finished. I walked into the College Center and Emil jumped off the couch, his lips curving seductively when he saw me. He grabbed two pool cues, handing me one. I put my backpack down and followed his lead, covering the end of the cue in blue chalk.

"So, do you know the rules?" he asked.

I leaned against the table. "Yeah. You use the stick to hit the white ball, and hope the white ball hits another ball into a hole. But you don't want the white ball to go in the holes, and the black ball needs to stay out of all the holes until the end of the game."

He laughed. "At least you have the basics. Why don't you take the solid balls for this game and I'll take the stripes. You only want to aim for the solids and get them in the pockets—or holes—as you call them." I seemed to be amusing him.

"Okay," I said. Aside from goofing off at the arcade when I was growing up, I didn't have much pool playing experience. I took the cue, holding it between my fingers like a cigarette. I lined the cue up with the white ball using my left hand to guide it and my right hand to move it back and forth like I'd seen people do on TV.

My attempt at trying to break the triangle of balls was a disaster. Instead of hitting the ball in the middle like I planned, I hit the table hard, scratching the green cloth. The cue went under the white ball, sending it sailing into the air, past the carpet the pool table sat on, and onto the tile floor, with a loud thumping noise.

I saw Emil chuckle as everyone on the first floor of the building turned to see the cause of the commotion. Emil walked over and picked up the stray ball. "Let's try again," he said, putting the white ball back on the table. "This time, with a little less aggression." The corners of his mouth were still quirked into a smile.

I glared at him, embarrassed and annoyed. I was only playing this stupid game to be closer to him; he didn't have to mock me. He sensed I wasn't having fun and gave me some tips for how to aim my cue. My second attempt was much more successful and I was actually able to break the balls, though they didn't roll far.

It was Emil's turn and I could tell he was holding back so I wouldn't feel bad. We talked while we played. He asked about my family, friends, and life in Montana. The conversation seemed eerily familiar—like the one I'd had with Alex early in the summer.

As we played, I couldn't help but notice the light glint off the ring he was wearing. The metal had been braided together, the black and silver interwoven. I wondered about it and decided to ask. "I like your ring, what kind of metal is it?"

He studied the table, deciding on his next shot. "It's mostly white gold."

I nodded. "The design is cool. I've never seen one like it."

"It's different," he agreed, leaning down.

I could get an accused murderer to give me more detail than Emil. "Most guys don't wear rings," I led, trying to get him to tell me why he had it on. He lined up his cue and took a shot instead. When he was finished I asked, "Does it have some special significance?"

He stood, watching me steadily. "It's symbolic. I never take it off."

"Huh." I braced my pool cue against the floor and leaned against it. "Symbolic of what?"

The corners of his mouth twitched in amusement. "Of my past and my family."

Finally! Some personal information. "Where did you grow up?" I asked.

He hit a striped orange ball into a pocket. "I've lived all over the place," he answered, lining up his next shot.

"Were your parents in the military or something?"

He took his shot, hit it into the pocket, and looked up at me. "No, the family business took us all over the world."

Emil wasn't giving me much to work with, but I forged ahead anyway. Growing up in a small town had made me a pro at being nosy. "Where does your family live now?"

"You like to ask questions," he observed.

"I thought the point of playing pool was to get to know each other. I'm sure your family will see our kiss on YouTube. I'd like to know something about them too. Plus, I answered all *your* questions."

He leaned over the table again and hit another striped ball, but the ball missed the pocket by a couple of inches. Emil might not have wanted to answer my questions, but he didn't seem uncomfortable with them either. One thing I was finding out about Emil was that he rarely lost control of his emotions. He stood and watched me as he held his cue. "My mom had a difficult labor and died when I was born," he said. "My dad died when I was eighteen. I have one brother, but he lives out of the country."

Now I felt like a jerk for asking. "I'm so sorry," I said.

"Don't be. It happened a long time ago."

"Eighteen isn't that long ago," I said. "You're only twenty-one right?"

Emil drew his lips back like he'd been caught saying something he shouldn't. "It was a long time for me. Plus, my dad and I didn't get along well. I didn't have much of a connection to him, so his death wasn't hard for me to deal with."

"Oh," I said, not knowing what else to say.

Emil pointed to a purple ball on the table. "This ball is right next to the middle pocket. If you hit it a little off-center, the ball will roll in."

I hit the ball like he told me to and it rolled slowly into the hole. He pointed out another shot for me to take. I wouldn't ever be an ESPN billiards champion, but with Emil's help, I might not give unsuspecting students concussions with the cue ball. We talked and flirted while we played for a couple of hours. After we were done, he walked me to my car.

"Same time tomorrow?" he asked.

I mentally checked my schedule. "I'll be done at four," I said.

"I'll meet you at the pool table." He stepped back so I could open the car door.

I got in and rolled the window down. Emil stared at me, a look of desire on his face. I attributed his expression to appreciation for my car. He whistled. "Damn, Evie." His eyes seemed to darken. "A hot girl in a hot car. You don't know what you're doing to me."

My mouth slid into a girlish smile. I looked down, shifting the car into reverse and trying to hide the blush flaring in my cheeks. Truthfully though, I was giddy he thought I was attractive.

"I'll see you tomorrow," he said.

I waved and drove off to get some homework done. If Emil and I were going to spend a lot of time together, I needed to make sure my schoolwork didn't fall behind. When I got home, Zach was watching TV in the living room and drinking a Pepsi.

"Hey!" I said. "Where's Jasmine?"

"Changing her clothes for the tenth time. Who knew going to a movie required so many costume changes."

I laughed. "You've been with her for over a year now, you should be used to it."

"The longer we're together, the less it makes sense."

I put my bag down on the table and started taking my books out. After a minute, Zach put the TV on mute and turned around. "How are your classes going?"

I shrugged. "Good. I need to get some homework done."

Zach seemed pensive. I could tell he wanted to say something but was holding back.

"What's on your mind?" I asked.

His eyebrows knit together like he was trying to figure out how to phrase what he wanted to say. Finally, with a look of worry, he said, "Alex seemed like a nice guy until he hurt you. Emil *seems* nice too, but who knows. Be careful, Evie."

I pulled my eyebrows together, confused. Zach had never given me relationship advice before. "I know Emil is forward, but it's one of the reasons I like him," I said.

I thought Zach would at least smile, but he didn't. "Evie, I know you were hurt and this feels like a good idea right now. I know you think this is a rebound relationship but . . ." he inhaled deeply. "I don't want you to get hurt again."

He was acting like some sort of big brother. I understood his concern, but wasn't about to stop dating Emil because of it. I gave him a sweet smile. "I know you're looking out for me, Zach. I won't get in over my head, I promise."

Jasmine came bounding down the stairs at that same moment. "Hey, Evie!" She turned to Zach. "How does this look?"

"Like the outfit you put on the first time you changed," he replied.

She looked at him like he was the most unobservant person in the world. "You're such a boy. This time the necklace is different and the shoes are red."

He snorted. "How could I have missed that?"

"We're going to be late," Jasmine announced. "Do you want to come with us, Evie?"

I motioned to my books on the table. "I have a lot of homework to do. Have fun though."

"Okay, see ya later." Jasmine grabbed her purse and bounded out the door.

Zach started to pull the door shut. "Don't forget what I told you, Evie." He closed the door and for the next fifteen minutes, all I could do was think about Zach's warning.

Over the next two days, my schedule with Emil remained consistent. As long as neither of us had class or work, we were at the pool table and my billiard skills were gradually getting better.

Thursday afternoon, Emil met me outside my class and he casually grabbed my hand as we walked to the College Center. We got to the pool table for our afternoon game, but the table was already being used.

"There are other pool tables in the dorms," I said. "We could sneak in and borrow one of those."

He thought for a moment. "I have a better idea." He led the way, pulling me to the cafeteria. Unlike most schools, Western State's food court was pretty diverse in the food it offered. Emil grabbed some plastic silverware, drinks, sandwiches, and apples. "Is there anything in particular you want?" he asked.

"Um, no, not really," I answered. "What are we doing?"

He just grinned.

"Where are we going?"

"It's a surprise," he said, still acting sneaky.

"I'm not a big fan of surprises," I told him, wincing as I remembered Alex's surprise earlier this summer that had been the catalyst for me having serious feelings for him. Really, I hate surprises in general. I like knowing what's going on, it makes me feel more in control of things.

My expression wasn't lost on Emil, but he attributed it to my comment about surprises. He grinned again. "I *like* surprising people, so get used to it." He paid for the food. "Come on," he said, holding the bag in one hand and slipping his fingers through mine with the other.

We walked across campus, making a familiar turn toward the botanical gardens. I followed Emil to a secluded grassy area surrounded by climbing roses and trees with leaves so thick they almost formed a canopy over our heads. The creek splashed over rocks a few feet away and the air smelled like honeysuckle and freshly turned soil. I sat next to Emil while he took food out of the bag.

"We're having a picnic?" I asked.

"Looks that way," he said, laying the food on the grass next to us. He handed me a sandwich, chips, and a drink.

I opened my can of soda and took a sip. "I have to admit, this is better than getting my butt kicked in pool."

"You're doing a lot better now than when you started," Emil encouraged.

"Yeah, now I can usually get two balls in the pockets before you win."

He laughed. "Well, at least people don't duck for cover anymore every time they see you trying to hit a ball."

I rolled my eyes. "Puh-lease, the ball only hit the tile floor once, all the others jumped off a couple of feet from the table onto the carpet."

"Obviously, you haven't noticed the people who deliberately move from the couches by the table whenever they see you playing," he teased.

I shot him a playful glare. "It's not my fault if the pool balls want to commit suicide," I justified, taking a bite from my sandwich.

Emil laughed and we ate in silence, listening to the calming sound of the water as it rushed over rocks. When I finished eating, I took a deep breath and smiled. I felt carefree. Being with Emil made me happier than I'd been in weeks.

I slid my gaze to the side where I found Emil watching me, his eyes hooded, intense. Something fluttered in my stomach as thoughts of Emil raced through my mind and color rose in my cheeks. Emil inclined his head as if sensing my emotions, his blue-grey eyes darkening like storm clouds. He moved closer and pulled me to him until my back was leaning against his chest. His fingertips trailed over my palms and up and down my arms like the tip of a feather. My head rested against his shoulder as he brushed his lips over my cheek.

"There's an old legend I'm fond of," he said, his

breath warm against my face. "In it, the world was created by Goddesses and their soul mates. The Goddesses
were all powerful, and with their mates, they performed
a ritual that created two souls—perfect matches for each
other in every sense. These souls were called divine
complements. But the souls needed to learn and grow,
so instead of keeping the souls together, they were sent
into the world, merging with the bodies of human babies
about to be born. The souls spend their lives looking for
their other half. When their human bodies die, their souls
are reincarnated to continue the search. Déjà vu, or the
instant connection people sometimes feel when meeting
someone new is said to mean their souls knew each other
in another life . . . and might even be that person's soul
mate."

I sat for a moment thinking about the story and
wondering why Emil would tell it to me. In the back of
my mind, I thought it was a little strange Emil would
bring up a story about soul mates when Alex had pro-
claimed he was mine a month ago. "It's a beautiful concept," I said finally, "But I'm not sure if I believe in stuff
like that." I turned my head slightly so I could see his
face. "What do you think?" I asked, a teasing smile curving my lips. "Did we know each other in another life?"

He gave a faint smile. "I can guarantee it."

I looked up at him, surprised by his seriousness.
"Oh really?" I said, cocking an eyebrow coyly, "So what
was I like, oh-expert-on-my-past-life?"

A smile touched his lips. As he thought, he seemed
to be in another place. When he came out of his trance,
he answered, "Similar to how you are now. Smart, funny,
stunningly beautiful . . . and you were a horrible pool
player then too." He laughed as I punched him in the
shoulder.

"Very funny," I said.

"Your punches used to hurt less though."

I fought the urge to stick my tongue out and tackled him instead, wrestling him to his back. It started with light-hearted tickling, but soon, our arms and legs were entwined tightly, Emil on top of me, his breath heavy on my neck. As our eyes met and held, the playfulness turned into something else entirely, something with a lot more heat. Emil leaned in, barely brushing his lips against my own he whispered, "We were good at this then too."

As his soft lips met mine, my entire body felt molten—liquid and hot, moving seamlessly with his. He parted my lips with his tongue and deepened the kiss. One hand cupped my face as the other ran a line up and down the side of my body. My hands explored his back, stomach, and shoulders. As I came to his bicep, my fingers brushed over a bump that I'd never noticed before and Emil tensed on top of me. He broke away from the kiss and moved off of me. Clearly he wasn't comfortable, and it had something to do with the bump I'd felt. I didn't want to push him if he wasn't ready to talk about it though, so instead, I waited. Though he'd moved away, he still held my hand in his and after several minutes of silence that I used to try and calm myself down, he finally said, "I'm sorry. I don't mean to rush things."

I rubbed his hand and met his eyes. "I wasn't complaining."

His lips curved. "No, I guess you weren't." He waited a few more minutes and took a cleansing breath. He changed the subject, unwilling to discuss the bump further. "We never decided when we're going hiking."

I nodded. "Yeah, we should do that soon. When do you want to go?"

"This week?" he asked.

"Sure," I said, gathering my trash and putting it

in the bag. "How about tomorrow?" Western State only schedules classes Monday through Thursday, so we have a three-day weekend every week.

"Sounds like a plan," he said.

"I have some homework to get through tonight, so I should go." I stood up and grabbed my bag. "But I'll see you tomorrow morning around eight?"

He nodded. "I'll pick you up at your house."

I smiled and waved as I walked to my car. I realized that I thought of Alex much less often now that Emil was in my life. Alex had at least agreed to my wishes. I hadn't heard from him since earlier in the week when he was jealously trying to convince me that Emil was dangerous.

There were still times though that something would remind me of Alex and I would be pulled unwillingly into a memory I wished I could repress. The thought of my upcoming hiking trip with Emil was one of those instances.

The relationship between Emil and meI was so different than my relationship with Alex had been. Emil was mysterious and charming. When we touched, it ignited a different set of feelings than I'd ever had before. Kissing Emil was like having a close encounter with a lightning bolt—and I liked it.

When I got home, there was a message from Jasmine telling me to call my mom. Most of my recent communication with my parents had been by email, so I grabbed the phone and dialed the familiar Montana number. Mom picked up after three rings.

"Hi, Mom," I greeted her when she answered.

"Evie!" she sounded excited. "Hold on, let me take

care of this customer." My parents own one of the gas stations in White Sulphur Springs. She came back on the line. "I'm so glad to hear from you. How's everything going? How's school?"

"It's great," I answered. "My classes don't seem like they'll be too difficult. How are you and Dad?"

"Good. Things are busy at the station. Your dad is getting the motorcycles ready for the sand dune trip. Let me know if you can come, we would love to have you there."

"I'll see how classes are going next week," I said.

Mom went silent for a few seconds. I could guess what she was going to ask next. "How are things with Emil?" She seemed concerned. My mom had been incensed at Alex's sudden break up. I had talked with her about Alex frequently when we were together, and my mom had been thrilled I was happy. When Alex and I broke up, I was confused and depressed. My mom threatened to come down and take care of me several times, but Jasmine was able to convince her I was fine. Needless to say, both my parents were upset with Alex for how he'd left me and were leery about Emil, but they were also glad I seemed to be moving on.

"Jasmine's note said you needed to tell me something," I led.

"Oh, well the nicest guy came into the station the other day looking for you."

I had no idea who would be looking for me in White Sulphur Springs. "Who was it? Someone from high school?" I asked.

"No, not at all. He wasn't from around here."

"That's strange," I said. "What did he say?"

"He said he knew you from college. He said you'd mentioned where you grew up and that your parents owned a gas station there." Now it was really getting odd. I rarely mentioned my hometown to people, let alone my parents' occupation.

"Huh. I don't remember telling anyone about that, but I meet a lot of people," I rationalized. "Did he say what his name was?"

"Yes, he said it was Caleb."

"He didn't give a last name?" I was racking my mind trying to remember any Calebs I'd met at school. I couldn't think of one.

"No, but he was very nice," she said. "He had your dad fix a flat tire for him and asked me a bunch of questions about you while the tire was being worked on."

An uncomfortable feeling started to build in the pit of my stomach. "What kind of questions?" I asked.

"He wondered if you were enjoying school. I told him you really liked Western State and how it was close to the mountains. He asked if you lived in the dorms. I said you lived with your friend in a house near campus. Things like that."

The knot in my stomach was getting bigger. "He said he knew me from college?"

"Yes."

If he knew me from school, he would already know the answers to most of the questions he'd asked my mom. "Did he say Western State specifically?"

My mom paused as she thought. "Well, no, I guess he didn't. I assumed since he knew you and was talking about school . . ."

I didn't know who Caleb was or why he was looking for me, but he had now met my parents, knew where their business was, could easily find their house, and knew more about me than I wished he did. Another problem with living in a small town: everyone thinks they can trust everyone else.

"Mom, if he comes back, you need to tell me right

away," my voice was tense. "And, don't give him any more information about me, or you and Dad."

Now my mom was concerned. "Why, Evie? What's going on?"

"Nothing, it's just a precaution," I said. "I don't know anyone named Caleb, and don't remember mentioning so much about where I grew up to anyone. Plus, he never said he went to Western State. It seems shady to me."

The other line was silent for a moment. "I'm so sorry, sweetheart! I didn't even think about it. He seemed to know you so well!" Her voice was getting higher, which meant her anxiety level was surging. "Should I call the police chief and let him know what's going on?"

Most people call the cops when something goes wrong, not my mom—she goes straight to the Chief of Police. "No, I don't think so," I said. "If Caleb comes around again though, it might not be a bad idea."

"Okay," she said, worry still in her tone. "What if he tries to find you though?"

I thought for a minute, unsure of what I would do. "I'll call the police," I said. "What did he look like?"

She thought about it for a minute. "He had auburn hair that fell past his ears and he was probably close to six feet tall."

That description fit about half the guys on campus, but I didn't want my mom to be even more concerned than she already was. "It's probably nothing. If a stranger who looks like that tries to contact me, I'll call the police and it won't be a problem." I knew my mom was worried sick. "It's fine, Mom, really. I'm always paranoid. You know me."

"I know, but I want you to keep me updated if anything strange happens," she said in a concerned voice.

I was as alarmed as my mom, but didn't want

to make her any more upset than she already was, so I changed the subject. "Emil's been teaching me how to play pool."

"That's great, Evie! So the two of you are spending a lot of time together?"

"Yeah, pretty much every day," I said. "We play pool or hang out after classes. He's really nice."

"I'm glad you found someone who treats you well."

"Me too," I said. "We're going hiking tomorrow. I'm excited."

Through the phone, I heard the bell on the gas station door ring. "Evie, I have to take care of this customer, but I'll email you the details about the sand dune trip."

"Okay, I'll talk to you later. I love you."

"Love you too," she said. "Your dad says to remember to check your brake fluid." The car maintenance reminders from my dad were his way of telling me he loved me without actually saying it.

"I'll check it," I said. "Tell Dad I love him too."

"I will. Love you," she said as she hung up the phone.

I put the phone back on the receiver and kept going over the conversation about Caleb in my head. The more I thought about it, the more the worry grew. Too many peculiar things were happening lately. Aside from the figure I'd seen over the summer, there was the guy in the park with the web scar on his arm, and the man I saw in the store while I was with Jasmine that had the same scar. Now there was a strange man tracking down my parents to get information about me.

I wanted to talk to someone about it. To ask someone for help, but who would I ask? Other than Alex, there was no one to tell. Regardless of where things between us stood, I was pretty sure Alex would still be concerned about someone stalking me. But I felt like I couldn't call him . . . shouldn't call him. I had moved on. Maybe it was a mistake, but I decided I would handle it on my own.

Chapter 9

I had a restless night, dreams of black figures and stalking strangers haunting me. Since I couldn't really sleep, I got up early and showered, brushed my hair and teeth, and pulled on a white T-shirt and jeans. I grabbed my hiking bag, rifling through it to make sure I had everything I needed. As I searched, I noticed my GPS, the same one I had forgotten that day in June, the reason I had met Alex. The memory jolted me. I wondered if there would ever come a time when I would stop being reminded of him.

A light knock on the front door broke me from my thoughts and I grabbed my bag as I bounced down the stairs. I ran through the kitchen grabbing water bottles out of the fridge. I opened the door and Emil was standing there in washed out jeans, a dark blue T-shirt and a black hoodie. He was holding coffee and a muffin.

"Hey, sexy." Emil grinned as he handed the food to me.

"You're a lifesaver!" I said, dropping my bag next to the door. "I didn't sleep very well last night."

"I can't go a day without coffee," he said. "It's a

caramel latte with extra caramel. That's your favorite, right?"

My mouth curved, surprised. "I'm impressed you remembered." I had told him about my preference for sugary coffee during one of our pool games.

He looked straight at me. "I remember everything about you."

The statement seemed odd. He hadn't known me that long so there wasn't much to remember, but I shrugged it off and asked, "Where's your food?"

"I ate already," he answered. "I'll drive so you can eat on the way there."

"Sounds good to me."

Emil noticed my bag sitting next to the door. "Is that your hiking stuff?

"Yep," I said, taking a drink.

"Okay." Emil picked up my bag for me. "Let's go."

I took my keys off the side table next to the stairs and Emil held my muffin while I locked the front door. He threw my bag next to his own in the backseat of his BMW.

"Where are we hiking today?" he asked, starting the car.

"Treasure Falls. Do you know where that is?"

"On Route 160, right?" he asked as he backed out of the driveway.

"Yeah," I answered, surprised he knew the area so well when he'd just moved here.

Each time I thought about how close Gunnison was to such beautiful mountains, I appreciated the beauty of my surroundings even more. I ate my muffin and drank my coffee while Emil drove and an old U2 CD played on the stereo. Sitting next to Emil, I couldn't help but realize how natural it seemed. I had started this relationship thinking he would be a simple rebound guy, but he truly seemed to like me. It had only been a week, but maybe this would turn into a real relationship and Emil and I would have a future together.

We got to the parking lot for the falls and grabbed our packs out of the car. I breathed in the fresh, earthy scent as Emil and I strapped our packs on.

"After you," he said, holding his hand out like he was giving me the right-of-way.

Surrounded by trees, we followed the narrow hiking path with me leading the way. I ducked under branches and climbed over boulders that bisected the path. We hiked for a while in silence until Emil asked, "So, why didn't you sleep very well last night?"

I'd forgotten I told him about that. What crazy person remembers anything that early in the morning? I took a deep breath and answered, "I keep having these weird nightmares." I maneuvered around a large tree that had fallen on the trail. "I usually don't remember my dreams, but lately they've been more vivid."

"What do you think is causing them?" he asked.

There was no way I could answer Emil's question honestly without getting into an old boyfriend discussion. I knew it would happen sooner or later. Jasmine had already made mention of "Ass Alex." Emil had politely ignored the name, but maybe it was time to tell him why Alex was such a jerk.

I stopped and turned slowly. "Well . . . we haven't talked much about this, but I guess now is as good a time as any." I took a deep breath. "The dreams started when I met a guy over the summer. We dated, but broke up about a month ago."

Emil winced and was quiet for a few seconds. "I would say I'm sorry your ex was stupid enough to let you go, but I'm not, because now I have you."

I smiled, however the way he said 'I have you'

made it sound like he thought he owned me. I hate that attitude. I don't belong to anyone and no one belongs to me, regardless of how committed we are to each other.

We started hiking again. This time Emil walked next to me so it was easier to talk. "So," Emil said, "who was the idiot who gave you up?"

I fingered the straps on my backpack, wishing I hadn't brought the subject of past boyfriends up. "His name was Alex." For a brief moment, I saw a flash of recognition spread across Emil's face, as if I had confirmed something for him.

"So he's the 'Ass Alex' Jasmine talks about?" Emil asked.

"Yeah, he is." I cringed at hearing his name and the feelings that flooded through me because of it.

"Does it bother you to talk about him?" Emil asked, noticing my expression and reaching for my hand. His touch was reassuring, making it easier for me to continue the discussion.

"No, it's hard, but it's good," I said. "It helps me deal with the memories better."

Emil was thoughtful. "So why did you break up?"

I sighed. "I don't really know. He thought it was better for me not to be around him. I didn't understand, and he wouldn't give me a straight answer about it."

Emil snorted. "Giving you a straight answer would have been the least he could have done."

I nodded my head and softly said, "Yeah."

"Has he contacted you since he left in July?" Emil was being very curious considering we were talking about my ex-boyfriend. The same guy I was once madly in lust with and still thought about more often than I should. I wondered if Emil enjoyed being tortured. I was about to answer when I got the feeling that maybe I shouldn't say anything about Alex accosting me in the school parking lot and warning me about Emil. I gave an edited version of the truth. "He pretty much disappeared after we broke up," I said.

The news seemed to make Emil relax a bit. "Was it hard when he left?"

My grimace should have been all the answer he needed, but I told him anyway. "Harder than I thought it would be," I confessed, more to myself than Emil.

I thought Emil would be uncomfortable hearing my admission of feelings for another man, but instead, I saw an unfamiliar expression on Emil's face; anger. The anger seemed to rise from his neck, up his face, and burned in his eyes. I thought Emil was mad at me, with how I'd felt about Alex. Suddenly I felt very guilty. I tried to backtrack. "It's in the past now though and I'm dating you, so something good came out of the whole thing."

Emil looked away for a moment like he needed a second to gather his thoughts. When he turned back, his expression was calm and he smiled half-heartedly. "I'm glad you think so."

We came to a cliff overlooking a breathtaking waterfall. The water cascaded down the planes of rock in a massive stream until it fell over the edge, plummeting to the reservoir below leaving clouds of misty water in its wake.

As we watched the water, I realized my admissions about Alex could have hurt Emil. Causing him pain was the last thing I wanted. Out of morbid curiosity, and to change the subject, I decided to ask Emil about his past relationships instead. "I spilled about Alex, now it's your turn," I said. "Do you have any old girlfriends?"

The expression on Emil's face was puzzled, but he quickly smoothed it away. "I've had my heart broken," he admitted.

"I'm sorry," I said, putting my hand on his.

He gave a slight smile that held no humor. "Don't be, it was my own fault."

"What happened?" I asked.

We moved away from the waterfall and started walking back to the car. "We had different lives," he said, clearly thinking back to his past. "We wanted it to work, and we tried, but too many obstacles stood in the way."

I stopped, my eyes sympathetic. "That must have been difficult."

Emil gave me a steady gaze. "I'm sure you could imagine it."

We started walking again as I grabbed my water from my backpack and took a drink. "What about other girls?" I asked. "Have you had feelings for anyone else?"

Emil answered immediately, "No. Only the girl I told you about."

"What was her name?"

He glanced at me, his eyes drooping slightly in sadness. In a reverent voice he answered, "Cassandra."

I rolled the name over in my mind and wondered what this woman had done to affect Emil so completely. "Have you talked to her since she left?" I asked.

He paused. "I've tried to stay out of her life."

I was surprised. "If she's the one you want to be with, why don't you get her back?"

He hesitated again. "It's complicated."

I was starting to feel like maybe I hadn't been the only one looking for a rebound relationship and Emil wasn't that serious about me. "If you're sincere, if your love is constant, nothing can stand in the way." I was adamant at first, then unsure why I was encouraging him to leave me and find his true love.

Emil studied the ground before meeting my eyes. "It would be nice if that were true."

I thought about what he'd said and as we walked I

was getting agitated. I realized I really *was* Emil's rebound relationship. After gathering my thoughts, I decided to test Emil's reaction. "So I'm your spare tire?" I playfully scoffed. "You're keeping me around, until the girl you really love decides to come back?" I nodded my head. "That's good to know."

Emil was stunned. "Is that what you think?"

He surprise shocked me. "Isn't that what you said?" I could tell I'd struck a nerve.

"You are *not* my . . . 'spare tire,'" he winced as he repeated the term. "You're worth a hell of a lot more than that to me."

I kept walking, not wanting to say anything to upset him again; obviously past relationships were a touchy subject.

"You don't have anything to say?" Emil asked.

"Not really," I answered as calmly as possible. "As interested as I am in the *real* love of your life, I think I'll just keep my opinion on the subject to myself."

Emil looked like he was biting his tongue but didn't respond. I noticed that he didn't try to correct me when I mentioned his real true love. In one short morning, I had jumped from thinking I could have a future with Emil, to realizing he was in love with someone else. I now knew that at any moment the woman Emil was in love with could be back in his life—and I would be out of it.

When we got back in the car, U2's song, "I Still Haven't Found What I'm Looking For" began playing. How appropriate, I thought. I enjoyed my time with Emil, but today's revelations about his emotional status made me leery. Emil attempted to keep things bright on the way home. I tried to play along, but the thought of both of us still having feelings for other people was in the back of my mind, even though I hadn't actually told Emil I still cared about Alex. When we got to my house, Emil walked me to the door.

"Thanks for hiking with me," he said.

"No problem, thanks for coming along." I gave an unconvincing smile. The outing with Emil had made my mind more muddled instead of clearing it like I'd hoped.

As usual, Emil leaned in to kiss me good-bye. I was surprised and wondered if he really wasn't aware of how distant I was being? The kiss lacked feeling—I was distracted, and he seemed to be also. When the short kiss ended, Emil said, "I hope I didn't make you mad today."

"No," I said. "It was good to find out more about you." It wasn't a complete lie.

Emil searched my face, looking for what I really meant, but I was careful to make sure the answer wasn't there. "I'll talk to you tomorrow," he said.

I nodded, and walked in the house, shutting and locking the doors. I was alone and couldn't stop thinking about Emil's true love as I dragged my bag up the stairs, threw my clothes into the laundry basket, and got in the shower. I let the water rush over me and steam fill the air, hoping it would help me clear my mind and make sense of how I was feeling.

If I thought there was a chance Emil and I could forget our past relationships and move on together, I would do it in a second. Emil was a good guy who treated me well. Aside from everything else, there was no denying the connection we had. I had wanted to make it work, but after today, I realized that probably wasn't possible.

Obviously, Emil was in love with someone else. And the more I thought about it, the more I realized I still had feelings for Alex and needed to deal with them.

I didn't know the best course of action to take. On one hand, I really liked spending time with Emil and didn't want to give that up, but he was emotionally unavailable, and so was I. Maybe that was a good thing, though? Maybe that would be the reason a friendship with benefits could work. If we both had feelings for other people, we didn't have to worry about hurting each other.

I got out of the shower and put on some pajama pants and a T-shirt. I grabbed my copy of *Gone With The Wind* from my bookshelf and started reading at one of my favorite parts. The last thing I remembered was Rhett and Scarlett arguing, reminding me of the men in my life. I drifted off into sleep, images of Alex and Emil clouding my dreams.

Chapter 10

The next morning I was in the middle of curling my hair when the phone rang. I walked to my room and answered, "Hello?"

"Hi, sexy," I recognized Emil's voice on the other end. Considering what happened on our hiking trip, I wasn't sure how to react.

"Hi." My voice was indifferent, but he didn't seem to notice, or ignored it if he did.

"How'd you sleep?"

"Good. I slept in this morning, it was nice."

"What are you doing this afternoon?" he asked.

"Just some homework," I answered. "Why?"

"I'd like to see you," he said. "I was thinking about going to a movie. Do you want to come?"

I did have homework, but it was only light reading and research for papers I was working on. I wasn't sure about seeing Emil, but decided that aside from the minor issue of us both having unresolved feelings for other people, there was no reason we shouldn't spend time together. "A movie would be good, what time does it start?"

"Three-thirty," he answered. "I'll pick you up around three."

"Okay. I'll see you soon." As I hung up the phone I wondered if spending time with Emil would be awkward now. The tone of our relationship had changed yesterday—for me at least.

I knew I was being hypocritical, given that every day, I secretly hoped Alex would show up on my front porch professing his feelings for me and giving me a full explanation. I knew his appearance in the college parking lot was probably as close as I would ever come to that fantasy. That day I had still been so furious I hadn't even wanted to talk to him. Even then, he wasn't asking me to be with him—he was asking me not to be with Emil. I sighed, thinking of what might have been with Alex.

I made a cheese sandwich and took it back to the table. I pulled my books from my bag and was engrossed in reading when I heard a knock. I glanced at the clock and realized it was later than I thought. I left my books on the table, and got up to open the door.

Emil's jeans hung low on his hips, a black t-shirt snug over his chest. One corner of his mouth curved up. "Hey, are you ready to go?" he asked.

"Not quite, I lost track of time." I pushed the screen door open and Emil walked inside. "I need to change clothes. I'll be right back," I yelled as I ran up the steps to my room. I quickly pulled on dark blue jeans, a white T-shirt, and sandals.

Emil whistled as I came down the stairs. "Damn, you're hot." I smiled, but it was more of a courtesy than an acknowledgement of his compliment. I grabbed my purse and keys from the side table and followed Emil out of the house. He held the screen door open while I locked the deadbolt. He rested his hand lightly on my back while we walked to his BMW.

Once we were on the way to the theater, Emil glanced over at me, concern in his eyes. "What's wrong, Evie?" I wondered how long it had taken him to realize the change in my mood. Had he been ignoring it since yesterday afternoon, or hoping it was something that would go away?

"Nothing," I answered in typical girl-speak.

His face was indignant. "Don't do that," he said. "You're not the type of girl who's afraid to speak her mind. Don't start holding back now."

I looked out the car window, silent.

"If you don't want to tell me what's going on, that's fine . . . as long as it doesn't have anything to do with me."

I raised my eyebrows. "Even if there is something wrong, what makes you think it involves you?"

He took a deep breath. "When I picked you up yesterday morning you couldn't wait to spend the day with me, but by yesterday afternoon, you acted like I had mono."

"How observant of you," I said, folding my arms across my chest.

"So your mood *is* because of me." The statement was not a question.

"I didn't say that," I answered. "I said you were oddly perceptive for being a guy."

Though he was trying not to show it, I could tell Emil was getting aggravated. He was silent as he found a parking spot and shut the car off. He turned his head toward me and looked me square in the eyes. "You *will* tell me what's bothering you at some point today." It was a command, not a question—and I don't handle commands well.

I opened the car door instead of answering. I heard Emil heave an exasperated sigh. I waited for him to get out of the car, and walked beside him into the theater. I wasn't sure why I was so upset with him. I had no reason to be jealous of Cassandra. I'd never met her, and I had feelings for someone else myself. The situation shouldn't have bothered me so much.

As I was thinking, Emil bought my movie ticket. I said I would get the popcorn since he got the tickets. After standing in line for our butter-soaked snack and drinks, we walked into the theater, sitting down about seven rows from the back wall. The movie wasn't a new release and it was the middle of the day on a Saturday, so the theater was relatively bare. Aside from a few people sitting in front and to the side of us, no one else was there.

We only had to wait a few minutes for the movie previews to start and I was grateful I wouldn't be having another discussion about my mood with Emil until after the movie. I had no idea what I should say to him. *I didn't understand how I was feeling, so how was I supposed to explain it to him?*

Halfway through the movie, I heard someone come into the theater. They must have sat behind us because I didn't see anyone walk up either aisle, and didn't hear the theater door open again. After the standard ninety minutes, the movie ended and the few people in front of us began filing out of the theater.

"Are you ready to go?" Emil asked, picking up his empty cup and some napkins. He was trying to pretend nothing was wrong.

"Yeah," I said, putting my trash in the popcorn bucket so I could throw it away. Everyone sitting in front of us had left and we were alone in the theater. I stood, and Emil followed me. As we walked toward the door, I saw someone step into the aisle from a shadow on our right. I gasped and froze. My thoughts immediately turned to the strangers with the red web scars on their arms.

I twisted to look for another exit and find out how far behind me Emil was. As I did, I saw Emil, still and staring straight ahead at the man in the aisle, his eyes on fire and his face fuming. The man in the aisle—still in shadow—turned his head toward me, then back to Emil, and started walking slowly forward. Emil did the same.

As the man got closer, he walked into the beam of one of the theater lights and my breath caught in my throat. I didn't know whether to be relieved, happy, or angry. I decided on a combination of all three. I was glad he wasn't one of my stalkers, and happy I got the chance to see him, but angry because he had followed Emil and me to the theater and I didn't know why.

Alex and Emil stopped within a few feet of each other, glaring. I was standing slightly behind Emil, watching and worried. Alex gave me a quick glance, his emerald eyes bright even in the low lights of the theater. His face was apologetic as he said, "I'm sorry, Evie. I know you told me to leave you alone, but this time, I can't."

I looked at Alex, confused, and saw the rage intensifying on Emil's face. I wasn't sure what was happening, but one thing was clear: Alex and Emil knew each other. I had no idea how, but their shared look of hatred made it evident. The conversation I had that day with Alex in the parking lot came flooding back to me. The questions Alex posed to me about Emil and the possibilities of him being dangerous, it couldn't be true, could it? Confusion was erupting as my eyes tracked from one guy to the other.

Alex and Emil stared each other down until Alex spoke. "It wasn't enough to hurt her with your lies once, now you have to do it again?" Alex's teeth were clenched, the question accusatory.

Emil glowered and shot back, "Like you didn't

leave her in shambles. How could you claim to love her, yet stand back and watch as she went through that kind of pain? Don't act so noble. You know you're the reason she came to me. To *me*, Night, *she* wanted *me*." Emil's entire countenance changed, even his voice. Everything about him became darker.

Alex fisted his hands. "She didn't come to you, Stone," he said, almost spitting the name. "You manipulated her. You're an expert at that."

Emil's eyes narrowed. "You have no idea what you're talking about. Make *no* mistake that *you* are the one who made her so vulnerable."

Alex seemed resigned and angry. "I know what my lapse in judgment caused, that's why I'm here now. You already know this, but I feel the need to make myself clear. I am watching."

Emil laughed dryly. "Of course you are." He inclined his head. "What were you thinking? Your relationship made the bond stronger and easier to track."

Alex gave Emil a pointed look, nodding toward me as if to say they weren't alone. I stood, watching, the confusion painted across my face.

"I didn't say I made the right decision, I said I'm going to make sure no more repercussions occur because of it." Alex's voice resounded in warning.

"I think it's a little late for trying to make amends in this situation," Emil said.

Alex stepped forward and in a low, threatening whisper I could barely hear, he said, "Make no mistake, Stone. If you hurt Evie, I *will* kill you."

Emil gave a hostile smile. "*I* wouldn't hurt her, and killing me is quite a threat considering the penalty for you."

Alex's eyes were ominous and cold as he told Emil through gritted teeth, "It's a sentence I'm more than willing to risk. I don't know what you're trying to do, but I will find out."

Emil scowled as Alex turned to me, his face pleading. "Evie, I'll take you home if you want me to."

I wasn't sure what I wanted. I didn't even know what had just happened. Before I could say anything, Emil answered for me, "She's been fine without you for weeks, she'll be fine now."

"She was never without me, and my question was for Evie, not you," Alex growled.

"I think Evie would argue about your presence in her life." Emil turned toward me. "She is *my* girlfriend. *I* will take her home."

Alex looked at me. "Is that what you want, Evie?" he asked.

I glanced at Alex, then Emil, both of their faces hard, waiting for my response. "Emil can take me home." I wanted to spend time with Alex, but thought I might have a better chance of getting answers about what was going on if I went with Emil.

Alex's face fell and Emil gave him a cruel smirk. "I guess you don't mean as much to her as you thought you did."

I wanted to protest, but I couldn't get the words to leave my mouth. Alex glanced at me again, pain in his eyes, and I tried to convey on my face what I couldn't say. Alex walked away, leaving me stunned and Emil still upset. Once he was gone Emil turned to me, frustrated. "Are you ready?" His voice was short and still dark. I didn't know if I wanted to go home with him given his current mood, but I nodded my head and followed Emil out of the theater to his BMW.

By the time we got in the car, I had regained some of my senses and wanted an explanation. I put my seatbelt on, laced my hands together, and stared at Emil. He put the key in the ignition and started the car. He pulled out of the parking lot, never meeting my inquiring gaze.

I thought he would say something, but we drove to my house in silence. We pulled into the driveway and Emil turned the car off. He gazed down before looking over to see my infuriated face. He took a deep breath and said, "Your ex-boyfriend is going to be a nuisance."

That was it? That was all he was going to say after everything Alex and Emil had said to each other? He wasn't even going to tell me how he knew Alex? There was no way he was getting out of this without giving me more details. "What the hell was that all about?" I asked, my voice much louder than normal, but not quite a yell.

Emil looked blankly out the window as if he hadn't heard me. "Nothing really. An old rivalry."

I was irritated and doubtful. "How do you know Alex?"

Emil gave me a strange, mischievous grin. "You could say we're part of competing fraternities."

I was confused. "Alex isn't in college anymore."

Emil laughed softly. "He certainly isn't."

"What did I have to do with your conversation?" I asked.

"It doesn't matter, Evie."

I was becoming more and more irate. "I just watched my current and ex-boyfriend almost get into a fist fight. You can sure as hell bet it matters. *Tell* me what you were talking about!" Emil was silent and I was mad. "So you aren't going to say anything?" I asked.

Emil draped his wrist over the steering wheel. "It's nothing you need to know right now."

My anger was growing into full-on rage. I decided I needed to leave or I'd say something I shouldn't. I opened the door. "My relationship with Alex ended because he couldn't be honest with me. When you decide you want to tell me what's going on, call me."

Emil didn't look at me as he responded in a sharp voice, "That's quite a demand from the girl who wouldn't tell me why she was pissed off earlier."

I was fuming. If he wanted a fight, he was going to get one, and I didn't care how hurt he was by it. "You want to know why I was mad?" My voice was low and callous. "Yesterday you informed me that you're still in love with another girl. I don't know why you're in a relationship with me when I'm obviously not what you want and you're just waiting for someone else to take you back." I watched as his face turned from dark to shocked. "Since you're having such a difficult time expressing your emotions to me today, let me make this easy for you. I refuse to be your second choice. We're done." I grabbed my purse from my lap and got out of the car, slamming the door shut.

I could see Emil's still stunned face through the windshield and I walked with authority to my front door. I expected Emil to get out of the car and try to stop me, but he didn't. I unlocked the door, walked inside, and locked it behind me. I was surprisingly calm considering I had just broken up with another boyfriend.

I put my purse down and walked aimlessly around the house, trying to get my mind off the theater and the demise of Evie and Emil. I finally settled on the couch playing the argument back in my mind. That wasn't how I intended our relationship conversation to go. During the movie I had planned it out, ending with something like, I want to be your friend, but think we both need to work through some things. Now, I wasn't sure I even wanted Emil's friendship. The way he had looked at Alex was dark, almost evil. I didn't ever want Emil to look at me that way.

I must have fallen asleep while my mind tried to

muddle through everything that had happened, because I woke to a knock on the door. I knew it would be Emil, trying to talk to me or change my mind. Maybe I'd over-reacted by ending our relationship, but I didn't want to deal with the drama right now. I let the knocking continue hoping that he would get the hint and go away. After ten minutes though, the knocking didn't stop and I decided it would be easier to answer it.

I dragged myself to the door and unlocked it. I braced myself for confronting Emil and threw open the door to find—Alex.

Chapter 11

My face registered the shock as Alex's gaze looked me over, assessing my demeanor. "Evie, are you okay?" He didn't seem to think I should be.

I nodded.

Alex looked at me intently. "Can I come in?"

I nodded again, suspicion in my gaze. I wasn't sure what he wanted, or why he was here. He walked to the couch and sat down as I shut the door and stood by a chair in the corner.

"Don't you want to sit down?" he motioned to the chair next to me.

"I'm fine," I said with more confidence than I felt. "What are you doing here, Alex?"

He waited a moment, choosing his words. "After the . . . altercation, at the theater, I wanted to make sure you were all right."

He looked up at me and I held his eyes. "What happened back there?" I sincerely hoped *someone* would finally give me an answer.

Alex exhaled an exasperated breath. "Evie, when

you started spending time with Emil I told you to be careful. He is more than he seems."

"What the hell is that supposed to mean?" I asked. I was upset and weary with the less-than-informative answers I was receiving from everyone.

"He doesn't have your best interest at heart," Alex answered.

I threw my arms in the air. "I'm sick of everyone always being so cryptic!"

Alex was quiet for a moment. "I'm aware it's frustrating for you."

"You have no idea!" I fumed. I was past the point of understanding and being nice. At that moment, all the rage I had when Alex left, the unanswered questions, flooded back to me.

Alex sighed, his expression tight. "If we're going to do this, you need to sit down." I eyed him warily as he motioned toward the chair next to the couch. I eventually sat. When Alex seemed satisfied I wasn't going to move, he said, "Evie, you have more history than you think you do." I stared at him. "I know you better than you realize."

This wasn't making any more sense than the things Alex had already told me. "What are you talking about?" I asked. "One month of dating doesn't make you an Evie expert." I was bothered that he was acting like he knew me better than I knew myself.

He seemed saddened at the mention of our past relationship. He forced the frown from his face, got up, walked toward me, and leaned forward until I could feel his breath tingling on my cheek as he whispered, "There are things you haven't thought of in *centuries*."

I waited for the joke, then realized he was serious. Apparently our break up had turned him into a raving lunatic. I should probably be flattered. "Really Alex, you don't have to act like an immature kid. It's fine if you want to see me again, but next time, just say so instead of making up asinine stories."

Alex looked exasperated. "I am *trying* to help. Emil is not who you think he is." I wrinkled my brow in suspicion, but Alex continued anyway, "He is *extremely* dangerous."

"Yeah. You've mentioned that before," I said. "What you didn't tell me was how you know he's dangerous, and why should I trust you?"

"I know because . . ." he drew his lips back, clearly debating whether to continue, "because I've seen things."

A short laugh burst from my mouth. Great. My insane ex-boyfriend was having visions now too. Maybe we could discuss the dream-like things I'd seen and compare notes.

My disbelief didn't seem to sway him. "I wanted to wait to tell you all this," he said. "I didn't want you to have to deal with it, at least, not so soon. And I still can't tell you everything."

"Deal with what?" I said through my teeth. I wanted to scream.

"That day I saw the man in the park . . . the one with the red web mark on his arm," he paused to see if I remembered. I nodded. "The web is a scar that indicates the man belongs to a group Emil is associated with. I knew the man's presence here might mean Emil was going to show up soon, but we haven't had a problem with Emil's . . . group for several years, so I hoped I was wrong. Emil showed up a few weeks ago. He didn't waste any time letting you know of his interest in you. I knew he had been sent to find you." Alex's face was almost tragic as he explained.

I tilted my head and thinned my eyes. I was pretty sure Alex had gone nuts. "You're losing your mind. Groups, delusions, and visions—you need a good psychiatrist and some drugs." I was pissed off and continued, "For clarification purposes: you think that because a new guy at school paid attention to me, the apocalypse is about to take place?" I was seething, mad at Alex, Emil—and the whole situation.

Alex rolled his eyes. "Don't overreact. You know I didn't mean it like that. I'm saying Emil has ulterior motives."

I leaned back in my chair, lacing my hands over my stomach. I gave him a calculating look. "All right. Say I believe your crazy story. You said you've seen things, so what exactly have you seen?"

He shook his head. "I can't answer that."

I pursed my lips and gave a knowing nod of my head. "Of course you can't."

"I *can* tell you that your safety is extremely important. If Emil knows I'm in your life and we're talking again, he'll be more careful. I can't watch you from a distance anymore. I need to spend more time with you." He said it like spending time with me was the last thing he wanted to do.

I put my hands up in front me defensively. "Don't do me any favors, Alex." He winced at my tone. "I don't understand what you want," I said. "You seem to be an expert at appearing when you think some sort of crisis is happening. You left me because you said it wasn't safe. Now you're telling me you have to be with me because it isn't safe. Which is it?"

Alex pushed his lips into a thin line. "I already answered this question. I had to leave because I'm your soul mate."

I laughed out loud. "Yeah, I remember that excuse. It doesn't make any more sense now."

"Just because it doesn't make sense, doesn't mean it's not true." Alex cocked his head to the side as he pegged me with a hard stare. "There's a lot you can deny, Evie, but our connection isn't one of those things."

"Listen, buddy," I said, pointing. "Just because we have," I waved my hands in the air trying to come up with a better word than 'feelings', "*hormones* for each other, doesn't mean we're soul mates." I paused, then added, "I've had *hormones* for a lot of guys."

He lifted a shoulder, his eyes sparkling. "If this was only hormones, it would be pretty easy to take care of the problem. Obviously, it's more than simple lust." His lips slid into a confident smile. "And while you might have had feelings for other *boys*, they'll never compare to me. Those *boys* are dalliances. I'm your other half."

I shook my head, completely stunned. "You're out of your freaking mind is what you are." I raised my eyes to the ceiling hoping for some answers, they weren't there. "Great," I mumbled. "Of all the guys on the planet, I've got the one who believes in soul mates stalking me. Regardless of what you seem to think, your soul mate rationalization still doesn't answer why you left."

Alex cringed. "I wasn't expecting our connection to be so strong that fast, Evie. I had to leave and get— counsel. But I told you, I was never really gone. I was stupid to think I could have a relationship with you and still keep you safe. My actions were irresponsible at best. Our physical relationship made it dangerous for me to be around you; so it will have to be managed—and I'm working on that. However, given other things that are happening right now, it's even more perilous for me to leave you alone."

I watched him closely. "Why should I believe you? You aren't giving me solid answers and the stuff you are saying is making you sound more insane."

He clenched his teeth, staring at me. "I know it's hard to believe, but I'm telling you the truth." His look turned calculating and in that moment, he seemed to decide something. "I can prove it."

I met his eyes, wondering what he could possibly say to convince me. "How?"

Alex reached out and caressed my hand. As he did, the lily shaped birthmark on my back got warm like it had every other time we had touched or kissed. "Do you feel that?" Alex asked.

I narrowed my eyes and gave him a barely perceptible nod. "You have a mark on your back, it resembles a lily. When we first met, the mark got darker. Now each time we touch, you notice the mark because it gets warm." My mouth fell open. He couldn't have known that. He had never seen me without my shirt and I hadn't told anyone about the strange sensations the mark had been causing, or the fact that over the last few months, the mark had slowly started deepening in color—it was now dark pink.

"How do you know that?" I asked.

He moved his hand away from mine. "Because everyone has one. They are soulmarks—a mark that travels with your soul into each new body your soul inhabits. Some people's soulmarks are more obvious than others. Most people explain them away as birthmarks, if they even notice them."

"What are they for?" I asked.

"They usually serve two purposes. They are a means of identification for a soul, and they also serve as a kind of matchmaker. When you first meet your soul mate, the mark gets darker. Once you have physical contact with the person, the mark becomes warm each time you touch and the color deepens. The heat and color intensifies depending on how intimate you become; that intimacy causes a bond to form between you and your soul mate. Some people are more sensitive to it than others."

I inclined my head wondering if he was joking. "Are you trying to tell me you truly think you're my soul mate?" I asked.

Alex gave me a conspiratorial half-smile. "Your soulmark seems to think so."

I thinned my eyes and asked, "What does *your* soulmark think?"

Alex grinned and didn't answer.

Aggravated, I shook my head. "Well, if a soulmark only recognizes its one true soul mate, my soulmark is defective. I noticed the same feeling from my *soulmark* when both you *and* Emil touched me."

From the hard set of Alex's jaw I knew he wasn't happy about my soulmark recognizing Emil. "Unfortunately, it's not defective. Though most people's soulmarks only recognize one other soul, yours seems to recognize two." He looked away for a moment and seemed to be gathering his thoughts. When he turned back to me, he said, "But that's not something we need to deal with right now."

I gave him a sidelong glance. "So if what you're saying is true, both you and Emil could be my soul mate?"

Alex bit his bottom lip, thinking. "I suppose *anything* is possible," he answered with annoyance. "Do you believe me now?"

I still wasn't convinced, but there were too many things Alex knew about for me to completely disregard him. I waited for a minute, thinking. Alex kept watching, never taking his eyes off me. I wanted to know what it was that made Emil so dangerous and who the men were who seemed to be following me. I wanted more answers, and I realized I had something Alex wanted. If he felt the need to be in my life and wanted me to co-operate, maybe we could reach a compromise.

"Okay," I said, playing along. "Since it seems

you've appointed yourself my personal bodyguard, how do you propose we go about ensuring my safety?"

He smiled a little, assuming he'd won a personal victory and I might be willing to acquiesce to his warnings. I smiled back, thinking of the deal he was going to have to make in order to get what he wanted.

"The biggest problem is the time you're spending with Emil. I'll try to shadow you as much as possible—like I started doing when Emil first arrived. But Emil isn't the only person I have to be aware of. I need you to tell me when you're going to be with him in case I'm not already there. And you're going to have to un-do your break up and fix your relationship with him."

I stared at Alex, open-mouthed. There was no way he could have known about the break up. It had barely happened—Jasmine didn't even know about it! "How did you know we broke up?"

Alex shrugged. "Lucky guess."

I narrowed my eyes as a knot started growing in my stomach. "No. It wasn't a guess. Just like you knowing about the lemonade I dumped on Luke's head wasn't a coincidence. Tell me how you knew."

Alex pinched his nose between his thumb and forefinger and sighed. "Of all the things you need to be worried about right now, that's not one of them."

"I can't think of anything else more important," I said, the knot getting bigger. "You're freaking me out. There's no way you could have known about the break up."

Alex's expression reflected a concern I didn't understand. "Someday I'll tell you all my secrets, Evie, but for now, we need to concentrate on your safety. You have to get back together with him."

I was still trying to figure out how he knew about what happened with Emil and almost didn't hear him.

When I realized he really meant what he said, I was mad. "No way!" I yelled.

"Listen to me," Alex said in a calm tone. "You don't have a choice."

I gave a staccato-like laugh. "Yes, I do. I choose not to date Emil. See how simple that was? I thought you of all people would be happy since you're the one who told me to stay away from him."

Alex ran his hand through his hair and surveyed the carpet. "I would have been happy about it a week ago, but now the two of you being separated is a problem."

"Are you going to explain that, or tell me it's better that I don't know?" I asked.

He looked at me reproachfully. "You kissed him and let him into your life without even knowing his name. Now, he has the advantage of knowing you, your friends, and anything else you've told him about during the past week. I already explained that he's dangerous. While you were together, there was a chance he wouldn't do anything stupid because so many people knew you were dating. By breaking up, you aren't connected any-more. Now he has no reason *not* to hurt you."

I gave him a doubtful look, but remembered the man who had been watching me in the store, and the guy who got information about me from my mom in Mon-tana. "I didn't tell you this before, but people have been watching me." I don't scare easily, but the realization that Alex might not be completely crazy and I could really be in danger made a shiver run up my back and down my arms.

Alex's eyes flashed to me. "What? How do you know?"

"There was a guy in a store at the end of August. I was waiting for Jasmine to try on clothes and he was watching me. He had a red web mark on his arm like the man in the park."

Alex's eyes became dark and hard, he was angry. "This is important, Evie. Was there anyone else?"

My voice shook slightly as I answered, "A guy named Caleb stopped at my mom and dad's gas station in Montana and told them he met me at college. My mom thought he was a friend and told him all about me, but I'd never heard of him."

Alex got up and slammed his fist against the wall, shaking the photos. "Dammit! I should have known they would go to any extent to find you."

"My parents said they'll notify the police if he comes back, so at least they'll be safe."

Alex kept his back to me. "It's not your parents I'm worried about, though I'm glad you told me in case they try to use your family to get to you."

"Who *are* these people?" I asked. "What do they want from me? What does Emil want?"

Alex walked back to the couch and sat across from me. He put his elbows on his knees, leaning his body closer to mine. "They want to use you, Evie, but I won't let that happen."

I measured him and had the overwhelming feeling that he really would protect me. "How much danger are we talking about?" I asked carefully. "What could they—Emil—do to me?"

Alex locked eyes with me. "They—he—could kill you. But that's not what they want you for. They think you can help them and they'd do anything to use your talents."

"What talents?" I asked.

Alex responded with a frown and shake of his head. "I can't tell you that either."

I sat motionless while Alex stared blankly into the kitchen. Fear was competing fiercely with my anger. I took several deep breaths as I tried to gather all the facts in my mind, becoming more alarmed as they came together. "Let me make sure I understand," I said. "You're telling me Emil, the guy I've been dating, is dangerous?"

Alex nodded, still looking in the direction of the kitchen table.

"That there's a group of people Emil is involved with who are following me, searching for me, putting people I love in jeopardy as well as myself?"

Alex nodded again.

"And you're saying that now, since I'm already dating Emil, or was until a few hours ago, I need to get back together with him?"

Alex's worry was evident by the deepening creases in his forehead.

"Are you insane?" I yelled.

Alex was resigned. "It's our best chance. He knows where you are. If you cut Emil out of your life now, it's more incentive for him to put his plan into motion immediately."

I stood in a huff and started pacing around the living and dining room. "If I get back together with him, then what?" I asked, frustrated. "Am I supposed to pretend nothing happened, and not worry about all the stuff you just told me?"

A groove formed between Alex's eyebrows as he thought. "I don't see any other way . . . unless you want to leave the country. But even that probably isn't safe enough at this point. There are groups like Emil's all over the world."

I considered that with a combination of confusion and worry. "I'll never be able to act like myself around Emil. He'll know something is going on."

Alex shrugged. "You're going to have to become a good actress."

I rubbed my arms like a sudden chill had descended on the room. I thought about the situation for several minutes. "If I do this," I said. "If I get back together with him, do you *promise* me that I won't get hurt?"

"Absolutely," Alex answered immediately, his voice confident. "Like I said, Emil isn't the only one I have to be aware of right now, but as long as I know when you're spending time with him, you will *never* have to worry."

"How can you guarantee that?" I asked.

"There are ways I can make sure you're safe, Evie." I opened my mouth to ask what he was talking about but he held up his hand. "I can't tell you how—at least, not yet. I hate to ask you to do this again, but please, please trust me. You'll have nothing to fear."

I sunk back into the chair. My face fell at the thought of going back to my relationship with Emil when I had Alex, sitting in front of me. If Alex said I was safer with Emil than without him though, I would listen to what he told me. I hadn't forgotten the last time I didn't, or the dark figure outside the kitchen window that haunted my dreams.

"So I'm just supposed to stay with Emil forever?" I asked.

A muscle worked in Alex's jaw. "No. But it will help if you're with him for the immediate future—until I can figure out what to do."

I frowned and quietly asked, "What if Emil isn't the person I want to be with?"

Alex looked at me steadily, a glimmer and question in his eyes. "Who else is there?"

I glanced down, not wanting to delve into the details of my one-sided infatuation for him. Instead of answering I said, "I don't know how I feel about this soul mate stuff, or what you've said about Emil, but I can't deny that there are things you've been right about.

Because of that, I'm going to err on the side of caution and do what you say, but just so you know, I still think there's a fifty-fifty chance you're certifiable."

He flashed a smug smile. "Only fifty percent now? Well then, my odds are improving."

I glared at Alex. "In exchange for my cooperation, you have to do some things for me." I hadn't forgotten the compromise I wanted Alex to agree to.

He regarded me with puzzled amusement. "And what would those things be?"

"I want some honest answers," I said, crossing my legs and sitting up straight. "What is it that you've seen? Why *exactly* did you leave me? How do you know Emil is dangerous?" I paused. When I continued, my voice was softer, almost a whisper, "Was this whole thing worth losing me?" I searched his face as I asked, hoping for an indication he still felt something for me.

He looked deep into my eyes. "I promise you, I will answer those questions, but not today. Those explanations will take some time and . . . understanding. We need to wait until we can talk it all through."

"I don't see any reason why we can't talk thoroughly now."

Alex sighed. "I think you've had enough to deal with for one night."

I wasn't happy about the response, but at least I knew answers were coming. I could live with that. "As long as you agree to answer my questions sooner rather than later."

"It will be sooner, I hope," he said, but his smile was unconvincing.

Alex left, giving me the assignment to get back together with Emil as soon as possible. I had no idea how I was going to accomplish that. I was still furious with him for the way he treated me and now I was scared of him too. I didn't claim to be a good actress and knew this wouldn't be easy. I flicked my fingernails against each other as I thought about what to do.

Even once we were back together, how was I supposed to pretend I had feelings for Emil when I was thinking about someone else? At least I hadn't told Emil about my feelings for Alex. I imagined that knowledge would be like waving a red flag in front of a bull.

I chewed on my lip as I thought about it, pacing the room. Emil, my sexy, potentially dangerous boyfriend. It seemed like the best course of action was to concentrate on the sexy bit, and pretend I didn't know about the dangerous part. At the same time though, I'd never had a bad feeling about Emil. He was attentive, caring, and seemed like he really wanted to make me happy. Alex's revelations had made me question that. I wondered if I was making a snap judgment based on fear—and that wasn't like me. The more I thought about it, the more I wanted to talk to Emil and give him a chance to explain his actions. Now that I knew Alex's reasons for distrusting Emil, I'd be more aware around him, but I wasn't going to follow Alex blindly and do what he said. Alex thought I'd be safer if Emil and I were in a relationship again, but I was going to make that decision on my own, not because Alex told me to. I would wait to decide until I'd talked to Emil. As I was going over the options in my head, I heard my cell phone chime notifying me I had a voicemail. The message was from Emil.

"Evie, I want to talk to you . . . about yesterday, about today, about everything. Call me."

At least he sounded like himself again, and he still

wanted to see me, which was a good sign. Maybe getting back together with Emil wouldn't be as difficult as I thought.

I woke up tired. Erratic dreams about a gang of men and dark floating figures had caused me to toss and turn again all night. After getting Emil's voicemail, I decided I needed to give myself a night to think about things before calling him.

Once I showered and got dressed, I went downstairs and picked up my phone. Emil answered on the first ring.

"Evie?" His voice seemed anxious, scattered.

"Hi."

"Evie, I'm sorry for everything that happened yesterday."

"Yeah, it was a rough afternoon."

"I want to talk to you," his voice took on a worried tone. "What are you doing today? Can I come over?"

I hesitated, thinking of Alex's warnings, but shook it off. "Yeah, you can come over. I want to talk to you too."

Emil seemed relieved. "I'll be there in ten minutes."

"Okay, I'll see you soon." I ended the call and put my face in my hands wondering what I was getting myself into. I texted Alex to let him know Emil was on his way.

I opened one of my psych books and started reading, but I couldn't comprehend anything that was written. I was re-reading one paragraph for the tenth time when I heard a knock on the door and got up to answer it.

Emil stood on the other side, bags under his eyes, his hair disheveled. I'd never seen him look so unkempt. He actually seemed depressed. I motioned for him to come in. When he did, I shut the door and he followed me to the couches. He sat down and I sat across from him on the overstuffed chair.

His expression seemed unsure. "Thanks for seeing me," he said. "I know my behavior yesterday was inexcusable and I want to apologize for it."

I crossed my legs in the chair. "What was going on?" I asked, pretending like Alex hadn't been sitting in the same living room last night telling me Emil was a bad guy.

"I snapped when I saw Alex at the theater," he explained. "There's no justification for it, I shouldn't have done that, especially not with you there."

I watched his face steadily for signs that he might not be telling me the truth. "What do you mean?" I asked. "What do I have to do with it?"

Emil ran his fingers through his hair. "Alex and I don't get along and I shouldn't have put you in the middle. The last thing I ever want is to hurt you, Evie."

I asked the question I hadn't gotten a detailed answer to yesterday, "How do you know each other?"

Emil scrubbed his hands over his face. "We met when we were younger. We didn't get along then. We don't get along now."

"Did you do something to him that would make him think you were dangerous?" I asked.

Emil gave a dry laugh. "Do I seem dangerous?"

"No," I said, noting that he answered my question with another question. "But at the theater, Alex seemed pretty convinced I shouldn't be around you." I didn't add in all the information Alex had told me last night.

Emil shook his head. "Alex has his own

opinions. What matters is how you feel. Do *you* think I'm dangerous?"

I assessed him for a long minute, thinking over what Alex had said and taking my own feelings into account. Alex had the tendency to overreact and he seemed to think I was incapable of taking care of myself. However, I'd always had good instincts and when it came to Emil, I didn't feel threatened. I wasn't discounting what Alex had said, but I wasn't going to let fear dictate my choices either. From here on out, I'd get both sides of the story. It didn't mean I was completely comfortable with Emil and I still had a lot of questions, but I had plenty of time to get those answers. Emil met my eyes with an unwavering gaze and I made my decision.

"No," I said with resolve. "I don't."

Emil's shoulders were bunched up, like he was waiting for the other shoe to drop. "That's good," he said slowly.

I put my hands in my lap and met his eyes. "I had no idea Alex was going to be at the theater. I'm sure it was a surprise for you to see him since he and I used to be together."

Emil's face fell like I'd punched him. "Yeah, it wasn't easy," he agreed.

I took a deep breath. "Well, I'm sure it won't happen again. Next time you won't have a problem telling me what's going on," I reasoned.

His face registered shock. "Next time?" he questioned.

I tried to act like it was obvious. "Yeah, next time. You apologized, I accept. Did you think we were going to break up because of a stupid fight over my ex-boyfriend?" I said the words, knowing how confusing they must sound, especially after how I had reacted yesterday when my main reason for breaking up with Emil had been that he was in love with someone else.

The surprise on Emil's face didn't subside. "I didn't know what you wanted. After you got out of the car. . . and the things you said, then you didn't return my phone call last night. I thought I would have to grovel for a few days at least."

I laughed. "I'm not that kind of girl," I assured him. "I don't like drama any more than guys do."

Emil grinned. "That's one of the many reasons I like you."

I smiled back and we sat in silence for a couple of minutes. I could tell Emil still wanted to say something, but he seemed to be having a difficult time putting it into words.

"Evie," he finally said. "There's something else I want to talk to you about."

Emil got up and came over to the chair I was sitting in. He knelt down in front of it so he was gazing up at me, his hands on the arms of the chair making me feel like I was captured—which, considering what Alex had told me, made me a little uneasy.

"You mentioned something yesterday that I want to . . . clarify. I don't know how to go about this and was up all night trying to figure it out. I'm not sure it makes any more sense now, but here goes. You said I told you I was in love with someone else, but I'm not. That's not what I meant. Cassandra was a part of my past, but our time together ended. The only person I want, the only person I *love*, is you."

My mouth dropped in shock. After our huge fight yesterday, after everything Alex had warned me about, Emil had said he loved me. And we'd only known each other a week. How was I supposed to respond to that? Emil was acting as crazy as Alex. I'm sure my expression once again betrayed me and Emil knew how I was feeling. When I didn't answer, Emil reached for my hand and kept talking.

"I don't think I explained my feelings very well when we were on the hike. I want to make it clear. I've fallen for you, Evie. When I thought I'd lost you last night, I felt like I was going to lose my mind. I've been waiting my whole life to be with you, and don't ever want to let you go. I need you. Even more than that, I love you."

I was completely stunned. After a few seconds, I broke the silence with a soft voice, "I . . . I don't know what to say."

His expression was full of compassion. "You don't have to say anything. I know it's a lot to take in. I just needed to tell you."

I nodded my head. "Thank you," I whispered.

Emil leaned forward and kissed my cheek. "No, thank you for listening to me. For giving me another chance."

I smiled as I noticed the dark circles under his eyes and wondered if he had slept at all. "You should go to bed, you look really tired."

"I am," he agreed. "I didn't sleep. I was too worried about you. About us."

"Well, now you don't have to worry about that," I said.

He rubbed his eyes. "I don't want to leave you."

I didn't want him to think I was trying to get rid of him, but it had been a long weekend and I needed some time alone. I made a split-second decision. My parents were going to the sand dunes in a few days. I needed to get away and think through everything. The camping trip was the perfect excuse. "I know, but I have a ton of homework to catch up on before I leave," I said.

Emil was confused. "Leave? Where are you going?"

"On vacation with my parents. We take a camping

trip to Idaho every year. I meant to tell you about it earlier, but I forgot."

He seemed bothered. "How long will you be gone?" he asked.

I hadn't thought that far ahead and made a quick decision. "I leave early Thursday morning and come back on Sunday." I said.

"Won't you get behind in your classes?" he asked.

I thought about it for a minute since I hadn't considered homework five seconds ago when I decided to go on the trip. "No, I only have two classes on Thursday and it's still early in the semester. Most of my assignments are reading and essays, but I'll take my laptop with me and work while I'm there," I said.

His face fell. "Will I see you before you leave?"

"I'm not sure," I said. "I'll let you know if I have time to get together."

His expression didn't change. "All right."

I smiled. "Go home and get some rest."

"Thanks." His lips shifted slightly in a tired smile and he leaned in to give me a light kiss. Despite everything Alex had told me, even a short kiss with Emil still made the connection between us surge.

"I'll call you when I get back," I promised.

He stood and walked to the front door. "It will be a long week without you," he sighed.

"I feel the same way," I said. "I'll see you soon."

I watched the door shut, locking it behind him. I leaned my body against the wood and took several deep breaths. All in all, the whole thing had gone better than anticipated and I was looking forward to leaving for a while and clearing my head. I picked up the phone and let my mom know I would be joining her and my dad camping this week.

Chapter 12

"How long will you be gone?" Jasmine asked. I was packing for my last minute trip. I had told Jasmine about the movie theater incident and my break up and reconciliation with Emil. I conveniently left out Alex's crazy talk. When I thought about it, it was no wonder I needed to get away.

"I'll be back on Sunday," I answered. I grabbed a stack of shirts and pants and put them in my suitcase. Earlier in the day I had changed the oil in my Mustang, checked the transmission and brake fluid, and filled the radiator to make sure the car was ready for the long trip to Idaho.

"I still can't believe Alex showed up," Jas said, watching me pack. "And what was Emil thinking telling you he was in love with someone else before turning around and saying he was in love with you?"

I lifted my shoulders as if to say I didn't know, but really, I had more pressing questions on my mind—like how did Alex know so much more about what was happening in my life than I did? What were Emil's real intentions? And most importantly, should I trust either one of them?

Jasmine glanced at the clock. "Crap, I'm going to be late for my human anatomy class, we're examining a cadaver today."

I wrinkled my nose. "Yuck. Have fun."

Jasmine smiled and left my room. I could hear her rummaging through her bag and soon after, she yelled, "Bye, have fun at the dunes! I'll see you when you get back." I heard the door close behind her.

I mentally tabulated everything I needed, knowing I would forget something. I was packing my hairbrush and makeup when I heard a knock on the door. I thought it was probably Jasmine; she had a habit of forgetting things at the house—including her keys. I ran down the stairs. When I opened the door, Alex had both hands on either side of the door frame and was staring at me, his eyes glowing brilliant green. He was gorgeous, but his expression was reproving. "Were you going to tell me about your vacation plans?"

I widened my eyes in fake surprise. "Oh, look! One of my soul mates is here."

"Not funny, Evie." Alex said. "Why didn't you tell me you were planning on leaving?"

I stood in the doorway and heaved a sigh wondering how long I'd have to involve Alex in every aspect of my life. "I'm going camping at the sand dunes in Idaho with my parents," I said. "I wasn't aware I needed to send out a news release."

He rolled his eyes and walked, uninvited, through the door. "Given the current situation, it would be an advantage to know where you are," he said, sauntering by me. "You know, just in case you'd like to continue being alive."

I shrugged, still not certain if the threat Alex was talking about even existed. Emil seemed head-over-heels in love with me when he came over to apologize. "Well, now you know where I'm going, so it's not a problem." I thought about that for a minute. "How did you know I was leaving anyway?" He flashed me a patronizing look over his shoulder that seemed to indicate I should already know the answer to that question. "Oh wait, probably the same way you knew about my break up with Emil, and the lemonade in my glass instead of Sprite. Am I right?"

He smirked. "You texted me before Emil came over. I was outside and heard your whole conversation. Why aren't you still keeping your windows closed?"

I was annoyed at his eavesdropping. "If you wanted me to continue keeping my windows closed, maybe you should have stuck around to give me further instructions over the summer."

His face fell and for a second I regretted saying something that hurt his feelings. "There are a lot of things I should have done differently," he offered as he sat on the couch and I followed, debating whether to sit next to him or not. Unfortunately, my cynicism hadn't affected my hormones; but since the feeling didn't seem mutual, I sat on the other end of the couch, leaving a cushion between us.

We were silent until he asked, "When are you planning to leave?"

"Tonight, well, early in the morning. The drive is better when it's not as hot outside," I said, remembering how much he didn't like my Mustang or its lack of air conditioning.

"Well, you won't have to worry about that. We'll take the Audi."

I bunched my eyebrows, confused. "What are you talking about?"

He leaned back into the couch and stretched his legs out on the floor in front of him. "I'm certainly not riding in your classic sauna for twelve hours all the way to Idaho," he scoffed.

I started to laugh. "What? You think you're coming with me?" My laughing became more hysterical.

Now it was Alex's turn to look confused. "Of course I am. You can't possibly think I'd let you go alone when you're being followed?"

I stopped laughing, realizing he was serious. "Oh no!" I said, waving my hands in front of me, shaking my head. "You are *not* coming on my family vacation."

"Yes. I am."

I laughed again. "You have got to be kidding." I stared at him, my mouth half open. Alex was giving me a no-nonsense look and I could tell he wasn't about to change his mind. I'd have to change it for him. "Listen— my dad doesn't have a gun, but if you set one foot near their motor home, he will find one for my mom so she can shoot you. I don't need my mom being charged with murder on top of everything else that's going on."

Alex wrinkled his brow, perplexed. "Your mom always seemed to like me when I spoke with her on the phone."

I looked at him with huge eyes, wondering how dense he was. "Yeah, when we were dating; *before* you left. Now she thinks you're the jerk who broke her only child's heart." There was no point in mincing words about it now.

Alex cringed and didn't say anything, but his expression shifted to determined again. "I can see how that would be a problem, but I think I can handle it. I'm pretty charming."

I snorted. "You obviously don't know my dad. Aside from the attempted murder, how am I supposed to explain to them why I brought you, instead of my *real* boyfriend, Emil? I'm pretty sure they'll think that's a little strange."

He thought about my points. I felt pretty confident I'd won the argument and could continue packing in peace, but he said, "We'll have to deal with those things when we get there. You *aren't* going alone."

That made me mad. I was *not* going to be told what to do. "Alex, I'm getting in my car tonight and I'm driving. By tomorrow afternoon, I'll be riding my four-wheeler, getting sand in my ears, and not thinking about you or Emil. I'm going alone, even if I have to tie you up and leave you in the basement of your mansion to make that happen."

Alex's expression was hard. "Fine. If that's what you want, I won't stop you, but you realize the danger you're putting yourself in?"

I raised my brow and put my hands out in front of me. "Actually, I don't. You haven't given me any details. If the people chasing me want to track me to Idaho, fantastic. Maybe they'll get some potatoes and a nice vacation out of it."

Alex gritted his teeth. "You are not grasping the reality of this situation, *Evangeline*. You need to be more concerned with your mortality than you are."

I lifted my shoulders, unconcerned. "If you want to give me some details, *Alexander*," I said his name with the same condescending tone he had used to say mine, "I would be more than happy to listen to your argument, but until you're willing to offer some specifics, you aren't coming with me."

He was angry and didn't respond. I took that as his answer. "Okay," I smiled, "I'll see you next week."

The irritation didn't leave his face as he got up and walked to the door. I followed him. He turned as he walked out, a devious smile flitting across his lips. "Have a good trip," he said.

"Don't worry about me, I'll be fine," I assured him. "I'll see you soon."

He mumbled something I couldn't understand as he walked away.

I left for Idaho late Wednesday night. I plugged in my iPod, singing along with Coldplay and Green Day while I tried to muddle through everything that was going on with Alex and Emil. The music and my thoughts kept me occupied during the drive and I got to the freeway exit for the St. Anthony sand dunes at eleven in the morning. As I turned onto the road that wound into the Egin Lakes campground where my parents were staying, I had an overwhelming sense of relief at the thought of being able to relax with people who loved me. I drove around the campground until I found my parents' motor home and enclosed cargo trailer that they use for hauling their four-wheelers, dune buggy, and my dad's motorcycle.

Some people think you aren't really camping unless it involves a tent, sleeping bag, the ground, and several bug bites. I've never been one of those people. I'm perfectly happy in my parent's thirty-five foot motor home complete with a microwave, TV, DVD player, bed, running water, bathroom, and heating and air conditioning. I like camping as much as the next person, but I don't see any reason to suffer for it.

As I got out of my car, I leaned against the door for a minute, taking the time to breathe in the rustic scent of sand, mixed with gas and motor oil. I smiled as I looked around at eleven thousand acres of yellow and gold sand cresting in every direction. In some spots, the dunes looked like they could kiss the clouds. Even with the noise of motorcycles, four-wheelers, and dune buggies, the sand dunes were still more peaceful than any other place I'd ever been. Most of my big life decisions had been made at the dunes. I felt like I could think here better than anywhere else.

I locked the car and started to get my bags from the trunk. The motor home had been leveled and the jacks set. The awning, folding chairs, Dutch ovens and all the other camping supplies were already out. I was getting the last few things from my trunk when I heard my mom yell, "Evie!"

I smiled, happy to hear her familiar voice and know that I was in a place where I at least felt safe, even if Alex said I wasn't. I ran to her and she opened her arms, hugging me tightly. When she let me go, I said, "I've missed you!"

"I've missed you more." She smiled and gave me another quick hug. "I'm glad you came."

My dad came around the corner. He smiled when he saw me. "How's the car?"

"Good. I haven't had any problems with it."

He nodded. "I'll look everything over for you while you're here."

"Thanks, Dad."

He took my bags and carried them into the motor home while my mom took my hand and guided me to the chairs under the awning. "I'm so glad you decided to come! You're sure you won't miss anything important at school?"

"Not this week. I brought my laptop so I could work on some essays and I have some reading to do, but that's all."

"Good. We're really happy you're here!"

"Me too," I said, leaning back in the chair. "I really

needed this."

Her expression turned to concern. "Is something wrong?"

I thought about what I should say. I'm in love with my maybe crazy ex-boyfriend who thinks he's my soul mate and insists on staying in my life to protect me from my current boyfriend who may or may not be dangerous. And I don't know if I can trust either one of them. Nothing wrong, nothing at all. I sighed instead. "Stuff with guys, you know. I was glad for the break."

"Oh, sweetie, is there anything I can do to help?" she asked. "Do you want to talk about it?"

I cringed, knowing there wasn't anything I could say without my mom thinking I'd lost my mind. "Not right now, maybe later though."

I knew I would probably have to talk to her about guys sometime during the trip, so if that happened, I could tell her about Emil saying he was still in love with another girl on the hike. On the way to the dunes I had thought about Emil and decided I still had questions about his feelings.

"Okay," my mom said as she patted me on the leg.

"How are things at home?" I asked, changing the subject.

"They're good. A few more of your friends are getting married; I brought the invitations for you." All of my friends seemed like they were in a race to get hitched. It was like they didn't realize they were only eighteen and would actually have to live with the person they were marrying for a good sixty years. My mom knew my opinion on the subject and continued, "The guy who stopped by the station looking for you never came back. No one around town saw him either. We let everyone know to be on the lookout." Only in a small town was that even possible. I wouldn't be surprised if my mom drew a sketch and posted it on the grocery store bulletin board.

I was relieved to hear he hadn't been back though. I hoped my parents would be safe. "That's good, it was probably a coincidence or something," I lied.

I didn't think she believed me, but she wanted to, which is what mattered. "Have you eaten lunch yet?" she asked.

"Not yet," I answered.

She smiled and jumped up. "I brought all your favorite foods. What do you want?"

My mom's life revolved around helping other people. It was one of the things that made me love her, but it also made me feel like I was taking advantage of her. "You don't have to make me anything, I can get it."

She frowned. "I never get to cook for you anymore, I'm going to make you lunch."

I nodded. "Okay, a sandwich is fine, I'm not too hungry."

She smiled, happy to be my personal chef. "That's good. We're having Dutch oven pizzas for dinner."

I laughed to myself, realizing she probably made the menu for the whole trip based on my favorite foods. She was the best mom. She disappeared into the motor home, re-emerging ten minutes later with a ham and cheese sandwich and my dad. My mom asked about Jasmine, Zach, and my classes as I ate. I was tired after the long trip and curled up in one of the lounge chairs under the motor home awning and fell asleep. I woke up an hour later and stretched my arms and legs. My dad noticed I was up and asked if I wanted to go for a ride with him. I couldn't wait to get on the four-wheeler and grabbed my helmet and gloves from the motor home. I waved to my mom and yelled, "We'll be back."

I walked to the side of the trailer where the black Yamaha Banshee four-wheeler, custom-built yellow dune buggy, and my dad's red Honda CR-500 motorcycle were resting. I was glad my parents had the extra four-wheeler and dune buggy that I could use when I came on trips with them.

I put my helmet on and started the four-wheeler; my dad did the same, kick-starting his motorcycle. The machines screamed to life. My dad took off and I followed him to the entrance of the riding area of the dunes. We sped quickly over small bumps in the sand that resembled ski jump moguls. The bumps were created when the water level rose in the lake and expanded to the riding area of the dunes. I crouched above my seat as I drove over the bumps so I wouldn't be thrown from the Banshee as the four-wheeler went up and down over the sand.

We drove toward the west end of the dunes. My dad rode in front of me to find the best routes for the four-wheeler. On a motorcycle, my dad can go anywhere, but the Banshee is wider and harder to navigate over steep and sloping dunes. As I followed him, I couldn't help but think about how much I enjoy riding with my dad. We don't have a lot in common, but Mustangs and motorcycles give us something to bond over. After an hour of riding, we stopped at the top of a dune across from Chokecherry Hill, a massive mountain of sand, peaking at over five-hundred feet, the tallest dune at St. Anthony.

At least thirty people were riding on the dune. The dune was so high that the riders resembled bugs scrambling across the sand. Several other riders were stationed at the bottom of the hill, watching people attempt to go up the dune. My dad zoomed to the top of Chokecherry Hill. I followed him a few times before parking at the bottom and watching as he flew past guys half his age to the top.

I took my helmet and gloves off and sat on the

Banshee to watch my dad and other guys try to beat each other to the top of the dune. There were a few other girls there, but it was clear they were more interested in flirting than riding. I felt my cell vibrate in my pocket and pulled it out. I had a new text message. I touched the screen to read it.

I didn't c you b4 u left. I miss u. Emil.

I smiled and thought it was sweet he was thinking of me. I knew my dad would be riding for a while and decided that to keep up with the relationship charade, I should call Emil.

The phone rang three times.

"Evie!" he answered, sounding a little surprised. "How are you?"

"Good," I said. The sound of the motorcycle and dune buggy engines almost drowning out my voice.

"Where are you?" he asked. "I can't hear you very well."

"Sorry, I'm at the sand dunes," I shouted back. Making a phone call right next to the busiest dune in the park probably wasn't the best idea, but it gave me the chance to reassure him about our relationship.

"What? Where?" Emil asked again.

"The St. Anthony sand dunes in Idaho." The noise died down a bit as one of the louder four-wheelers left the area and zoomed up Chokecherry.

"Oh, how are things? Have you been there long?" he asked.

"I got here a few hours ago. I'm out riding with my dad."

"That sounds fun," he seemed like he was trying to be enthusiastic. "So you'll be there a few more days?"

"Yeah, until Sunday" I answered. "I got your text. How are things in Gunnison?"

"Same as usual," he said. "It would be better if you

were here."

I smiled in spite of myself. He was really trying to make sure I knew he cared about me. "I won't be gone long," I promised, trying to say it in a way that would indicate I missed him too.

There was a lull in the conversation as a few of the four-wheelers sitting next to me roared to life and I could barely hear anything. "It's pretty noisy, I should go," I said.

He said something I couldn't decipher because of the noise, so instead I yelled, "I'll see you soon! Bye." And ended the call.

I watched my dad fly up the mountain and jump. It was fun to see all the younger guys with newer motor-cycles nervous to take the jumps my dad was making. They were more reckless, but it seemed experience was winning out over stupidity. When my dad finished rid-ing, we left to go back to camp.

We got to the motor home at about four in the after-noon. I pulled up next to the trailer and took off my hel-met and gloves. I heard my mom talking; it sounded like she was on the phone. I walked around to the front of the motor home and noticed someone sitting under the awning with her, their back toward me. My mom looked up at me, anxious. I wrinkled my brow wondering what the problem was. It was probably someone visiting from a neighboring camp.

"Evie! You're back!" she said with marked enthusi-asm. "You have a visitor." Her eyebrows went up, mak-ing a sharp crease in her forehead as she inclined her head toward the person in the chair across from her.

I should have recognized him before I even saw his face, but the large camping chair obstructed my view. He turned slightly, the sun glinting off his dark hair, emerald eyes glittering. I was furious.

"Hi, Evie," he said, trying to be charming as he flashed a broad grin. I had no doubt that charm was the only reason my mom had allowed him to stay at camp once she found out who he was. As far as my parents knew, Alex hadn't been in my life since we broke up.

My voice was low and angry, my eyes squinted into a furious line. Through my teeth I asked, "Alex, What. Are. You. Doing. Here?"

His mouth curved in a knowing smile as he recognized my tone. "I had a friend driving this way and remembered you told me you'd be camping at St. Anthony and I should stop by to see you and meet your parents."

I had to bite my tongue not to yell out, "Liar!" and a few other choice words. I continued to glower at him, an expression that was not lost on my mom. "Fine. This is my mom, Karen." My dad walked around the corner as if on cue, still in his intimidating black leather pants, heavy black boots, and a red Thor riding shirt. He was carrying his red and black helmet. "And my dad, Denys." My dad assessed us, trying to figure out what was going on.

"Dad, this is Alex Night." At the mention of Alex's name, my dad's face settled into hard lines. Alex stood and reached out his hand toward my dad. "It's nice to finally meet you, sir."

My dad shook Alex's hand with a tight grip, but Alex didn't flinch. "I've heard a lot about you," my dad said, his voice guarded.

"Likewise," Alex smiled. "Evie has the most popular car in Gunnison because of your help." I knew Alex well enough to know that wasn't a compliment, but it made my dad's mood lighten a bit, and he released Alex's hand.

"Did Evie invite you here?" my dad asked.

"Yeah," Alex lied. "She mentioned where she was

going and said I should come by if I had time."

My dad's expression held the same concern my mom had shown when I first arrived back at camp. He addressed Alex again. "You can stay, but only if Evie wants you here."

I sighed. "It's fine, Dad. Thanks."

I could take care of myself, but knew my parents were aware of exactly who Alex was and what he had put me through. They were trying to protect me, but if I wanted Alex to stay, they would respect my decision and try to get to know him. That didn't make the atmosphere any less awkward though. My dad watched us with a disapproving look and my mom tried to make conversation. "Have you been riding before, Alex?"

"Not at these dunes," Alex answered.

"But you know how to ride?" my dad asked.

"Yeah," he said, "I have some experience." He smiled, turned, and *winked* at me! My mouth fell open at his blatant disregard for my anger.

"You could take a ride with Evie," my mom suggested. My dad shot her a warning look. My mom noticed and added, "If Evie wants to, I mean." I'm sure she was thinking a ride would be a good way for Alex and me to be alone and talk.

Alex grinned. "I'd like that. It would be nice to explore a little. I noticed a sign that said Egin Lakes and people driving by in swimsuits."

"The lake isn't far from camp," my mom piped up.

I nodded, still hostile. "That's right, Alex, do you want to jump in it? I can show you where the deepest spot is, I can even drag you there behind the four-wheeler."

Alex gave me his trademark sarcastic smile, my mom looked at me reproachfully, and my dad grinned, amused. "I know you're an expert at finding the deepest part of the water," Alex taunted. "I bet a lot of people like to drive their four-wheelers through the lake."

I knew where he was going with this and gave him a warning look. I hadn't explained my mountain lake buoy experience to my parents.

"Is that where you got the idea from?" Alex asked.

"What idea?" my dad wondered, still suspicious of Alex.

"Evie didn't tell you about our adventure at the lake?" Alex asked, acting confused. My parents didn't hold back their interest. "We went riding in the mountains one afternoon in June. Evie drove out in the middle of a lake, but the water was higher than she anticipated. The engine died and she got stuck."

My dad, the traitor, started to laugh. I glared at him. "Dad!"

"What?" he said innocently. "You should've learned your lesson the first time you did it."

"The first time?" Alex asked, interested. The day in the mountains, I had mentioned to Alex that it wasn't the first time I'd been stuck in a lake. He was just using the story as a way to bond with my parents.

My dad smiled. "Yeah, Evie got stuck in the middle of the lake here a few years ago. She didn't want to get her shoes wet, or deal with the bugs in the water, so she sat there, feet up on the seat, waiting for help."

Now Alex and my mom were laughing too. I was embarrassed and aggravated. "Ha ha ha. I drove through that same spot a couple of weeks earlier without a problem. I didn't know the water level would change so much; at least when it happened in the mountains, I knew how to fix it."

"I bet that mountain lake was cold when you had to get off and push the four-wheeler back to shore," my dad teased.

I spoke before Alex could. "I didn't have to push

the four-wheeler." My dad's eyebrows shot up in curiosity. "Alex didn't follow me into the water because he thought it was too deep. He had a rope and tied it on my four-wheeler. He pulled me back in when the engine died." My dad was impressed, making me even more bothered. "He's a real hero," I said, sarcastically. "My shoes were totally safe this time."

"Good thing you were there, Alex," my dad said. "Who knows how long she would have been in the middle of the lake if she'd been alone."

I shot my dad a look that could have killed, but having received the look hundreds of times over eighteen years, he had grown immune to it. I turned to Alex. "Want to take that ride now?" I walked into the motor home to grab the dune buggy keys.

My dad gave Alex a cautious glance. "She's not someone you want to make mad," I heard him tell Alex as I came down the steps.

"I've learned that lesson too." Alex grinned and followed me.

Once we were on the other side of the motor home and alone, I asked in a hushed voice, "Where's your car and when are you leaving?"

His eyes glittered. "I told you, Evie, I had a friend drop me off. I'm not leaving. Your mom invited me to stay and use the spare tent."

Holy treason! I mumbled a string of profanities under my breath. My mother and her ludicrous manners. She always insisted on bringing the tent in case anyone showed up and needed to borrow it. Her vigilance had finally paid off.

"I hope you get eaten by a snake," I sneered.

His smile lingered and he shrugged. "I don't have a problem with snakes."

I threw a jacket at him, hitting him in the stomach.

"How long were you talking to my mom?" If she'd offered him a place to stay, he must have been there a while.

"I don't know, an hour maybe."

I realized that he had come up with his cunning little plan before I even left Gunnison. He probably followed me here and when I left with my dad, Alex used the opportunity to talk to my mom. This knowledge only made me more upset. "And how did you manipulate her into thinking you weren't the devil?"

He lifted a shoulder innocently in a kind of half-shrug and hitched one corner of his mouth. "I didn't get the impression she thought I was evil at all. She seemed to like me quite a bit."

"She doesn't," I countered. "She's just being nice. Let's go."

I got in the driver's seat of the dune buggy. Alex climbed in the passenger side. I grabbed the headphones off the top of the dune buggy and gave a pair to Alex. The headphones would allow us to hear each other over the dune buggy engine in case we needed to talk on the ride. I knew exactly where to take him. As soon as we got to the secluded little lake in the middle of the dunes where it was quiet, Alex and I were going to have a long talk, and I was going to get some answers. I felt I had been more than patient. If he was going to ruin my vacation, solid answers were the least he could give me. If he didn't . . . I hoped he could doggy-paddle.

Chapter 13

We didn't talk during the ten-minute ride to the water. The tiny blue lake was sometimes deep, other times shallow, and occasionally even disappeared depending on the amount of rain the area had. The lake was hardly noticed by most people as they zoomed by it on their way to bigger dunes. The private location was ideal for what better be a very informative discussion.

I pulled up on a flat area near the lakeshore and cut the engine. I unstrapped my seat harness, took off my headphones, and pulled myself out of the dune buggy. The combination of hot sand and water made the air smell a lot like the beach. I walked to a swath of dry sand near the shore. Alex followed me and sat down a couple of feet away.

We didn't say anything at first, instead staring at the mountains of sand that towered in every direction. After about five minutes, I broke the silence. "Do you want to tell me how you found me when I explicitly told you not to come?"

"I followed you," he admitted without remorse. My

face flushed hot with anger. Alex was quick to note my reaction. "You don't understand—it's my job. I couldn't be sure you were safe unless I was here."

"Your *job*?" My question was laced with outrage. "Who appointed you my keeper?" Alex was quiet but I decided it was about time for him to enlighten me. "Listen Alex, I've trusted you since June, but I need to know what's going on. If the people chasing me are dangerous enough to potentially follow me through three states and put my family in danger, I need specifics. You said you'd give me the answers I wanted when you had time to explain. We have plenty of that, so start talking."

Alex sighed, clearly less than willing to share information with me. I turned away from him, listening to the engines of motorcycles race across the dunes. It had been silent for so long that I jumped when I heard him speak. "I'm not sure how to begin," he said. "I know you'll think it sounds crazy, but bear with me."

I didn't believe anything could be more insane than the things I had already seen and experienced, but his preface made me even more curious.

"The people looking for you are part of a group committed to finding people in love and killing half of the couple," he stalled to gage my expression. "These are not your average murderers. They're powerful, Evie." The ire in his voice was thick.

I considered him, unwilling to believe what he was saying, trying to take it in. This is what he started with? I hoped this was the worst of it and he'd been giving me the bad news first. Without being totally aware of it, I shuddered. I asked the question that seemed to be the most obvious. "What would they possibly want with me?"

Alex took a deep breath. "You are an anomaly, Evie." His brow knit together as he attempted to clarify himself. He turned toward me. "What do you know about the concept of eternity?"

Eternity? What? I didn't understand how this would explain why a bunch of psychopaths were looking for me. "It means forever, that things don't end after you die."

Alex moved closer to me, never taking his eyes from mine. "What if your eternity doesn't start when you die?" he asked carefully. "What if your eternity has been going on since before you were born?"

I stared at him with a blank face, wondering what drugs he was on.

"Do you remember when I told you I've seen things?" he asked. I gave a reluctant nod. "That gift comes from the institute I belong to, the Amaranthine Society. I'm one of their Protectors. The things I know about," he explained slowly, "are things that have happened in your *past* lives." He watched me closely, searching my face for a reaction.

I sat unmoving, trying to grasp what he had said. "Like reincarnation?" I said it mostly as a question to myself.

Alex answered, "Kind of, though it's a bit different from the definition of reincarnation you're probably familiar with." He continued to stare so hard I felt like his eyes could knock me over, even though I was sitting down.

"What's different about it?" I asked, confused.

"Most people believe reincarnation is directly linked to your actions in your previous life. They think that the life you're currently living is a tool for you to learn something and grow. For example, if you did something in a previous life, like abusing someone, you may come back in your next life as an abuse victim. It's a way for your soul to mature.

"While that aspect of reincarnation is a part of the belief system of the Amaranthine, there is another, much stronger facet to it. Love," he said, still watching me closely. "Reincarnation is a means for finding your soul mate. Souls spend hundreds, even thousands of years living and dying in search of their one true love. The Amaranthine Society works to ensure that everyone has the opportunity, the best chance possible, of finding their soul mate and being together forever."

I had so many questions I didn't know where to start, but Alex took a breath and continued.

"In addition to the Amaranthine Society, there are others who belong to a sinister organization, the Daevos Resistance." He looked at me pointedly. "Emil is one of those people."

I inhaled a sharp breath. Alex had said Emil was dangerous, now it seemed I'd finally get an explanation why. "The members of the Daevos are committed to exterminating souls, leaving a person's soul mate to wander eternally without their other half. Every soul has the choice to become good or evil, but finding your soul mate makes you happy and balances your emotions so you're less apt to choose a negative path. By targeting soul mates and taking half a person's soul, the remaining soul mate is much more likely to join the ranks of the Daevos Resistance. The goal of the Daevos is to bring as many souls into the Resistance as possible, and grow their army.

"While the Daevos have the power to take souls, they don't have the power to sense the bond that indicates people are soul mates. For that, they need a Tracker. Some Trackers join the Daevos willingly, but most are abducted and forced to help them. When the Daevos Resistance was organized, the Amaranthine took on the responsibility of protecting Trackers. Dealing with the

Daevos is a time-consuming process, but it's not usually difficult. Daevos Resistance members have a knack for evasion, but other than that, the Amaranthine Society holds all the powers."

He pulled his knees up and rested his arms on them as he studied the dune on the other side of the water. "Remember when I told you about soulmarks?"

I nodded.

"Your soulmark is a little different. While it still acts as a marker for your soul and reacts to your soul mate, your soulmark is a variation of the trinity knot, which represents life, death, and rebirth. It's the mark of a Tracker, and it stays the same through each of your incarnations."

I absently reached behind me and rubbed the lily on my back.

"Trackers have the ability to locate any bond. They can find soul mate bonds, but they can also track the bond between a Protector and Tracker. They're invaluable to the Daevos Resistance for both reasons."

"What do you mean?" I asked. "Why do Protectors and Trackers need a bond?"

"Because Trackers are like any other soul. They live and die through many incarnations. Once the Amaranthine Society knows a soul is a Tracker, the Tracker is assigned a Protector. The Protector and Tracker form a bond that allows the Protector to follow that soul through each incarnation."

"What about when the Protector dies?" I asked.

"The lifespan of a Protector isn't the same as a normal human," he explained. "I mentioned that my society has many powers, one of them is that I live for a very long time. Once we're assured a Protector is no longer needed for a soul, we have a choice: become human again, or be assigned another case."

"So you never get older?" I asked.

"Not while we're Protectors. When we reach the age of twenty-one, we stop aging. If we ever choose to leave the society, the aging process starts again."

"So, how old are you really?" I wondered, but an even more pressing question came to mind, "Wait! How old am I?"

Alex lifted his eyes and he watched the surface of the lake. "I've been your Protector for two hundred and fifty years, but I imagine your soul is much older than that. I don't know what happened in the lives you had before I became your Protector."

I tried to do the calculations in my head. I'd never been very good at math. When I realized how old Alex actually was and how long he'd been protecting me, I stuttered, "You're at least two hundred and seventy years old!"

He cringed. "Two hundred and seventy one, actually."

The number was too difficult to wrap my head around. "You don't *seem* that old."

He smiled and cocked his head to the side. "We adapt for each new life cycle. We don't want to draw unnecessary attention to ourselves."

I thought for a moment, but everything was so new and hard to grasp. It seemed Alex had another revelation for me every time he spoke. "Is the lifespan of Daevos members similar to the Amaranthine?

He nodded. "They stop aging at twenty-one also."

"Can Daevos members be killed?"

Alex picked up a small red and white shell that was lying next to him on the sand and rubbed it absently. "They can be, but souls are given many lives to redeem themselves. Some souls eventually become so evil that their souls are taken in the same way that Daevos members take souls. Their memories are stripped and they are sent to the Nothing where they spend eternity unable to retain any of their memories. It's a horrible death. The Amaranthine are forbidden from taking a soul without orders."

I stretched my legs out in front of me and rubbed my hands down my thighs as I took a deep breath. "Okay," I said, turning my head toward him, "say I decide to believe all this. How does it work? The reincarnation I mean? I'm not the same person every time I come back. I can't be, can I?"

"Your physical appearance changes with each incarnation, but your personality is similar," he answered. "You aren't exactly the same, but you keep a lot of the same characteristics."

"Huh," I said, wondering what aspects of myself had traveled with me through time.

"Trust me," Alex said. "You were just as stubborn, opinionated, and outspoken two hundred and fifty years ago as you are now. It constantly amazed me no one tried to behead you."

I fought the urge to stick my tongue out at him. Though, truthfully, it gave me a strange satisfaction to know that despite all the years and different bodies, I'd never lost myself. I picked up some sand and let it run through my fingers. "Explain the bond we have. How do you find me once I die, before my soul is reborn?"

"When you die, your soul's past is judged. If it's decided your soul isn't ready to move on to the afterlife, your soul immediately moves into the body of a child about to be born. During the death and rebirth process, your soul leaves a marker that can be followed by some-one with a bond to your soul. It's kind of like a trail."

"You don't ever worry about getting on the wrong trail?"

The corners of his mouth twitched. "No, the marker and bond is specific to your soul."

"So you meet me in each life, or what?" I asked.

"No," he answered. "I only become involved in your life if there's a direct threat to you. For the past few months, Trackers have gone missing, even Trackers with Protectors. The Protector / Tracker bond is severed somehow and the Trackers can't be found. Because of that, the Amaranthine ordered all Protectors to become a physical presence in the lives of their Trackers. A Protector can't defend a Tracker remotely; we have to be a physical presence to do that."

"You're not with me every second, so how do you protect me?"

A smile touched his lips as he held up his right hand. The sunlight reflected off the black stone ring on his index finger that I'd noticed when I first met him. "This ring is connected to our bond." He reached over and put it in front of me placing the thumb of his left hand on the ring. When he did, a symbol appeared. It resembled a circle and two half moons on each side of the circle. He ran his thumb over the symbol in three swift motions, first to the right, then to the left, then straight up. Suddenly an image appeared on the ring.

I looked closer and my chin dropped. It was an image of Alex and me sitting in the sand on the shore of the lake. I waved my hand in the air and the image waved also, like a live video feed. Alex brushed his thumb three more times in the opposite direction; the image faded. "The rings are given to Protectors as a way to watch our Trackers and make sure you're always safe. I don't watch you all the time, but I check in. The ring also allows me to transport to you immediately, so if you need my help, I can be there in an instant. I asked you to tell me when you'd be with Emil so I could make sure I was watching every second during the times you were together."

"So that's how you knew about the lemonade and the break up?" I asked, stunned. That was one of the questions I'd wanted answered the most. And if he hadn't had the ring to show me, I'd have been the one calling the mental institution.

He nodded. "Luke deserved every drop of lemonade he got."

We sat for a few minutes as more questions and realizations kept popping into my head. As I thought of the Van Gogh painting at Alex's house, I put my hands over my eyes and shook my head. When I opened my eyes, Alex was watching me with a puzzled expression. "When you showed me *Starry Night*, I should have known it was more than a coincidence you had my favorite painting hanging on your wall."

"I had to call in a lot of favors, but my family name is well-known for our art collection so I was able to bring it back in time for our dinner."

Alex mentioning his family made me wonder about them too. "The things you told me about your past? Your family? Were they all lies?"

"No, I tried to be as truthful as possible with you. I didn't inherit my house, though; I bought it when you decided to go to Western State for college. My family was part of the London aristocracy during the 1700s. My father was a land owner and was very wealthy. We had estates in France, Italy, and London, where I was born. When I was fourteen, my parents drowned in a boat accident. I was an only child and their only relative, so I inherited all of their assets—including the art collection that I've continued to add to. I was fortunate enough to be alive in London during the industrial revolution. I invested some of my inheritance and I've continued investing well ever since. After I finished my education, I was approached by some family friends who asked if I'd be interested in joining the Amaranthine."

I couldn't begin to comprehend what Alex must have gone through losing his parents, let alone making a life altering decision to join the Amaranthine Society.

"Why did you decide to tell me all of this now?" I asked. "You've always been so careful about what you say."

He exhaled. "For a couple of reasons. You were getting frustrated. Your annoyance and curiosity was making it difficult to get you to listen and trust me."

"Imagine that," I said, rolling my eyes.

"I needed you to take me seriously and understand that Emil is a member of the Daevos—and that makes him very dangerous."

I fidgeted, still uncomfortable with the idea of Emil as a bad guy.

"I couldn't risk you talking to Emil, or anyone else, about your theories regarding me. I needed you to believe what I was telling you about him, but you weren't willing to do that without a full explanation."

I studied the sand for a moment, thinking about the Daevos and Emil. Finally, I glanced up. "I have a hard time believing he's part of such a horrible organization, or that he wants to hurt me."

Alex looked at me severely. "The Daevos are master manipulators," he said. "That's why I showed up at your car last week and told you to stay away from Emil. There's also the chance that he was only sent on a mission to find you. I'm not certain what his intentions are. He could have abducted you the first day he kissed you, or any time since."

"Why didn't you tell me this sooner?" I asked.

"I warned you to stay away from him, but that was as much as I could do at the time. I couldn't tell you anything else until I got permission from the Amaranthine leadership. When they said I could talk to you, I decided your sand dune trip would be a good opportunity."

I watched the water lapping against the sand while I tried to deal with Alex's assertion that Emil was not only dangerous, but evil.

I could see Alex watching me from the corner of my eye. "Do you believe me, yet?" Alex asked.

The things he'd told me were far-fetched, but it was hard to deny what I'd seen with my own eyes—like the powers of his ring. "I need some time to think about it," I answered. "You might still be crazy." My tone was teasing, though I kind of meant what I said.

Alex's smile held a hint of disappointment. "What's my percentage now?"

I bit my bottom lip, considering. "There's a twenty percent chance you're nuts."

Alex laughed. "You haven't called the insane asylum yet, so I'm taking that as a good sign."

"You have to admit, it doesn't sound like a story a rational person would come up with. How did you think I'd react?"

"You were more hostile than I thought you would be," he said with a slight smile.

"What? Did you think I'd run to you with open arms, unable to keep my hands off you?"

Alex cringed. "Hugging and kissing me would have been a bad idea."

I sucked in a harsh breath and felt like he'd slapped me. I turned away so he couldn't see my reaction. I could feel the tears pricking my eyes and I was determined to stop them. Why did I keep allowing him to hurt me like this?

I no longer felt strapped to the sand. I got up in a huff, moving toward the dune buggy. Alex could see I was upset and followed me. "Evie, what's wrong?" he asked obliviously.

I fisted my hands and gave him a hard look.

"Evie?" he questioned again.

"Add it to the list of times you've hurt me, Alex," I said through my teeth.

His face fell in shock. "I didn't mean it like that."

I gave an offhanded laugh. "Does it really matter anymore? You've made it excruciatingly clear. You're here to do a job; that's all."

"Let me explain," he said, putting his hand up. "There's a reason—"

"Let it go," I said, cutting him off. I was more hurt than angry, and he could tell. "If you want a ride back to camp, you should get in. It'll be easier to convince my parents I want you here if I don't come back alone. And that's the only reason you're here, right? To put on an act so you can make sure I'm safe? We better get back to it."

Alex seemed surprised at my reaction, though I didn't understand why. If he couldn't tell I still had feelings for him, he was an idiot. He got in without saying another word. The dune buggy roared to life as I prepared myself for the performance I would have to give when we returned to camp. As we drove, I pushed all the things Alex had told me to the back of my mind to deal with later.

When we pulled up to the motor home, I could see my mom outside, already cooking dinner. "How was the ride?" she asked with a smile as we walked over to her.

"Great!" I said, with mock enthusiasm.

Alex recounted the entire trip for my mom, even

adding in some information about a few of the dunes we didn't visit. When he told my parents he'd never been to these sand dunes, that wasn't entirely true. He'd tagged along using his ring every freaking time I'd been here.

I was bitter and hurt . . . and the worst part was I knew it wouldn't be the last time it happened. I wished I didn't have to be around him, but that wasn't a possibility. So, I'd deal with the knowledge that he was constantly there by trying not to think about it. I consoled myself with the thought that as soon as I died a normal death, I probably wouldn't remember Alex's reincarnation revelations in my next life.

"Where's Dad?" I asked when Alex decided to shut his mouth.

"He went out for another ride, but he'll be back soon," my mom said. "Here's some dough for both of you, put whatever you want on it and we'll start cooking your food."

Alex followed my lead and topped his pizza with sauce, meat, cheese, and vegetables from the table in front of the RV. When we were done, we put the lids on the eight-inch Dutch ovens. My mom organized the charcoal into various patterns to ensure even cooking.

We had to wait about thirty minutes for the pizzas to cook. I used the time pretending to do homework and glaring at Alex as often as possible. We ate in relative silence except for the questions my mom asked. When my dad came back, my mom went in the motor home to eat with him and shut the door, leaving Alex and me outside where I could scowl at him in private. When we were done eating, Alex got up. I put my arms on the table and watched him grab the tent my mom had left sitting next to the drink cooler. He started to walk away. "Where do you think you're going?" I asked.

"To set up for the night," he said. "There's only

one road into the campsite. The best vantage point is two campsites down, so that's where I'm pitching the tent. I'll be back in a while." Alex disappeared around the front of the motor home.

About five minutes after Alex left, my parents came outside and sat across from me at the picnic table, shuffling Uno cards. "Deal me in," I said, gesturing to the cards.

"Where's Alex?" my mom asked as she made three stacks of cards, one for each of us. She flipped over the first card on the deck. It was red.

"He's setting up the tent," I answered, picking up my cards. My hand wasn't great, but I'd managed to get a draw four wild card.

My mom and dad looked over their hands as well. My mom plopped down a red nine to start the game. "He seemed a little depressed when you got back from your ride," she said.

My dad put down a card next; I followed. "Alex doesn't know what makes him happy," I answered.

"Hmmm," my mom hummed, her lips pressed together like she wanted to say more. She waited a few beats until her inquisitive nature got the best of her. "What's going on with him?" she asked. "I didn't know you two were friendly again."

I drew a card from the deck. "We weren't, but he apologized for everything. I think we're trying to figure out how to be civil. I was surprised he showed up here."

"Evie, if you don't want Alex here, I'll take care of it." My dad nodded once, indicating his authority on the matter as he put another card down.

"It's okay, he's fine, Dad," I said, trying to be as convincing as possible.

My mom watched me over the fan of cards in her hands, her eyes narrowed in concern. "How are things with Emil?" she asked. "Are you still together?"

I should have been prepared for this question, but I wasn't. Yes, we were still together, but it was on a trial basis until I found out if he was a soul killer. I couldn't exactly explain that to my parents though, so instead I shrugged and said, "Yeah. We haven't been dating long, but we both like each other a lot."

"What do you think Emil will say when he finds out Alex came camping with you?" my mom asked.

I lifted my shoulders as I put a draw two card down. "I'm sure he won't be happy about it, but there's not much he can do. I invited Alex in passing," I said, angry that I had to lie to my parents because of the cover story Alex made up. "I really didn't think he'd stop by."

"Why do you think Alex came here to see you?" my mom asked, putting another draw two card on top of mine, forcing my dad to draw four.

"I don't know," I said.

My mom's eyes were huge and her eyebrows shot up again. "If you don't know, you aren't looking hard enough."

I was confused. "What do you mean?" Though my relationship with Alex was sometimes baffling, I felt he'd made it clear he wasn't interested in being anything other than my Protector . . . if that's even what he really was.

"Evie, I've only spent a few hours with the two of you and I can feel the chemistry from fifty feet away. I've seen the way he looks at you, the longing in his eyes. That's not how you look at someone you only want to be your friend." She made the statement like I was the most naïve person in the world.

My mom's perspective and opinions about Alex shook me. Did Alex really still feel something for me, or was he just being a good actor? At this point, I couldn't tell and didn't know what to believe. I decided that to prevent my heart from breaking into even more pieces, I would only count on what I knew, and what I knew was that Alex was excellent at creating illusions.

I shrugged. "Well, he hasn't said anything to me about how he feels."

"Maybe that's why he's here," my dad suggested.

"Maybe," I said, trying to sound like my dad's theory could be right even though I knew Alex's real reason for inviting himself on my trip.

After a few more rounds of cards, I heard Alex come up behind me and say hello to everyone. I didn't turn around to look at him. I hoped he'd been using his ring and had heard my conversation with my parents. If his feelings were hurt, it served him right for eavesdropping.

"Did you get the tent set up all right?" my mom asked. My dad got up to start the fire for the night and Alex sat down next to me.

"I did. Thank you again for letting me use it," he said. "It's nice to be able to stay and spend some time with your family—and Evie especially." Alex looked directly at me, his expression intense and eyes shining. My breath caught in my throat. I hadn't seen a look like that on his face since the night I went to his house and we danced in his ballroom.

The air fell into silence as Alex and I stared at each other, but I could feel my mom's eyes on us, watching closely. She broke the quiet. "Well, we're happy to have you." I turned away from Alex. "Do you want to play Uno?" she asked him.

"Sure," he said, "deal me in."

That night, I slept in the motor home with my parents and Alex climbed into the tent without saying a word about the look he gave me. I tossed and turned thinking about the impossibility of everything Alex had explained to me. And in the back of my mind, a thought lingered—what if Alex had lied?

Or even more frightening, what if everything he said was true?

Chapter 14

When I woke up, my mom had already put away breakfast. I took a shower, not the least bit concerned that we were camping in a pile of sand. I had made it clear to my parents years earlier that I wasn't going to be smelly just because we were camping. Luckily, the motor home had a seventy-five-gallon water tank so my showering obsession wasn't a threat to our water supply.

By the time I made it out of the bathroom, Alex and my dad were already gone. My dad had decided to take Alex out and show him the big dunes. I hoped Alex wouldn't kill himself on the four-wheeler; I really didn't know how much experience he had driving one. But I remembered that even if he did crash, he probably couldn't get hurt, or so he had hinted. It was somewhat disconcerting to me that I was logically considering things that defied all logic.

My mom was reclining in a lounge chair reading the newest Mercy Thompson novel. She nodded to a plate of food she'd saved for me. I sat at the table with my breakfast and textbooks, using the time as an excuse to get some homework done. More people started trick-ling into the campground throughout the day to take advantage of the weekend recreation.

By about one in the afternoon, I was ready to take a break from studying and go ride. Since the four-wheeler was still out with my dad and Alex, I grabbed the dune buggy keys and took off.

I prefer the four-wheeler to the dune buggy since the four-wheeler is smaller and easier to handle, but the dune buggy is better than nothing. I slowly cruised over the small moguls in the dry area of the lakebed to make sure I didn't ruin the dune buggy shocks. Once I got past the lake and onto the dunes it was more fun. I drove around, putting everything out of my mind for the time being. I concentrated on enjoying the sand and the beauty of the landscape.

I ignored my thoughts about Alex and Emil, the Amaranthine and Daevos, murderers and reincarnation, for as long as possible, then drove to the smaller lake I'd been at the previous day. I got out of the dune buggy and sat under a tree in the shade.

This mystical world Alex had told me about bor-dered on lunacy, yet I couldn't quite disbelieve him. I thought through everything he had said, analyzing it, trying to make sense of it. I had so many questions. The more I thought about it, the more questions I came up with. I wanted to know more about my past lives, includ-ing the life Alex met me in and how he'd become my Pro-tector. Alex said my soulmark meant I could track bonds. If that was the case, why did I feel a connection to both Alex and Emil? Why couldn't I tell which one of them was my soul mate?

I'd also been thinking about the dream-like visions I'd had when I touched Alex and Emil. If everything Alex had said was true, maybe the visions weren't visions at all, maybe they were memories? If they were, what life did the memories come from, and why had I remembered them when I touched Alex and Emil? I sighed. There was still so much I needed to know. The conclusion I came to was that Alex had no reason to lie to me about this. In a weird twist of insanity, everything he told me yesterday helped me understand his previous actions.

This did nothing to quell my hurt or confusion over his feelings for me. I could spend hours trying to figure out what was going through his head and still come up blank. I couldn't decide whether his reaction to my relationship with Emil was jealousy, or his innate need to protect me from what he thought was a bad situation. If he was jealous, it meant he had to have romantic feelings for me on some level. My mom's revelation and Alex's reaction to the overheard conversation last night didn't give me any answers either. I only ended up more bewildered.

I sat on the sand replaying actions and conversations in my head for what seemed like hours. Finally, I decided I should go back to camp and see if my mom needed help with dinner.

When I got back, Alex and my dad were already there.

"Hey, Evie," my dad said. "How was your ride?"

"Great, how about yours?"

"Good. I took Alex to Chokecherry and a few other places. He's a pretty good rider." I raised an eyebrow, knowing his experience might have come from memorizing the riding style of every person he had seen on the dunes over the years.

"Yes, it seems Alex has a lot of talents," I implied. Alex caught the insinuation, but my parents were oblivious.

"What's for dinner?" I asked.

"Taco salad," my mom said. "The food is almost done."

I turned to Alex. "How long have you been back?"

"An hour or so," he answered. "I was given the assignment to find you so you wouldn't miss dinner. I was about to leave when you got here."

I picked up an olive from the bowl on the table and popped it in my mouth. "Well, it's a good thing I came back when I did. I wouldn't want to waste your time."

He locked eyes with me. "It wouldn't have been a waste."

Comments like that puzzled me: it wouldn't have been a waste because he wanted to be alone with me, or it wouldn't have been a waste because it was his job?

Dinner was ready soon and we sat down at the picnic table under the awning to eat. My dad told us about some kids who catapulted off the top of a dune thinking there was sand on the other side when there wasn't. He lamented the inexperienced riders and how they were making the dunes more dangerous for everyone. Alex kept looking at me throughout dinner with a thoughtful expression.

After we ate, Alex and I helped clean up. When we were done with the dishes, I sat back down in one of the folding chairs outside to do more reading for school. I was a few pages into the chapter when Alex walked over and stood beside me. "I'm going to take a walk. Will you come with me?" It seemed like there was something on his mind.

I was intrigued. "Uh, sure." I put my book down and stood up.

My parents were sitting outside, talking. As I got up to follow Alex, I heard a car door shut somewhere near the motor home. We started toward the dirt road, me in the lead with Alex following close behind. We weren't even out of the campsite when a familiar face appeared around the corner in front of my parents' motor home. He saw me and grinned, but the smile quickly turned to anger as his eyes shifted behind me. Dammit! Why was he here now too? And how in the hell was I going to explain this? I took a deep breath and pasted on my best smile.

"Emil!" I said with noisy enthusiasm as I hugged him. "What are you doing here?" I stepped back. Alex's demeanor had completely changed; his face had turned to stone and he was staring at Emil. Emil's face could have been a reflection of Alex's as he glared back.

Emil finally looked away from Alex, toward me. "I wanted to surprise you," he said. "I guess I should have called first."

"You're not the only one who's been surprised in the last couple of days, trust me," I grumbled.

"Stone," Alex acknowledged in an angry voice.

"Night," Emil said through his teeth.

Alex and Emil's hands were balled up, the veins in their arms bulging. I didn't know which guy would take a swing first, but decided I should probably stop the fight before it happened.

"Emil, come with me, I want you to meet my mom and dad." I took Emil's hand, pulling him away from Alex. I knew getting distance between them was the most important thing. My parents had been watching the exchange with interest, though we had been far enough away that they couldn't hear and had no idea who the new guy was.

"Mom, Dad, I want you to meet my boyfriend, Emil." My voice went up an octave when I said the word boyfriend. At the same time my voice shot up, so did both of my parents' eyebrows. They recovered quickly. "Emil, this is my mom, Karen, and my dad, Denys."

"Emil," my mom smiled, "we've heard so much about you."

"Nice to meet you," my dad said, trying to hold back a laugh at the predicament I was in now that Alex and Emil had both crashed our camping trip.

Emil seemed more composed now. I turned my head slightly, enough to get a quick glance over my shoulder and see that Alex was still standing there, leaning against the RV with his arms crossed, a sneer on his face.

"It's great to meet both of you. Evie talks about you all the time," Emil said.

My parents both smiled. "What brings you up this way?" my dad asked.

"Evie told me she would be here, so I thought I'd surprise her. I also wanted to follow her home. I know she likes to drive at night and was worried about her being alone."

I gave him a sidelong glance thinking that was a strange reason for Emil to show up. His rationale seemed to impress my parents though. "Well, it's nice to know Evie is being taken care of even though she lives far away from us. We had no idea she had such devoted—friends." My mom glanced toward Alex as she spoke.

"Yeah, we won't have to worry about you getting home safe," my dad said to me. "Between Alex and Emil, you'll be fine."

At the mention of Alex's name, Emil bristled.

"So are you staying here until Sunday, Emil?" my mom asked.

"That was my plan," Emil said, looking back at Alex.

"Well, I'd offer you our tent, but when Alex showed up without anywhere to sleep, we gave it to him. It's big enough for two people if you want to share," my mom offered, not realizing what a horrible idea that would be.

I saw Emil's eyes darken with anger. The last thing I needed was Alex and Emil sleeping in the same tent together. It would be better if they weren't even on the same continent. I was trying to come up with an alternative when Emil said, "Thanks for the offer, but it's all right, I brought my own tent."

My dad grinned and nodded in my direction. "Look at that, Evie, Emil is actually prepared."

"Speaking of that, I should put the tent up," Emil said. "Evie, do you want to help me?" The look he gave me indicated he wanted to get me alone where we could talk.

"Yeah, let's find a good spot for it," I answered. "We'll be back."

We turned around and walked past Alex. "Can I help you with anything?" he offered in a way that meant he wouldn't take no for an answer.

"We're taking care of it." Emil's voice had an air of authority to it that dared Alex to challenge him.

"I'm sure you are." Alex smiled and waved at my parents as we all walked around the RV. "Where's your vowmark?" Alex asked Emil casually.

"Covered up," Emil answered.

"How did you manage that?" Alex asked. "You're supposed to have it visible."

Emil smiled in a way that wasn't friendly at all. "There are a lot of things you don't have a clue about, Night." My gaze tracked one guy to the other, a little buzz settling in my stomach. Vowmarks? Yet another thing that needed an explanation.

Even though Alex had clearly been uninvited to the tent set-up, he followed behind Emil and me. As soon as we were on the other side of the motor home, Emil swung around in front of Alex, planting his feet and crossing his arms. Alex stopped within inches of him. "I said we don't need any help," Emil's voice was low, threatening. "So, you can go back to the motor home, or better yet, you can go back to Gunnison."

"Trust me, I'm not going anywhere. Especially now that you're here," Alex warned.

Emil fumed and stood up straight, like he was trying to lean over Alex even though they were about the same height. "Like hell you aren't."

Alex started to laugh. Their egos were taking over again. I knew it wouldn't be long before Emil would throw a punch, and it wouldn't take much longer than that for Alex to knock Emil down. I moved between the two of them and stood sideways, looking at them both.

"What does it matter, Emil?" I asked. "Even if Alex left, he wouldn't really be gone."

Emil's expression registered shock that swiftly turned to anger as he shifted his attention from me to Alex. "What does she know, Night?" Emil asked.

Alex decided to use my knowledge to his advantage and smirked. "She knows enough."

"That doesn't answer my question," Emil said, his tone dark.

"And I have no reason to answer it."

Instead of continuing to speak to Alex, Emil turned to me. "Evie, I wish I didn't have to involve you in this disagreement, but I need you to tell me, what has Alex said to you about me?"

Alex's expression was unmistakable; he didn't want me to say anything. I tried to think quickly and cover up my earlier slip. "Nothing, really. He said some people have been following me so he's watching me to keep me safe. He told me he used to be a part of the military and has a lot of unique skills from his experience as a soldier."

Alex looked relieved while Emil studied my face, suspicious of my explanation. With a release of tension, Emil sighed. But it was clear it wouldn't be the last time we discussed Alex's revelations. Even though I knew I shouldn't bring it up, part of me wanted the chance to talk to Emil and find out if Alex's story was true. Especially since Emil and Alex seemed to be sharing a lot of secrets.

Calmer now, Emil opened the trunk of his car and took out his tent. He found a spot on the other side of the cargo trailer near some vegetation. I helped him set it up while Alex watched with his arms folded across his chest, a sneer on his face.

In the middle of hammering a tent peg, Emil stopped and looked up at Alex. "Do you want to tell me exactly what you're doing on a camping trip with *my* girlfriend?"

Alex gave a brazen smile. "Maybe she invited me."

Emil scoffed. "Right. Why would she want the jerk who broke her heart to come on vacation with her?"

Alex made a "tsk-tsk-tsk" noise. "Someone's throwing stones while living in a glass house." The lines of Emil's face became hard. Alex continued, "Just because she doesn't *remember* what happened, don't for one second think that I won't remind her."

I put my hands on my hips. "If there's something you need to tell me, you better get it out of the way."

Alex and Emil both ignored my comment. The veins in Emil's neck throbbed and I could tell he was furious. "*You* don't know *what* happened, Night. Stop acting like you do."

"I know everything I need to. Make one wrong move, that's all it will take for Evie to find out."

"Find out *what*?" I was ticked off no one was listening to me or answering my question—again.

"Are you threatening me?" Emil asked Alex, the anger in his voice palpable.

"No," Alex said. "I'm giving you my word, and a warning. I'm not leaving. I would advise you not to be as brainless as usual."

I was riveted as I watched Alex and Emil and my stomach felt like it was in my throat. Emil's reaction to Alex's threats seemed to confirm that Alex hadn't lied; at least part of the insane story he had told me about the Amaranthine and Daevos must be true. I realized the fighting between them was only going to escalate. I considered asking them both to leave, but knew neither of them would be amenable to that plan.

At that moment, my dad came around the corner and asked if he could help with the tent. I wondered if he or my mom had heard the fighting between Alex and Emil. The tent went up quickly. My dad said he needed to get the fire going and asked Alex to help him. Alex reluctantly agreed, knowing he would have to leave me alone with Emil, but if Alex wanted my "relationship" with Emil to work, he would have to give me some time to explain things. As soon as Alex was far enough away, I grabbed Emil's hand. "I'm so sorry, Emil. I had no idea he was going to show up here on Thursday. I wasn't happy about it."

Emil dropped my hand. "Thursday?" I thought his eyes might pop out of his head and play in the sand. "Why didn't you tell me he was here when you called me?" His voice was accusatory and he seemed to be losing the level of calm control that he usually had.

"I didn't know he was here until I got back to camp," I defended.

"Why did he come?" Emil asked, as if he already knew the answer and was testing me.

I lifted my shoulders. "I think he wanted to make

sure I was safe, that's all."

"Why wouldn't you be safe? Who are these people he says have been following you?" Emil asked. I realized he might think Alex had told me more than I insinuated.

I tried to answer the question with as much truth as possible. "Alex said he noticed some guys had been interested in me recently and he wanted to make sure they didn't bother me. Plus, he's never liked my car. He always worries about it breaking down or me getting in an accident. Jasmine told him where I was and he got here a few hours after me."

Emil considered that for a moment. "If someone was following you, why didn't you let me know?"

"Because I didn't know about it until Alex showed up here and told me." I was calm, convincing, and pretty impressed with myself and my lying abilities.

Emil watched me, trying to decide if he should continue the interrogation. "When did you decide to start hanging out with him?" The creases in his forehead were getting deeper. "After what he did to you, I didn't think you'd ever speak to him again, let alone allow him to come on your family's camping trip."

I threw my hands in the air. "It's not like I invited him!" I was becoming angrier by the minute.

"You didn't ask him to leave either," Emil said, his voice low.

I learned a long time ago that the best defense is a good offense, so I replied, "How do you know? You weren't here, and speaking of that, did you really drive twelve hours to accost me, or is there another reason you decided to show up? You can hardly get mad at Alex when you did the exact same thing as him. Neither of you were invited. I'd rather have you both back in Colorado."

"The difference," he said, aggravated, "is that *I* am your boyfriend and Alex isn't. Not only that, but Alex is your *ex*-boyfriend! How do you think that looks?"

"I don't give a damn how it looks. You know how I feel." Truthfully he didn't know *exactly* how I felt, but I was too angry to bother with semantics.

"I thought I did, but I might have made an error in judgment," Emil said, his voice sharp.

"You're not the only one," I spat. I started to storm off when Emil caught my arm.

"Wait." I glared at him. He closed his eyes while he took a few deep breaths. When he spoke again, he was calm. "I wanted to see you, especially after everything that happened last week. There are some things I want to talk to you about and I thought we'd get to spend some time alone together. It didn't make me happy to find out Alex was already here with you. I'm sorry." His smile was apologetic and I could see sincerity in his eyes.

I exhaled a long breath. "Yeah, it would have been nice to spend some time with you too, but really, all I wanted from this trip was to be alone and have some time to think. The two people I was trying to get away from in Gunnison followed me here."

"I'm sorry, Evie. I'll leave if you want me to." At least Emil had offered to leave, unlike Alex who had told me the opposite—that he would never be gone.

"No, now that you're here, you might as well enjoy yourself until we leave Sunday morning. Come on," I said, smiling. "I'm sure the fire is going and we can make some s'mores." I held out my hand. He laced his fingers through mine, and I felt a rush of heat inflame my birthmark as we walked to the fire.

My dad had put two chairs out for us and we sat down. Alex was sitting about four feet to my left. I thought it would be best to put myself between Alex and Emil, keeping them as far away from each other as possible. I didn't really look at Alex until Emil and I had settled in our chairs, but when I finally glanced at him, the fire wasn't the only thing burning. Alex's eyes were blazing, focused squarely on Emil's hand braided through my own, his expression livid.

The night wore on as the heat from the fire warmed my legs. Smoke hung heavy in the air. Emil made jokes and talked to my parents while I pretended to listen to what they were saying. However, my attention was focused not on the predicament I was in with Alex and Emil, or on the people allegedly trying to abduct me. Instead, I couldn't stop peeking at Alex. I was consumed with trying to figure out what was going through his head. I didn't understand why he was so upset or why the anger seemed to be directed at Emil and me as a couple. Alex was the one who wanted me to be in a relationship with Emil. Unless something had changed, I didn't see what the problem was.

My focus on Alex made me lose track of time. After a while, my parents left to go to bed for the night. Instead of being the centerpiece of another argument between Alex and Emil, I decided to go to sleep as well. "I'm going in too," I said. "Have a good night, guys."

"Good night," Alex smiled at me.

"Sleep well, sexy," Emil said. He smirked at Alex like he had challenged him.

"I'll see you in the morning," I assured them both, hoping that they wouldn't kill each other during the night.

Alex gave Emil a firm glare in answer to the dare. "I *will* see you soon," he assured me. I caught the double meaning, knowing that Alex wouldn't leave me alone for a second with Emil here. Judging by Emil's hard eyes and the taut line his mouth formed, I knew he understood what Alex meant as well.

My parents were amused at the two guys who had

driven twelve hours to spend some time with me. My mom couldn't get over how gorgeous they both were. My dad refused to tell me his opinion. I had a pretty good inkling of how they'd react if they knew the alleged truth about my romantic interests. I was really glad they didn't.

Chapter 15

I slept fitfully, worried about the fight that might start at any moment outside the motor home. I woke up earlier than usual, took a shower, and got dressed. When I went outside, I was relieved to see everyone had survived the night without a scratch.

Alex and Emil still didn't seem to be speaking to each other, but Alex smiled and Emil's mouth quirked into a grin when I came out of the motor home. There was more drama going on in our little campsite than in a high school girls' locker room.

"Glad you're awake," Emil said.

"Good morning," Alex smiled.

"Hi," I said to both of them. "Morning, Mom and Dad."

I got some cereal for breakfast. While I was eating, my dad asked if Alex, Emil, and I wanted to go for a ride with him.

Alex and Emil seemed to hedge, waiting for my reaction. I felt like any activity was better than sitting around watching Alex and Emil scowl at each other all day, so I said, "Sure, when do you want to leave?"

"Right after breakfast." My dad raised his eyes to the sky as if trying to gauge the weather. The weather fairies don't talk to me, so I thought the sky looked fine. "It might rain later, but we'll see."

Alex accepted my dad's invitation. "I'll come too."

"That's great," my dad said. "Emil, how about you?"

Emil seemed wary for a second, but agreed. "Yeah, I'll tag along."

For a brief moment, I wondered if Emil had any experience driving a four-wheeler or dune buggy, but decided he wouldn't come if he didn't know how to ride. Plus he was rugged, sexy, mysterious Emil—of course he knew how to ride something as basic as a four-wheeler. He probably had a Ducati sitting in a garage somewhere. The thought stuck in my head though. Riding a four-wheeler or motorcycle was one thing, successfully navigating dune after dune, when you had no idea what or who might be on the other side, was another story completely. You had to be prepared to gun the engine to get up a steep hill, but stop on a dime at the top if you hit the crest of a dune. The worry nagged me through breakfast.

Everyone seemed to be waiting on me, so I finished my cereal quickly and grabbed my riding gear. I met the guys outside. I wasn't sure what the best seating arrangement would be since two of us would be in the dune buggy and one of us on the four-wheeler. My dad came around the corner, holding his helmet.

"Who wants to ride the quad and who wants to ride in the dune buggy?" my dad asked.

Alex preempted everyone. "I'd like to try driving the dune buggy, if that's okay."

"Sure," my dad said.

I narrowed my eyes at Alex, knowing he chose first deliberately. He knew I wouldn't let him ride with Emil in the dune buggy. "I'll ride with Alex." I looked at Emil, trying to convey that I was sorry, but he didn't seem to notice and instead wore a concerned expression.

My dad and Emil put their helmets on. Alex and I belted our harnesses and put on our headphones so we could talk over the engine. As we prepared to leave, I watched Emil closely. He got the four-wheeler started without a problem. I decided his concern must have been over the fact that I was in such close proximity to my ex-boyfriend. I laughed a little to myself, if Emil only knew how little he had to be worried about.

Things started off smoothly. For a while I was even enjoying myself, which wasn't easy; I liked the dune buggy even less when I wasn't the one driving it. Then, Alex started interrogating me.

"What did Emil say yesterday when your dad pulled me away?"

I gave short laugh. "I think you can probably guess."

"I don't *want* to guess, I want to know exactly what happened."

"Of course you do," I said. "I'm sure it was rough on you, not being able to utilize your usual voyeur skills through your magic ring."

The corner of Alex's mouth went up in a smirk. "It's nice to know what you really think of me. Now what did Emil say?"

I gave him a dirty look. "He wanted to know what you're doing here."

"And what did you tell him?"

"I told him you stopped by the house looking for me and Jasmine mentioned I was driving to Idaho. I said that you were worried about the guys who had been following me, so you drove up with a friend to make sure I got here safe."

Alex furrowed his brow. "And he believed you?"

I shrugged. "He seemed to."

Alex was quiet for a minute. "How are things between the two of you?" He tried to cover his curiosity with a tone of indifference.

"Fine. I think."

For the shortest second, Alex's face became hard, the same look he had when he was upset about something, then his expression smoothed back to normal. "What was his reason for crashing your camping trip?" Alex asked.

"He wanted to talk. He felt distant because of what happened last week and wanted to spend some time alone with me."

"What happened last week?" Alex asked, confused.

I looked at him in disbelief. "Don't give me that Alex. Your ring probably showed you everything I did last week, from the TV shows I watched, to what I had for dinner."

Alex shook his head as he drove up a dune, slowing down as he came to the top. "I watch you, but not that closely. Last week I was a little pre-occupied trying to find the Daevos members in Gunnison. I'm only one person. I couldn't see you every second."

"Oh." I was relieved that I did have some times that were my own, even if there weren't many.

"Evie, last week? What happened?"

"Well, aside from you being at the theater, there were some things Emil told me that made me pretty mad. It was part of the reason I broke up with him."

Alex's temples pulsed. "What did Emil say that made you so angry?"

I didn't feel like I should be talking about something this personal with Alex, but knew he would be unrelenting until I told him. I took a deep breath. "We were talking about past relationships. He said there was only one girl he had ever truly loved. Someone named Cassandra." At the mention of her name, Alex's eyes thinned and his grip on the steering wheel hardened until his knuckles turned white. I wasn't sure why Alex was having such a strong reaction to the information.

"Why would that upset you?" he asked, trying to keep his tone even.

Alex was an idiot. "Because I was really starting to like Emil when he dropped the bomb that he would never love anyone as much as this other girl. If I stayed with him, I would always know I was only second best, and he would probably always wonder about Cassandra." Duh.

Alex's answer was not what I expected, but nothing ever is with him. "I can't believe you had feelings for Emil."

"Why not?"

He shot me a sidelong glance as we drove around a huge bowl of sand. "I could give you a list a mile long, but for starters, he's evil and that's not really your type."

I gave him a sardonic laugh. "You don't know my type, Alex."

He lifted his brow, amused. "I've watched you date for more than two hundred and fifty years. I'd say I know your type better than you do."

"I really doubt my type stays consistent through all of my lives," I rationalized.

Alex held his mouth tight as he mumbled, "You'd be surprised."

I wondered what that was supposed to mean, but he didn't elaborate, so I decided to tell him exactly why Emil was attractive. "Emil is mysterious, he challenges me, he listens to me and cares about what I think, and he's really hot. He is *definitely* my type."

The grimace on Alex's face became more pronounced with each characteristic I listed. He was quiet for a minute, then started, "Evie, I need to tell you . . .."

It was at that moment, the worst possible moment, it happened. I waited for Alex to continue what I hoped was a sentence explaining he still had feelings for me, but he had stopped short, looking intently in front of us. I followed his gaze.

The conversation with Alex had left me paying little attention to Emil or the landscape. Apparently Alex was more aware, which was good, since he was driving. I turned in time to see Emil gun the four-wheeler to get up a big dune, but he was going too fast to stop at the top. Emil shot over the peak of the dune like a cannon. Both Emil and the four-wheeler caught air, the problem was that they did it separately from one another. The four-wheeler made it a good four feet off the ground, landing somewhere on the other side of the dune. Emil was at least six feet in the air and flew about ten feet before a puff of sand exploded from where he landed. I didn't see my dad anywhere, though I knew he would turn around when he realized we weren't following him anymore.

I was out of the dune buggy in a flash, running to where the sand had ruptured. In that instant, I realized I wasn't just running because Emil had crashed, I was running to make sure someone I cared about wasn't hurt. Regardless of how dangerous Alex said Emil was, I knew I did care about him and my feelings for Alex and Emil would always be conflicted. Alex followed me at a slower pace, unconcerned. I turned, yelling, "What are you doing? Emil crashed, aren't you worried?"

Alex shrugged. "No."

The disbelief came across in my voice. "He might be seriously hurt."

Alex sighed. "If only we could be so fortunate. We

won't be, though. He's fine."

My voice shot up. "How do you know? Were you watching a different four-wheeler than me?"

"Amaranthine and Daevos members are basically immortal, Evie. We heal fast."

I thought about that, but didn't slow my pace. I found Emil lying on his back in the sand. Just like Alex had said, nothing looked broken, scratched, or even bruised. He was unconscious, though. I leaned over him and put my hands on his cheeks hoping the contact would wake him up. Nothing. "I thought you said he couldn't get hurt?" I hissed at Alex.

"He's recuperating. Give him a second."

"Can he hear what we're saying?" I asked.

"Not until he wakes up," Alex answered.

I sat back on my calves and watched Emil, thinking about what Alex had said. "If Amaranthine and Daevos members are so unbreakable, how does anyone ever die?"

"I told you, we don't take souls unless we're ordered."

"Yeah, but you do get orders occasionally. So, how do you do it?"

"It's complicated."

I waited, but when Alex didn't continue I asked, "Are you going to tell me why it's so difficult?"

"Immortals are hard to kill," Alex said in a condescending tone. I glared. "The Daevos are resilient, though they're not nearly as indestructible as Protectors. Protectors can't be killed while we're in service to the Amaranthine Society because the Protector vows are spelled to shield our minds from the Daevos. However, killing a Daevos member takes a certain amount of skill."

"What kind of skill?"

Alex rolled his eyes. "It's not like I can shoot Daevos

members with a gun or stab them with a kitchen knife. It takes time, energy, and concentration."

I was about to ask Alex to elaborate when Emil started moving his head and I could see his eyes fluttering under his eyelids.

"Emil?" I said, touching his cheek with one hand and his chest with the other. "Emil? Are you all right?"

Emil opened his eyes. "Don't move," I warned, "you might be hurt."

Emil laughed and sat up. "I'm fine. Thanks for worrying though." I glanced at Alex and his expression said, "I told you so." I shook my head. This was getting complicated.

Emil moved his head, searching. "Where's the four-wheeler, is it okay?" I'd noticed the four-wheeler when I first came up over the dune. It was at the bottom of the hill, miraculously unharmed and idling.

"It survived the crash better than you did," I assured him.

"I shouldn't have been so stupid," Emil said.

"It's not surprising," Alex gloated. I punched him in the leg.

"Don't worry about it," I said. "It was just a little accident. It happens to even the best riders."

Emil winced, but not in pain. "Yeah, I'm not one of those. I should've asked for some lessons. I've only been on a four-wheeler a couple of times and have never driven one on sand."

"Why did you come today if you didn't know how to ride?" I wondered.

Emil snorted. "Do you honestly think I was going to let you spend all day alone with *him*?" He asked, nodding toward Alex.

"You should have ridden in the dune buggy," I said.

"That was my plan, until Alex decided to drive."

Alex smirked and I gasped. "Alex, did you know Emil couldn't ride?"

Alex gave me a sly smile. "Not really. I mean, I had an inkling, but wasn't sure until I saw his reaction when he realized he would have to ride the four-wheeler."

I gaped at Alex, stunned. "Why didn't you stop him?"

"Why would I?" Alex asked without a hint of apology. "It's not my job to take care of *him*."

I glowered at Alex. I was about to tell him exactly what I thought when I heard an engine and saw my dad pull up over the dune to the west of us. Emil was standing now and seemed to be fine, but I wasn't convinced.

My dad stopped his motorcycle and took his helmet off. "I lost you guys."

"Emil crashed, but he's okay," I explained.

My dad studied Emil with a wary expression. "You sure you're all right?"

Emil nodded. "Yeah, I came up over the dune too fast."

"It happens to everyone. Do you still want to ride, or would you rather go back to camp?"

"No, I want to ride," he smiled, but I could see the hesitation in his eyes as he looked toward the four-wheeler.

"I'm going to take him in the dune buggy," I told my dad and gave Alex a pointed look. Emil's expression said thank you. "Alex can ride the four-wheeler." I was still unhappy with Alex and would rather ride with Emil anyway. Alex's face turned hard at my suggestion, but no one else seemed to notice.

"Okay," my dad agreed. "Are you ready to go?"

"Yep," I answered.

I left Emil and Alex standing at the crest of the

sand. I jogged back to the dune buggy, started it, and drove over to the waiting men. Emil got in the passenger seat as I shoved a helmet harder than I needed to into Alex's stomach. He snorted like I was wasting my time trying to hurt him. He looked at Emil as he said, "I'll be following you.

The rest of the ride went by quickly. We drove to Chokecherry and watched Alex and my dad race up the mountain. I stayed below to be with Emil and make sure he was okay. When we were ready to go, Emil rode back to camp with me in the dune buggy while Alex followed us.

We were both wearing our headphones. After awhile, Emil said, "It's peaceful here, Evie. I understand why you like it so much."

I glanced at him. "It's always been one of my favorite places. I get a lot of clarity here."

"I'm really sorry about crashing the four-wheeler," he apologized for the tenth time.

I waved a hand in the air. "Don't worry about it. You have no idea how many people have crashed it— only they end up doing a lot more damage to the four-wheeler and themselves. I'm glad you weren't hurt. I didn't believe Alex when he said you'd be okay."

I knew Alex didn't want me to tell Emil about all the things he'd said at the lake, but it was obvious Emil and Alex both knew some of the same information. Having Emil confirm Alex's story would help me figure out how much of it was true. Alex wouldn't be happy, but I decided to take a chance. "Do you want to tell me what vowmarks are?"

Emil pursed his lips. "You caught that yesterday, huh?"

"It was kind of hard to miss."

Emil sighed, exasperated. "What has Alex told you?"

"A lot of crap that sounded like it came from a fantasy novel. Since the two of you seem to be reading from the same book, I'd like to know your perspective."

Emil considered the situation and made a decision. "I assume you know about the Amaranthine Society," he said. I nodded, surprised he was being so forthcoming when I'd had to drag the information out of Alex. "So, I'm sure Alex told you about the Daevos Resistance as well?" I nodded again. "Did he tell you anything about the history of the Daevos and Amaranthine?"

"A little," I said. "He told me the Amaranthine Society keeps people—especially Trackers—safe from the Daevos. He said the Amaranthine are good and the Daevos are bad."

Emil sighed and scrubbed his hand over his chin. "It's more complicated than that. Do you remember the Goddesses and soul mate legend I told you about?"

I nodded.

"That wasn't just a legend, Evie. It's part of the Amaranthine and Daevos history." My mouth dropped as Emil kept talking. "Soon after the Goddesses started sending souls into the world, they realized some souls had a natural inclination toward evil. Once souls found their soul mates though, those tendencies were balanced. The Goddesses decided they needed a group that could help people find their soul mates, as well as act as the enforcers of the Goddesses when evil souls needed to be dealt with. So, they organized the Amaranthine Society. Amaranthine members work on many levels. Some, like Alex, are Protectors and keep Trackers safe. Others are part of the army that takes the souls the Goddesses have deemed too evil to continue living. Then there are others who work with Trackers to help people find their soul mates and try to influence souls who have evil tendencies.

"For centuries, the Amaranthine helped the Goddesses and things were peaceful. Until the soul mate of the Goddess Callista decided he didn't want to be with her anymore and left her alone, half of a soul. She was crushed. Finding your soul mate doesn't make everything perfect. The relationship still takes work. Callista's soul mate decided it was easier to leave than put more effort into their bond. After some time, her sadness turned to fury and she became bitter about love. Callista decided no one should have the chance to be with their soul mate. She left the Goddesses and started the Daevos Resistance—her own personal army. Their purpose was to find soul mates—preferably using a Tracker—and take one of the couple's souls. Without their mate, the remaining soul would become unbalanced and the Daevos could recruit them to the Resistance and enlarge Callista's army. She believes that with a large enough army taking souls, she'll be able to obliterate love and destroy the Amaranthine.

"Part of the reason the Amaranthine are so strong is because they get their powers from the combined strength of the Goddesses. Alone, Callista has limited power to offer her army. She can only gift Daevos members with two things: the power to take souls, and limited immortality—because their soul can still be taken by the Amaranthine."

"Why would someone choose to be part of the Daevos? The Amaranthine seems like it has a lot more perks."

Emil lifted his shoulders. "Every person who joins has their own reasons. Some have a tendency toward evil, and some become that way because the Daevos have taken their soul mate. Others just care more about chaos than happiness. Some join because they don't believe in love, and some . . . have other motives. Each case is different."

I took a moment to wonder what Emil's motives had been. "How are souls taken?" I asked.

"Throughout all of a soul's existence, even though they don't remember, the memories, thoughts, and actions of their previous lives are still with them, helping them form the person they are in their current life. When a person dies a mortal death, the soul is judged on its past. Once a soul has learned enough, it can move on to the afterlife. When a soul is killed, its thoughts, actions, and memories are taken. Without its past, a soul has nothing to learn from, nothing to guide it, nothing to anchor it. A body is merely a shell for the soul. Once a soul is dead, its body dies with the soul's lost past." He turned away, staring out over the sand like he was lost in thought. After a minute, he shifted his gaze back to me. "As part of the Amaranthine Society, Protectors are gifted with the ability to shield their minds, making them impossible for the Daevos to kill. The Daevos don't have that capability."

I thought about what Emil said as we drove up and down dunes, following my dad back to camp. Everything Emil was telling me confirmed what Alex had already said. I took a deep breath as the realization sunk in; Alex hadn't lied to me. I still had so many questions, though. "What about the vowmark Alex mentioned? What is that?"

Emil unconsciously rubbed his left hand over the bump on the bicep of his right arm—the same place I'd touched in the botanical gardens when he'd suddenly stopped kissing me. "The Goddesses believe souls should be able to choose their path. So when Callista created the Daevos Resistance, the Goddesses allowed it to remain in existence—as long as the Amaranthine were there to help combat them. To do that, the Amaranthine would need to know who the Daevos members were.

"In order for a Daevos member to get the powers Callista offers, the member has to take the Resistance vows. The Goddesses put a spell on the vows so anyone who takes them is immediately marked with a red web scar on their bicep called a vowmark. The mark gets larger with each soul the Daevos member takes, and wraps around the member's right arm. The mark is the only way Protectors can truly tell who a Daevos member is. The size of the mark lets the Amaranthine know how dangerous the person might be. My mark isn't as big as Alex assumes it should be, and it's usually covered by the shirts I wear—so that's why Alex can't see it."

If Emil was telling the truth—and it seemed like he was since he was confirming the things Alex had told me about the Amaranthine and Daevos—could I trust him? The mission of the Daevos was horrible, and Emil had admitted he was a part of them. But why would he have told me so much about the Resistance if he wanted to hurt me? I needed to know what role Emil played within the Daevos, and I needed to figure out why I didn't feel as scared around him as I probably should. "When I first met you, Alex warned me that you were dangerous. He still thinks that." I waited, expecting Emil to say something, but when he didn't, I continued, "So are you?"

Emil pulled his lips into a thin line. "I know Alex probably told you some shocking things about the Daevos—about me," Emil said, "but I want you to know, I'm not like that. I've done things I'm not proud of, but they've been done out of necessity."

"So you aren't part of the Resistance anymore?" I

asked.

Emil drew in a breath. "That's . . . complicated. I'm still a member, but I'm not like the rest of the Daevos."

Ugh. I'd heard that before. "Between you and Alex, I feel like I'm constantly trying to figure out a riddle. I don't understand why you would remain in the Resistance if you've changed and aren't like the other members anymore."

Emil grimaced. "There are reasons I've done what I have, Evie. And there are reasons I can't leave."

Wrangling a rhinoceros would be easier than getting information from either Alex or Emil. Why couldn't they be completely honest with me? "When will you be able to tell me what those reasons are?" I asked.

Emil ran his hand through his hair. "I'm not sure."

"Patience is not one of my strong points," I said.

"It will be worth it, I promise." Emil reached out his hand and put it on my leg. Right after he touched me, I heard an engine grow louder behind us. Alex pulled up to the side of the dune buggy shooting a steely scowl at Emil. Emil sneered and Alex dropped back, but not far.

Emil grinned. "It's driving him crazy, you know."

"What is?" I asked, oblivious to what Emil was talking about.

"Me being here with you."

I laughed. "Yeah, he's worried about you dragging me off in the sand to take my soul or something. He's just doing his job."

Emil looked at me doubtfully. "His job isn't his only motivation."

I glanced over my shoulder at Alex. "It's pretty clear his only incentive is to keep me alive. Though I don't even know why he's doing that; being a Protector must get really tedious."

Emil opened his mouth to say something, but shut

it, probably deciding not to get into an argument with me and put any more strain on our relationship.

"Thanks for telling me about the Daevos," I said. "I understand you're still a part of the Resistance, but for some reason I don't feel like you're here to hurt me. Am I wrong about that?"

Emil answered immediately. "No, you aren't wrong. I will never hurt you." His voice was strong and his eyes sincere.

I thought about what he said for a few minutes, and turned to him. "I don't understand why you haven't left the Resistance yet, but against my better judgment, I'm going to trust that you'll tell me when you can."

Emil gave me an appreciative gaze. "You have no idea how much your trust means to me. I won't let you down," he promised.

As we drove back to camp, I thought about all the things Emil had told me. Emil didn't know what Alex had said to me. There was no way his explanation and Alex's would be so similar if it wasn't true. In a rush of clarity, I felt like I could move past the point of suspicion and deal with the reality of what had seemed to be an impossible truth. I was relieved to have so many secrets out in the open. Now I wouldn't have to spend so much time obsessing about what was really going on with the men in my life.

The conversation had also made me view Emil differently. I was still wary of the things he couldn't tell me, but there were things Alex was keeping from me too. The Daevos Resistance might be evil, but I truly didn't feel threatened by Emil. It didn't mean I was going to let my guard down, but I wasn't as worried about Emil now as I had been when Alex warned me he was dangerous last week. Despite everything I'd learned about Emil, and even knowing there were things I wasn't aware of yet,

I still felt a bond with him that I couldn't explain. It was becoming apparent that I really did still care for Emil. I hoped my feelings weren't affecting my common sense.

When we got back to camp it was late afternoon and we all helped my mom make dinner. I was glad the day was almost over and I'd be leaving in the morning with my little entourage. Trying to appease two guys was exhausting.

We joked with my parents as we ate, then I decided to go to sleep early since I knew it would be a long drive home. Alex and Emil agreed and went to their tents. I settled into the motor home and fell asleep, dreaming of a war that had been going on forever. All the people in the war were fighting over something. As I got closer, the object in the middle that everyone wanted wasn't a thing at all—it was me.

Chapter 16

woke up to my mom's voice calling me for breakfast. I was glad I'd been able to see my parents on the trip. I wished I could have spent more time with them alone. After my shower, I packed all my things and carried them to my car, turning down offers from both Alex and Emil to take my bags for me. Both guys followed me to the car anyway.

"Are you ready to go?" Emil asked.

I opened the trunk and put my bags inside. "Yeah, I need to say good-bye to my mom and dad."

"Okay, I'll follow you home in my car," Emil said.

I nodded, rearranging the bags so everything fit. "That sounds good," I said.

Emil's eyes found Alex. "When are you leaving?" Emil asked.

Alex nodded in my direction, answering, "When Evie does. I'm riding with her."

I wasn't excited about the prospect of twelve hours in my car with Alex. I really wanted to be alone but knew that even if I thought I was alone, I wouldn't be—Alex would just be watching me with his ring.

Emil laughed until he realized Alex wasn't kidding. The smile on his face washed away; in its place was a calm, determined expression. "That's not happening."

Alex smiled in challenge. "Try to stop me."

The tension between Alex and Emil escalated until my mom and dad came around the corner. The guys told my parents thank you and left me alone to say goodbye; though, I couldn't help but notice Emil's frustrated expression as Alex got in my Mustang. I hugged both my parents and my mom made me promise to call as soon as I got home. My dad told me to be careful and said he had checked my car earlier in the morning so I should get home without a problem. I waved, watching my mom and dad disappear in my rearview mirror as we drove off.

We turned onto the main road when Alex decided it was time to chat. "That was an interesting trip," he said.

"I would call it awkward."

Alex laughed. "Your dad seemed to like me a *lot*," he mused, "your mom too."

I rolled my window down and rested my arm on the door. "Don't flatter yourself. My mom likes everyone. My dad liked that you could keep up with him on the four-wheeler."

Alex was quiet for a minute. I noticed a smile playing on his lips. "Regardless, I don't think they liked Emil *nearly* as much as me."

I looked over at him, trying to figure out what game he was playing. "They didn't get to spend as much time with Emil. You had a whole day of them to yourself before Emil showed up," I said. "Why does it matter who they liked more anyway?"

Alex ignored my question and studied me, his expression a mixture of annoyance and concern. "Why are you being so defensive of Emil all of a sudden?"

I could get whiplash from Alex's mood swings. "Telling you my parents don't have a preference for either guy who decided to crash our camping trip is not being defensive."

Alex shifted in his seat watching the fields, houses, and random potatoes on the side of the road as we drove by. He stewed for a while. When he finally spoke, his tone was frustrated. "You're making it difficult for me to keep my promise."

"What promise?"

"I told you that you would never have to worry about your safety with Emil as long as I was here."

"Do you plan on leaving?" I asked, confused.

"Not exactly," Alex hedged. "But you being alone with him in that dune buggy for half the day while I had to follow behind you wasn't helpful. It's not like I could use any of my powers to keep you safe. We were in public and your dad was fifteen feet in front of you. I didn't know what the two of you were talking about, or what was going on. If he had tried something, if he had wanted to hurt you, Evie, I might have been too late."

I ran a hand through my hair. "I wasn't worried about him doing anything to hurt me. I talked with him on the way back to camp. I really don't think he has any malevolent intentions toward me."

Alex thinned his eyes and frowned. "He's a master manipulator, all Daevos are. Of course he would make you feel like that."

I was quiet for a few seconds. "Maybe you don't know him like you thought you did. Maybe he's different," I defended.

The hard set of Alex's jaw made it obvious he was rankled by my comment. "I've seen what he's capable of. If you only knew . . . trust me, he's as bad as the rest of them."

We'd barely been on the road thirty minutes; I wasn't going to start an argument with him this early into the trip, so I decided to stay quiet. I could feel the air in the car become thicker, almost rancid, but Alex didn't push the conversation. I turned on the radio and we rode in silence until we had to stop for gas.

Emil pulled up at the pump next to mine and came over while my tank was filling. He moved in next to me, leaning against my car. "Hey there, sexy girl."

I could feel myself blushing and turned away.

"How's the Mustang handling?"

I wasn't sure if the blood had drained from my cheeks, but I looked at Emil anyway. "No problems so far. We're just listening to some music."

"Well, let me know if you need anything." He leaned in close, brushing my hair with his cheek. "Why don't I give Night the keys to my BMW so I can ride with you for a while?"

I wrinkled my brow, wondering if he was crazy. "I don't think that's a good idea. Alex would crash your car out of spite."

Emil grinned slyly. "It would be worth it."

I laughed softly. "He won't let us ride together," I said. "His inability to leave me alone is becoming irritating."

"You're not kidding," Emil agreed.

I put the gas cap back on. "I'll see you on the road," I said to Emil as I got in the car. Alex had moved to the driver's seat and cracked the window open; I knew he'd been listening to my conversation with Emil. As he turned the key and started the engine I said, "I thought you didn't like my car, so why are you driving it?"

"I don't," he answered, pulling into the intersection, "but it's safer with me driving it than you."

I glared. "Next time, ask before you commandeer my vehicle."

We rode in silence for a few minutes until Alex sneered, "You and Emil seem to be getting along well."

A crease formed between my brows as I tried to figure out what I'd done to piss him off this time. "What are you upset about?" I asked. "You're the one who wanted me to be in a relationship with Emil."

"I wanted you to *act* like you're in love with him, not actually be in love with him," Alex said.

I sighed. I didn't want to have this conversation, but Alex seemed determined. "I'm not going to lie to him. He told me a lot of stuff about the history of the Daevos yesterday. He said he's not like the other Daevos members anymore. He said he's changed—and I believe him."

My assessment of Emil got Alex's rapt attention and fury flashed across his face. "Evie, you don't know . . ." he stopped mid-sentence, seething. "Whatever happens, you *cannot* fall for his lies. If you . . ." he hesitated like he shouldn't say anything, "decide to be with him based on lies he tells you, there's not much I can do. I need you to step back and really look at this situation before you believe anything Emil says." Alex's fingers were held so tight around the steering wheel that I could see the veins pulsing in his hands and arms. I couldn't understand why he was reacting this way when it was clear to me that Emil wouldn't hurt me. Maybe I hadn't communicated that well enough to Alex.

"Alex, I just don't see Emil ever doing anything as awful as you're suggesting. I'll be objective, but he won't hurt me, I—"

Alex put a hand up and cut me off. "You have *no* idea what you're dealing with."

I opened my mouth to protest. Alex stopped me. "Evie," he said my name louder this time. "If you knew about his past, you would be a lot more careful."

I frowned at him. "Then enlighten me, because I don't see it. Emil said he's different. He hasn't given me a reason to doubt him."

Alex didn't hide his anger. "There are still some things you don't know."

I raised an eyebrow thinking that seemed unlikely. "Considering everything I've learned over the last few days, I think I could probably be an Amaranthine and Daevos scholar."

"I didn't want to overwhelm you, but apparently I need to go into more detail." He paused like he was collecting his thoughts. I was getting impatient.

"Well," I said, gesturing with my hand for him to go on. "Don't let me stop you."

He took a deep breath. "The Daevos Resistance works by breaking members into smaller groups called Clans. The Clans operate in locations around the world and Daevos members can move among the different groups." He stopped talking and looked at me. "Every Daevos clan wants a Tracker. Emil's Clan is no different, but there's another reason they want you." He sighed. "You were almost one of them."

I gasped in disbelief. "What? Why would I ever join the Daevos?"

"Two hundred and fifty years ago, you were eighteen in London. It was your debut season and you were quite popular at the parties that were held. You had many friends—some of whom were members of Emil's Daevos Clan. The more time you spent with them, the more you became involved in their lives, but you had no idea what they were doing or who they really were. Your Tracker abilities hadn't been activated. You didn't know you were a Tracker—neither did they.

"You were spending a lot of time with Emil's Clan. They were courting you, tempting you, hoping you'd take the Daevos vows. Eventually, you learned about the Amaranthine and Daevos. You were horrified at the evil things your friends were doing. You knew they wanted you to join them, but that wasn't your path. Instead, you turned to the Amaranthine, hoping they would be able to protect you. You left the Clan late one night, running to the shelter of a safe house where I was assigned as your Protector."

I leaned back in my seat, thinking about Emil's clan and wondering about the history of my past lives. "Once I was at the safe house, what happened?" I asked.

"The Amaranthine Society moved you to another location. They told you someone would be watching to ensure your safety. You went on with your life. Emil's Clan probably would have left you alone if they hadn't already put so much time and effort into recruiting you. His Clan searched frantically for you, even attempting to attack the safe house, but you had already been moved and they couldn't find any information about you. After many years, you died and your soul moved on to its next life. When Emil's Clan realized you were gone, they vowed that they would find you one day."

Alex's face was grave as he stared out the window. He turned his attention back to me. "The problem, Evie, is that Emil's Clan still wants you."

I was motionless, my mind trying to take it all in. A week ago, I didn't even believe in reincarnation. Now I was being told that not only does it exist, but I have an insane Clan hunting me, not just across the miles, but across centuries, hell-bent on finding me and making me part of their evil group, or taking my soul.

"So, you're saying Emil helped recruit me?"

"Not only that, he was also the reason you stayed as long as you did."

"What do you mean?"

Alex's arms tensed. "You were enamored with him and he didn't dissuade your interest. He pretended to care about you and even made you believe he was your soul mate."

I laughed; the irony of the situation was lost on Alex. "So Emil told me he was my soul mate—like you told me that you were mine?"

Alex blinked in surprise. "No. I told you the truth. Emil manipulated you into believing he had feelings for you."

I wasn't sure what to believe. "Maybe he did have feelings for me? Obviously my soulmark recognizes him, so maybe his recognizes me," I rationalized. "If I'm a Tracker, shouldn't I be able to tell who my soul mate is?"

Alex shifted in his seat, his left leg resting against the door. "Your Tracker abilities have to be activated for you to use them. They weren't activated two hundred and fifty years ago, and they aren't activated now. You'll only know who your real soul mate is once you meet another Tracker who can awaken your abilities with their own power."

"Why can't I remember any of the things you're telling me about?" I asked. "What happens to the memories of past lives?"

"Most memories are dormant until the soul is ready to move to a higher plane. However, there have been cases where some people have remembered their past lives. It's rare, but sometimes events can trigger those memories."

I watched the road in front of us as I again wondered

if the dream-like visions I'd seen had actually been memories. If so, what were they memories of and how did they fit into the story of my soul?

Neither of us spoke and the silence felt like a heavy blanket weaving its way through the car. I wanted to know how I'd really felt about Emil when I met him so many years ago. I wished that I could see my past, see what had really happened. I was so sure my instincts had been right and Emil wasn't a threat. "I don't understand why he's always been so worried about me and my feelings if he was only using me," I said. "He's one of the *better* guys I've dated."

Alex frowned at my opinion of Emil as a boyfriend. "I wouldn't lie to you," he said. "I told you from the beginning that Emil had ulterior motives."

That was exactly what I needed at the moment, Alex rubbing his superior knowledge in my open wound. Anger rose from the bottom of my stomach. "Yeah, maybe you should've given me a heads up about the Daevos and your theories about Emil. Then I might have taken your warning a little more seriously instead of thinking you were jealous."

Alex smirked. "Is that what you thought?" His expression made me even more upset—as if jealousy would be such a difficult thing for him to experience. "Besides, you know about him now and are still having trouble believing he's a bad guy, so it wouldn't have made a difference what I did or didn't tell you, would it?"

I leaned back in my seat, turning away from Alex. I rolled my window halfway down and breathed in the smell of newly turned soil and fresh harvested fields. It was all so much to take in. I felt completely alone. It didn't matter that my parents would always support me no matter what, that Emil and Alex both knew about the craziness of past lives and secret societies, or that Alex was there twenty-four-seven to watch me and keep me safe. None of that made a difference. I felt like the only person who could take care of me, could save me, was myself. I'd always thought my independence was one of my strongest attributes, but at the same time, the sheer knowledge that I was utterly alone sent me into an emotional tailspin. I turned toward the passenger window, slumping down in the seat until I finally fell asleep.

Chapter 17

When I woke up, we were pulling into a rest stop about an hour away from Gunnison. I rubbed my eyes. "How long did I sleep?"

"About three hours." Alex assessed me with concern, similar to the way my mom looked at me when I was sick. "How are you feeling?"

I wrapped my arms around myself like it would protect me from my thoughts. "Overwhelmed."

Alex nodded in understanding. "Considering everything you've learned this weekend, I'm surprised you're taking it as well as you are." He unbuckled his seat belt. "I needed a break so I pulled over."

I nodded and opened my car door. Still tired, I stumbled into the rest stop bathroom. I stood at the sink looking at myself in the mirror, finger combing the knots from my hair. I took a few minutes to compose myself and breathe before going back out to face Alex and Emil.

There were tables between the rest stop building and the car; Emil was sitting at one of them. "Hey," he said with a grin.

I smiled back. "Hi."

"Did you have a good nap?" Emil asked.

"Yeah, I guess I was tired. I need to practice resting when I go on vacations instead of getting stressed out."

"Why are you stressed?" Emil asked, perplexed. This question confirmed it for me, guys really are idiots.

I laughed. "Having you and Alex show up wasn't helpful."

"Sorry," he frowned. "I wasn't trying to cause problems. I just wanted to see you." He seemed sincere and it was hard to believe he had ever wanted to use or hurt me in any way. In fact, I wasn't sure I did believe it. Even knowing what Alex had told me didn't dissipate my gut feeling that Emil cared for me.

I smiled. "No, it's okay. I'm glad you came."

Emil flashed a boyish grin. "So, do you want to ride with me yet?"

I smiled, managing to get a jab in at Alex. "Wish I could, but you know the warden won't let me."

Emil glanced away for a beat before turning back to me. "Alex has control issues," he said with the hint of a smile.

Alex walked up behind me. "Are you ready to go?"

I nodded. "I'll see you at the next gas station, Emil."

"I'm looking forward to it," Emil said as we walked back to the cars.

I yawned, still trying to wake up. Alex noticed and said he'd drive again. We drove out of the rest stop and back onto the freeway. "You handled the conversation with him well. I couldn't tell you were uneasy," Alex said.

I hadn't thought about Alex watching me, but of course he was. He wouldn't have left me alone. "Because I wasn't," I said. "I know you're on an evil-Emil kick, but I have pretty good instincts and Emil doesn't make me nervous." Alex tensed and instead of getting in yet another argument, I decided to change the subject.

"Don't you ever get tired of constantly having to watch over me? You're almost three hundred years old—you're like a geriatric babysitter."

The muscles in Alex's face relaxed. "I never get tired of being with you." Comments like that infuriated me. Alex was so fickle about his feelings. Why did he have to keep leading me on when a few hours earlier he was balking at the idea that he would ever be jealous? I was sick of it and decided to confront him.

I took a deep breath, turning in my seat to face him. "I need to ask you something." I was quiet while I decided what to say. "Why *exactly* did you decide to leave in July? You said you left to stop the Daevos from tracking our bond and finding me, but was that the whole reason?"

The smile dropped from Alex's mouth, a sullen look replacing it.

I continued, "I thought there was a connection between us from that first day in the mountains, but then you were a jerk. I wasn't surprised—you're a guy after all—but when you came back into my life again, acting like you still cared, I was . . . confused. I understand that you being in my life is part of your job, but it seemed like there was more to it than that. I mean, you said you were my soul mate." I looked away, waiting for his response.

When he started talking, I turned back to him. His hands tensed on the steering wheel. "I wasn't *acting* like I cared. I did—I do, care. I left because I had to. I knew my feelings for you were affecting how well I could protect you.

"Once I realized Daevos members were in Gunnison, I left to talk to the Amaranthine leaders about how strong my connection with you was and my theory that our soul mate bond had drawn Emil's clan to us. They advised me to watch you remotely for a few weeks to see if the Daevos threat continued. When Emil came into your life, I had to come back. But since our bond caused the problem in the first place, I knew I wouldn't be able to have a physical relationship with you. Now you know what's happening and even though you're sitting a foot away, we still can't be together because Emil's Clan is too dangerous.

"For me . . ." the words seemed difficult for Alex to find, "getting to stay with you, to spend more time with you . . . to love you the way you should be loved, it's all I live for."

Alex's words shocked me so much I forgot to breathe; when I finally remembered, I gasped a little. Since the day he had shown up at the theater he'd been so aloof about his feelings that I wasn't even sure if he liked me anymore, but now he was telling me he loved me? Alex searched my face for a reaction that would give him more information than my inability to take a breath. "You . . . love me?"

Alex smiled like I was an idiot. "I thought my feelings for you were pretty obvious."

I threw my hands in the air in complete shock and felt like I was reliving our previous conversation at his house when we first started dating. "How could I have possibly known that? You're the king of mixed signals! One minute you're insulting me, the next minute, you're declaring your undying love."

The muscles at his jaw contracted for a moment. "Sometimes I have a difficult time expressing my emotions."

I replayed Alex's words in my head. His feelings didn't seem like a recent development. I wondered how long Alex had been in love with me. "What did you mean when you said you want to love me the way I should be loved?" I asked.

"I can't really be with you like I want to be, or show you I love you until I become human again," Alex explained.

"So, if you were human, we could be together?" I asked. He nodded. "So why would you choose to remain my Protector?"

He looked like he wanted to say more than he should. "I was there the night you came into the safe house. I asked to be put on your case."

"Why would you do that?" I asked.

Again, the look. "We have a history, Evie. I knew without a doubt that I was supposed to be with you—whatever you needed, I knew I would be there forever—and I took steps to make sure that would happen. I wanted to take care of you, to make sure you would be safe—in the hope that one day, one life, we could be finally be together."

I took a moment to process what Alex had told me. I was surprised, happy, and above all else, flattered. Most people have a hard time finding a person they can stand to be with for twenty or thirty years, yet Alex had loved me for centuries. As Alex and I looked at each other, it felt like nothing in the world could tear us apart. He turned his attention back to the road and I said, "I guess it's not all bad. I mean, in some ways it must be nice being a Protector. You have everything anyone could ever want," I pointed out.

"Not everything." He turned away, but I could still see the pain flash across his face. "Protectors are chosen for their strength: both mental and physical. Protecting souls is our job. We have a choice, of course, but being a Protector comes at a *huge* cost."

"What cost?" I asked. "I don't understand."

"In my case, not being able to touch you, or interact with you the way I wanted to. Having to love you in silence for so many years was harder than you can imagine," Alex explained. "When the Amaranthine gave all Protectors orders to guard their Trackers in person, it meant I needed a reason to be in your life every day. I appeared to you in the mountains because you were hopelessly lost and needed help finding your way back to the trail. My plan was to get to know you and be your friend, but once I was in your life again, I couldn't stop there. I let things go too far. When the incident on your living room floor happened, things went downhill rapidly. I shouldn't have touched you, let alone become that intimate with you." He gritted his teeth, disappointed in himself.

I thought about us kissing on the floor and failed to understand Alex's concern. I pushed my brows together and asked, "Why aren't you supposed to touch me? What's wrong with that?"

Alex sighed and smiled. "I tried to tell you about this a few days ago. Remember the bond that allows a Protector to track their client's soul after they die a mortal death?" I nodded, remembering his explanation. He continued, "In addition to our Protector / Tracker bond, your soulmark and mine recognized each other, which made our bond even stronger—and more dangerous. Our bond becomes more intense depending on how intimate we are—that connection makes it easier for a Daevos Tracker to find us. Our connection happened faster than I anticipated it would. Touching you was bad enough, kissing stepped *way* over the line, and anything more than that, well, I might as well have set off fireworks inviting Emil's Clan over."

I grinned, realizing I wasn't as repulsive as I'd thought. If it weren't for the soulmarks and the Daevos, Alex never would have left.

Alex noticed my smile and gave me a curious look.

"What are you thinking?"

I glanced over at him. "About the soulmarks—and that I'm glad you really did want me. I thought you were making excuses."

Alex laughed. "No, I was practicing centuries of active restraint. Even that was hard when we kissed. It took everything I had to stop things from getting more heated, and your eagerness didn't help."

"Speaking of kissing," I raised my eyebrow, "You're pretty good at it. Exactly how many girls have you practiced on?"

He licked his lips and answered, "Just one."

My mouth fell open. "Are you telling me that in the two hundred and seventy one years you've been alive, you've only kissed one other girl?" He nodded. "How is that possible?"

He shrugged. "Things were different then." He could tell I didn't believe him. "Think about it—I spent a lot of my life in boarding schools. When most of my peers were going to parties and meeting their future wives, I was busy running the estates my parents had left me and managing investments. Soon after that, I decided to become a Protector."

Alex's quick summary of his life coupled with the solitary existence he'd lived as my Protector made me think he must have been very lonely. "So you aren't allowed to have a significant other when you're a Protector?"

He lifted his shoulders. "It's not prohibited, but it's not advised either. You're always gone. Unless your partner is also part of the Amaranthine, you can't tell them what you do. Protectors usually resign from their position soon after they get romantically involved with someone."

I was bewildered, still thinking of what an amazing

kisser he was. "One other girl doesn't give you much practice."

Alex's grin was smug now. "Years of watching you kiss other people was a frustrating tutorial. Plus, the chemistry we have helped."

Now I was irritated and uncomfortable wondering what he'd seen. "You watched me?"

"Not often," he said. "I didn't enjoy watching the person I loved look at someone else, let alone kiss them."

I wasn't sure how I felt about that and stared out the window. I recognized the familiar mountains and stores of Gunnison. I was glad we'd be back at my house soon. After about five minutes, Alex sighed, but in a good way. "Do you have any idea how long I've waited to tell you all of this? It has literally been centuries that I've had to keep quiet and not tell you I love you. You can't possibly understand how difficult it's been to watch you date, kiss, fall in love with, and marry other men for so long. Men who could never be right for you because I'm the one who's right—I am your soul mate.

"Everything changes, but my love for you never will. I've fought myself on this too long and I can't pretend anymore. I can't feign that I don't want to talk to you, to reach out and brush the hair out of your eyes, or wipe a tear off your cheek. I want to hold you, to tell you how much I love you, to kiss you without repercussions." His voice grew softer, electricity sparking in the air. "I've loved you since I met you, Evangeline, and I will love you for all of eternity."

He looked at me through hooded eyes. There wasn't anything I wanted more in the world than to feel his hands caress my body and his lips press against mine. I could see my own expression reflected on Alex's face and the car seemed to sizzle with our connection. He slowly moved his eyes from mine so he could drive, but my gaze lingered on his profile, my thoughts focused on the things I wanted from him. I placed my hands in my lap and sighed in frustration.

Alex turned into the driveway of my house. He stopped the car as Emil pulled in behind us. Alex didn't seem any less frustrated than me as he glanced over to gage my mood. He was determined, as if he'd made a decision. "I can't do the things I want to yet, Evie. But I will. Somehow, I'll figure out a way around this so we can be together."

Chapter 18

It had been a week since we'd gotten home from the sand dunes and the entire time I'd been playing referee between Alex and Emil. Despite what Alex had said, I trusted Emil—he hadn't given me a reason not to. Both of them refused to leave me alone. The only reprieve I got was when I went to class. Truthfully, I didn't know what I wanted. If I was being honest with myself, I probably wasn't ready for a relationship with either of them. But I cared about them both more than I wanted to admit.

I was walking to my car after class one afternoon, looking forward to watching movies, ordering pizza, and relaxing at the house. I hadn't invited Alex and Emil along, but I didn't doubt they'd end up there anyway. As I contemplated their excuses for showing up tonight, I didn't notice where I was stepping and tripped. I laughed, pushing myself up and leaning back on my knees. My backpack had fallen open when I landed. As I attempted to gather my books and my dignity, I heard a bemused voice. "Have you always been this clumsy?"

I looked up, but sunlight was reflecting off several

windows on one of the dorms making it difficult for me to see the person speaking—the voice sounded vaguely familiar though.

I grabbed the rest of my belongings and stood, throwing my bag over my shoulder. From this angle, I could see the guy. Recollection, then surprise flashed through my mind and I almost dropped my bag again. He'd looked a lot younger the day I'd met him in the Black Canyon parking lot—the same day I'd met Alex. He'd asked about my car and been persistent when I said I wouldn't go on a date with him; other than that, I had no idea who he was. I wasn't sure if I should pretend I didn't know him, or admit to remembering him. I decided ignorance was best.

I smiled politely, answering, "Not usually."

His face was a picture of calm and he spoke in an eerie tone. "You never called me." So much for acting like I didn't recognize him. Being direct didn't work in our previous conversation, but there was no point in lying.

I wrinkled my brow like I was trying to place where I knew him from, and pretended to realize who he was at that very moment. "I thought I recognized you. I met you in the mountains at the beginning of the summer. Do you go to school here?"

"No. I was looking for you," he said without the slightest hint of teasing in his tone. A chill ran through me like cold fingers had wrapped around the base of my neck. I instinctively wrapped my arms around myself.

I tried to act like it was all a big joke. "That's funny."

He lifted his brow. "What's funny about it?"

"It's strange you would be looking for someone you barely know."

He stepped closer and gave a haunting laugh. "Who says I barely know you?"

I was getting worried, but tried not to let it show. I

didn't have my pepper spray with me. "I've only spoken with you once. Even that didn't last longer than a couple of minutes," I pointed out.

He leered at me and the noise that came out of his mouth could only be described as a cackle. "Evie, Evie, Evie," it sounded like he was saying tsk, tsk, tsk. "Let me ask you a question. What happened to the paper I gave you in the parking lot that day?"

"Umm, I'm not sure," I hedged, "I probably threw it out." I said the words, thinking about the note he'd given me. What had I done with it? I remembered ripping it up and putting the pieces in my pocket.

"Did you read it?" he asked.

I tried to evade him by answering, "I don't remember."

His smile became dark. "Oh, Evie, you *really* should have read that note," he paused as if contemplating something. "Throwing it away was a big mistake."

I tried my best to look amused instead of afraid. "And why is that?"

His smile was menacing and his dark expression seemed to communicate my ignorance. "With enough initiative, that note might have helped you gain your freedom," he said.

"I don't understand."

His maniacal laugh was the last thing I heard.

When I woke, my head hurt and I was curled in a ball on a cold, stone floor. The air was cool and smelled like a combination of wet dirt and mold. I heard tiny splashes as small trickles of water cascaded down the sides of the room I was in. I sat up, the pounding at the

back of my head becoming more painful with each movement. I reached my hand around to rub the aching spot
and a sharp pain shot through my skull. When I brought
my hand forward again, it had blood on it. Unsure how
bad my injury was, I took my jacket off, pressing it against
my wound to stop the bleeding.

I tried to control my panic as my eyes adjusted to
the darkness. I took in my surroundings. I was alone in
what seemed to be some sort of room inside . . . a cave?
The walls were made of jagged, layered rocks in various shades of blue, grey, and black. The crunch of rocks
beneath me echoed off the dense stone in ominous whispers. The room was about ten feet long and twenty feet
wide. A distressed wood table sat in the corner of the
room, the only light coming from one candle sitting on
top of the table. There was one chair next to the table
and the candlelight illuminated some sort of door across
the room. I knew the door wouldn't be open, but had to
check anyway.

I got up slowly, in case any other part of my body
had been injured, and was relieved when my head was
the only thing in pain. I took the candle from the table,
walking across the room. The door was thick, freezing to
the touch, and felt like metal—definitely not something
you would find in a cave. There was no handle on the
door and I assumed the only way to get in was to open
it from the other side. I pushed and rammed my body
against the hulk of metal, but the door wouldn't budge.

I sat down in the chair going over the details of the
abduction in my mind. The last thing I remembered was
talking to the guy from the Black Canyon parking lot and
being scared. Somehow, the guy had knocked me unconscious, but I couldn't remember him hitting me. It didn't
make any sense, but nothing in my life the last couple of
months could be considered normal.

I wasn't sure what the auburn-haired guy wanted. I remembered him saying I should have read the note he gave me . . . what else had he said that day in the parking lot? Most of it was about my car, then he'd asked me to go out with him. He hadn't seemed to like Alex, but Alex hadn't been concerned.

I didn't know what he could possibly want from me. Furthermore, I didn't know where Alex had been earlier, or why he hadn't stopped the guy from taking me. I realized I had come to rely on Alex's protection far more than I thought, and obviously, to my detriment. Thinking Alex could always see me and would be able to stop someone from hurting me had not helped my situation. I knew Alex would be searching for me, but I also knew there was a chance he wouldn't find me. I couldn't count on anyone else to get me out of this mess. Somehow, I had to figure out a way to save myself.

There were no openings in the room other than the door, which I couldn't get out of unless someone came in. I knew enough about defending myself that I might be able to escape the room successfully, but not knowing what I would encounter once I left was the problem. I would fight, if it was the last thing I did, I would make sure this wasn't easy for the people holding me captive. Now I needed to figure out why they had taken me.

As if on cue, I heard someone on the other side of the door. The door opened and the guy with auburn hair sauntered in. He was wearing black pants, a long-sleeved red shirt, and a black tie. "Evie, it's nice to see you awake," the guy said with mocking concern.

I tried to remain as calm as I could, even though I was seething. "My head hurts. What did you do me?"

He leaned against the wall a few feet in front of me, smiling darkly. "You didn't like that? The skill took quite some time for us to acquire."

My eyes felt like they were throwing daggers. "It isn't that hard to knock someone out. Come over here. I'll demonstrate."

The guy tilted his head like he was humoring me. "There's no reason to be flippant. I'm being very civilized considering what I'm capable of. As for knocking a person unconscious, it's not difficult if you use your hands. Assaulting someone with your mind is significantly more complicated," the guy said smugly, the corner of his mouth rising in an abnormal grin.

I stared at him. "That's not possible."

He laughed. "By now, I thought you would be an expert on the impossible."

I furrowed my brow. "Why would you think that?"

"Considering the company you keep, this shouldn't seem strange at all."

I narrowed my eyes at him in suspicion. "I don't know what you're talking about."

He smiled slyly. "Come now, Evie. You were intimately involved with an Amaranthine Protector, and you recently dated a member of the Daevos."

Clearly, this guy had more information than I thought. I turned away, not wanting to admit anything about Alex and Emil. Ignoring him didn't seem to help though because he kept talking, "People like to explain things they don't understand by calling them odd occurrences or impossibilities; really the rationalizations are coping mechanisms people use when they can't deal with the truth. You seem to have adapted well, which is one of the reasons we thought you'd be a helpful addition to our group. We've been watching you for a long time."

I rubbed my hands over my arms in a self-soothing gesture, stunned and disgusted that he'd been spying on me. I also wasn't sure how he knew about the

Amaranthine Society and Daevos Resistance. "What do you want?" I spat the words out through my teeth.

"I think you can be of assistance to me and my group," he answered matter-of-factly. "Before we found out who you really are, we intended to abduct you as a way to force your Protector, Alex, out of hiding. But when Alex appeared to you, it made drawing him out unnecessary. We were trying to decide how to infiltrate Alex's mind right around the same time you and Alex touched. Your connection was much stronger than we anticipated. Alex's bond with you was useful in finding out some of the information we needed, but not all of it. Between your bonds with him and the time you've spent together, you should be able to act as the vessel to help us get into his head and find the information we need."

I furrowed my brow, confused. Alex had told me he couldn't be hurt by the Daevos. "Alex's mind is shielded," I said. "You can't hurt him, and you can't affect his mind."

He gave me a slow, patronizing smile. "His mind is shielded to Daevos members, but not the woman he loves. We can use your connection, to access his memories."

Panic started to race through me. I didn't want Alex hurt because of me. I stepped away from the guy, wanting to run, but I had nowhere to go. I took a deep breath and held my ground, looking him straight in the eyes. "I won't let you kill him," I said.

He shook his head, chuckling. "We don't want to kill him. We want to use him to find out what he knows. We've been watching your schedule and were pleased to find you alone today." He moved with a lethal grace, stepping behind me. I shifted my head to look at him over my shoulder as I felt a tug on the shirt shrug I was wearing and heard the snick of a switchblade. I held my breath, wondering if my throat would be slit, or if I'd be stabbed. Before I could figure out an escape plan, I heard a ripping sound and felt threads fraying from my shrug. The damp cold of the cave hit the warmer flesh of my back causing instant goose bumps. I was grateful he'd only ripped the shrug and not my pale pink camisole. The guy walked to my left side where he could see my back, as well as my face. "We have many plans for you, my little Tracker."

I shivered when I heard the name. I had no idea how they knew I was a Tracker, especially since I'd only recently found out. I also couldn't figure out why these people would want to provoke Alex since he seemed more powerful and indestructible than anyone I'd ever met. "Who is your group?"

The guy looked at me, mystified. "You don't know?" I stared back, unanswering. "We're one of the Daevos Clans."

Of course they were, and Alex had been right all along. Emil's Clan had found me and now they were going to do what they'd been threatening for two hundred and fifty years. But what were they waiting for? And what information did they want from Alex? "I don't know what you think you can learn from Alex. Taking me will only make him angrier when he finds you."

"*If* he finds me," the dark smile was back as he continued, "And the anger is what we're counting on. Alex is quite the historian. He knows a great deal more about the Amaranthine and Daevos than most. You do know how the Daevos came to be?" he asked. I gave a slight nod of my head. "There are secrets the Protectors have about their powers, things I want to know. We're going to learn as much as we can from him, through you."

They obviously didn't know Alex very well if they thought he gave me anything more than obscure explanations. "I won't tell you anything," I said, while trying to hide the fact that I really didn't know anything I thought would be of value. If they believed I had the information they wanted, they might be less likely to hurt me.

The guy smiled, patronizing me, and I noticed his crooked teeth for the first time. He reached a hand toward me, brushing his fingers roughly through my hair. "Truly, I could care less whether you are willing to help or not. We aren't giving you a choice. You will help us, regardless of how much you fight it."

I surveyed the floor like I was thinking, but wanted to scream.

"Rest assured, Alex will not be able to help you unless we let him. Regardless of what you know about Alex, there are many things he doesn't know about *us*." The guy stood, reaching into his pocket with his left hand and pulled out a small vile. He carefully unscrewed the lid from the top, stepping back as he poured it on the floor. Red and black smoke rose from the puddle as it expanded and I started to feel dizzy.

"This should keep both of us entertained. I call it Sync. It requires an established bond between two people in love. Your Protector / Tracker bond with Alex makes it even more powerful. Sync opens up a door into Alex's mind that allows my Clan to view his memories and find out the information he has about the Amaranthine. The potion is spelled so that as long as you're synced to Alex, we can access his memories and copy them—like a computer backup. Your bond opens the channel to his mind, the information flows into the liquid on the floor, and we have it forever. We'll be copying his knowledge, but he won't know it. While we duplicate his memories, you'll be able to see and hear everything he's experiencing, though I doubt you'll remember much."

I looked back at the puddle of what I thought was water, but now appeared to have a sheen over it, like oil.

As I watched, the colors of the puddle started changing in a dizzying rainbow of purples, blues, greens, and reds, hypnotizing me. I tried to look away, but couldn't. It was like I had lost the ability to control my mind and my choices. I got the impression the substance could envelop me in a black hole of darkness if I fell into it. The puddle was no bigger than a dinner plate, but it seemed like it was slowly drawing me in.

I was completely absorbed in the colors and darkness, only vaguely aware of the guy still in the room with me as my mind kept spiraling deeper into the black mass. The guy's voice came like an echo in the back of my mind. "By the way, my name is Caleb." He gave me a chance to recognize the name through the haze in my head. "If you live, you can tell your mother I said hello—or maybe I'll tell her myself." My stomach dropped in terror as the door shut heavily. I heard a key turn to engage the lock, but all I could do was stare in fuzzy horror at the puddle.

My breath came in quick gasps and my head started to pound. It felt like I was being pulled into the hole, but my body remained firmly on the floor of the cave. The feeling was spreading throughout my head. My mind became increasingly foggy and seemed to be somewhere else. Out of nowhere I could see flashes of images, like I was watching them through someone else's eyes. My own thoughts became hazy as I realized my mind was somehow merging with Alex's.

Chapter 19

As I came out of the fog of my mind, the first thing I noticed was the pounding. The loud thumping was coming from a large redwood door with a heavy iron handle at the end of a hall. I wondered why no one was answering it. I looked around at the familiar black marble countertops and stainless steel appliances. I heard a groan coming from the floor and noticed keys scattered haphazardly on the ground like they'd been dropped.

I followed the chaos with my eyes, watching as Alex moved slowly to sit up. Had he been attacked? Was he hurt? I moved my mouth to ask him but no sound came out. I thought maybe I could touch him to get his attention, but I realized I didn't have hands to touch him with. It felt like I was watching a movie and couldn't interact with the people on the screen.

The knocking on the door continued as Alex rubbed his head with both hands like he was trying to calm the pain. His clothes were rumpled, dark circles rimmed his eyes. He placed his palms on the ground, shifting to his knees. As if testing his strength, he gripped the side of the countertop and stood. He walked with hesitation to answer the banging coming from the front door. Heavy footsteps sounded across the wood floor as he ran a hand through his disheveled hair.

I tried yelling his name again, but the sound still wouldn't produce. Alex didn't know I was there, and frankly, I wasn't sure if I was. I felt like I'd disconnected with my body somehow and was an invisible spectator in Alex's life. I took a moment to wonder if I'd died. I didn't feel like a ghost, but I didn't feel like myself either. I could observe what was happening around me, but the things that made me *me*, were missing. It was like my soul had stayed with my body while my mind synced with Alex's. Now I seemed to be stuck in some sort of limbo where I could see and hear everything going on, but no one knew I was there.

As Alex took slow steps down the hallway, I could sense his confusion and frustration. Alex unlocked the door and twisted the handle, opening it slowly. Emil stood in front of him with his hands on the door frame, his face a mask of cold calm. His knuckles were white and the veins in his neck bulged. His gaze tracked over Alex's tight lips and angry expression.

Before Alex had a chance to speak, Emil said, "Where the hell is she?"

Any hints of the pain Alex had endured that caused him to crash to the kitchen floor vanished with Emil's question. Alex widened his stance and crossed his arms over his chest, blocking the doorway. "What are you talking about?"

Emil's eyes were dark and I could see his pulse pounding. "Evie's been missing for six hours. Why the hell haven't you found her yet?"

Alex's eyes went huge with shock and he stumbled back. "What? She's been gone for six hours?"

Emil ground his teeth, then pushed past Alex into the house. "Been sleeping on the job, Night?" Emil glanced down at his watch. "The Tracker you're supposed to protect has been gone for six hours, fourteen minutes, and thirty-two seconds. Clearly, you haven't been paying attention. Use your bond and find her. Now!"

Alex stared at Emil for a few beats. He pressed the tips of his fingers against his head as he closed his eyes. It only took five seconds for him to double over, gasping in pain. When he regained his breath, he stood and mumbled, "This can't be happening." He lifted his hand, touching his thumb to his ring. The circle and half moon symbol appeared. He rubbed his thumb once to the right, then to the left, then straight up. When he'd done that at the sand dunes, he'd been able to see me. This time, there was nothing. He tried three more times with the same result. His breath became labored, unbridled anger flashing in his eyes. He stalked to a statue and threw it across the hallway, imbedding it in a wall. Alex turned on Emil, his expression furious. He mumbled a string of curses. "I find it hard to believe you're not involved in her disappearance, Stone. Tell me what the hell happened to her."

Emil gave a humorless laugh and looked Alex up and down, assessing his disheveled clothes. "Of the two of us, I'm the one who stayed awake long enough to know she was gone. *I've* actually been searching for her during the last six hours. So tell me, Night, how was your nap?"

Alex clamped his hands into tight fists. He looked like he was ready to kill Emil. "I wasn't asleep you jackass. I checked on Evie and she was leaving school. I was going to meet her at her house. The last thing I remember is picking up my keys. I woke up on the kitchen floor to the sound of you beating the door down."

Emil glared. "I'd like to beat more than the door.

I've been here pounding on the door three times since she went missing. How could you lose her like that?"

Through his teeth Alex said, "Are you kidding me? It's not like I did it on purpose. My bond with her is gone." He crossed his arms over his chest, regarding Emil with suspicion. "How did you even know she was missing?" It was more of an accusation than a question.

Emil clenched his jaw. "Like it or not, Night, Evie and I have a bond too. I can't feel it anymore either. It seems both of our bonds with her stopped working at the same time."

Anger and desperation warred on Alex's face.

Emil studied Alex and took a deep, calming breath. "You're going to need help finding her. I'll do whatever it takes to get her back."

I expected more bickering, but instead, Alex assessed Emil and after a minute, nodded his head in a come-with-me gesture.

Emil followed Alex to the sitting room and sat on a large, dark brown leather couch. Alex poured two drinks from a sideboard that sat under a massive portrait of a man in a dark brown suit, and a woman in an emerald dress from another era. I hadn't noticed the picture when I'd visited Alex's house, but we never spent time in the sitting room either. I examined the portrait and noticed the name Mercier scribbled at the bottom of the painting. I remembered the same name next to some of the masterpieces in Alex's art collection. The man in the portrait had dark hair and a chiseled face. The woman's skin was ivory, her features soft, but there was fire in her green eyes. Between the two of them, the family resemblance was unmistakable: Alex's parents.

Alex turned and walked back to Emil, handing him a glass. Emil took a sip and held the glass as Alex lifted his drink to his lips and swallowed the contents with one swift tilt of his head. He walked back to the sideboard to refill his drink. "Where have you searched for her?"

Emil lifted his head watching Alex. "Where haven't I? Her house, the college campus, every store, restaurant, and park in town. Her Mustang is still at the school. From the moment my bond with her was gone, I've been searching for her," Emil said. "Where was she when your bond was severed?"

Alex poured more amber liquid into his glass. "She was walking to her car after class. She fell and when she got up she seemed to be talking to someone I couldn't see. At that point, she disappeared and her bond went with her. I've never felt anything like it. I have no idea what happened."

"So it's similar to the other Tracker abductions that have been going on?" Emil asked.

Alex gave Emil a long, surprised look. "What do you know about the abductions?"

Emil put his glass on the coffee table in front of him. "Enough," he said, lacing his fingers together, resting his elbows on his thighs. "The Daevos leaders are as confused as the Amaranthine."

Alex curled his lip in a sneer like he didn't believe a word Emil was saying. "Well, someone is taking Trackers, so someone has to know what's going on." He sat down in the chair again, this time holding his drink instead of tossing it back immediately. "I've been watching the other Daevos members in town. I assume you're here with them. What do you know?"

Emil looked up sharply and froze. "I didn't know there were other Daevos members in Gunnison."

Alex couldn't cover his surprise. "They've been all over town! They showed up right after Evie and I kissed. I assumed your Clan was using a Tracker and had followed my bond with her. I thought you were trying to seduce Evie into joining your Clan . . . again."

Emil shook his head slowly. "That's not why I came. And I'm here alone. My Clan is still in Greece."

Alex swirled the liquid in his glass, watching Emil carefully. "Why would you come here without your Clan?"

Emil moved his gaze to the floor as if deciding what to say, then met Alex's eyes with a steely determination. "I knew about the Tracker abductions. I thought the more people Evie had watching out for her, the better," he paused as if weighing his thoughts. "But that wasn't the only reason. I came because I had to see her. Regardless of what you believe, I love her as much, if not more than you," Emil said with resolve.

Alex's face burned red with anger and his eyes flashed. The alcohol wasn't helping the situation. "No! You. Do. Not."

Emil pegged Alex with a hard stare. "Yes. I do. I always have. It was as difficult for me to be away from her as it was for you. At least you had the advantage of always getting to see her. I didn't even have that."

Alex took a deep breath so ragged with anger that it seemed like the air was scorching his lungs. "Don't you dare compare your feelings for Evie with my own. You have no idea how much I love her."

Emil lifted his shoulders. "Believe what you want, but I know how I feel. I came here to find her, to be with her again and make sure she's safe from the Daevos."

Alex ground his teeth and flames blazed in his eyes. Emil held his ground as Alex threw his glass against the wall and yelled, "You are the Daevos! You're the person she's being protected from. Don't try to tell me you're worried about keeping her alive."

"Someone has to be worried about that," Emil spat. He gestured toward the sideboard and the amber liquid now dripping down the wall and winding its way through broken glass shards on the floor. "You certainly aren't doing your job."

Alex recoiled like he'd been hit and Emil stood. "Arguing isn't going to help get Evie back," Emil said. "We need to work together."

I could see Alex didn't want to admit that Emil was right. Taking a few cleansing breaths, he composed himself and asked, "If your Clan didn't take her, who did?"

"I don't know," Emil said pacing back and forth in thought. "You said you saw other Daevos members in Gunnison?"

Alex nodded. "I noticed them for the first time in July."

"July? So that's why you left?" Emil asked.

Alex nodded again. "I thought it would be safer if the Clan couldn't track our soul mate bond."

Emil snorted. "The damage was already done. You shouldn't have left after the Daevos members already knew where she was and that you'd been spending time with her."

"I left because I put her in more danger by being around her—especially because of our soulmarks. If anyone should understand that, it's you."

Emil laughed. "No wonder Evie was mad. You told her she was in danger and then you ran away."

Alex ground his teeth. "I did not *run away*. I was still watching her, but she didn't know it."

Emil was quiet again for a moment, thinking. "If you're sure it's the Daevos, I'll find out what I can. We'll get her back."

"*I* will bring her home safely."

"We both will," Emil corrected him. "And just so we're clear, you should know this doesn't change anything. I'm doing this for Evie, not for you. When we find her, I'm still going to fight for her."

Alex nodded in acknowledgment of the warning, and the fact that he couldn't do this alone. "You're probably our best chance for locating her."

Emil walked out of the sitting room and stopped before turning the front door handle. "I'll contact you as soon as I hear anything," he said. The door shut loudly behind him.

I hovered in the corner of Alex's room, watching him. It seemed I had to stay wherever he was—probably a side effect of the mind sync. I watched as Alex ran his fingers through his hair and pulled on a fresh red T-shirt and crisp jeans.

Alex spent the rest of the night and the next day searching for me, for Daevos members, or any other clues that would lead him to me. When I disappeared, the only thing that had been left behind was my backpack. Alex had recovered it and found my house keys inside. He used the keys to get into my bedroom and search there too.

He thumbed through my bookshelves, and flipped back the quilt on my bed. He examined tidy dresser drawers, and fanned open books I'd used recently. My desk was the only thing he hadn't searched yet. The top of it was clean, like everything else. Photos and knick knacks were scattered around the edges. A large calendar was centered in the middle of the desk. Alex examined the calendar, but nothing seemed suspicious. I had almost given up when Alex noticed a few pieces of ripped paper sticking out from under the calendar. I wondered what the scraps of paper were. It wasn't like me to leave trash lying around.

Alex lifted the corner of the calendar and found several more pieces of paper. As I watched him gather the pieces, a memory clicked in my mind and I knew what it was. I couldn't believe I'd kept it! I wanted to scream at Alex to puzzle the shards of paper back together. Alex had the same idea as me. The pieces were large and it only took a few minutes for the message on the jagged edged note to come into focus.

I know who you are. Do you?

– Caleb 555-3845

Alex rubbed the back of his neck like the hair was standing up. I hoped that meant he knew it was a clue. He quickly taped the note back together with supplies from my desk, and left.

Alex met Emil in the parking lot of the Gunnison grocery store. He handed Emil the note, which Emil took with a raised eyebrow. As Emil read, his expression became more concerned. "I remember when Evie got this," Alex explained. "It was the first day I met her in the mountains. A group of guys were standing around her car, all wearing dark grey long-sleeved jackets even though it was the middle of June. I was too preoccupied with Evie to notice how familiar the guys seemed. The ringleader of the group had auburn hair and was a few inches shorter than me. He wrote something on a piece of paper and gave it to Evie. At the time I thought it was a phone number.

"Evie ripped the paper up without looking at it and put it in her pocket. She probably emptied her pockets when she got home that night and forgot about the scraps of paper on her desk. The pieces must have been pushed under her calendar, or she would have thrown them away by now."

Emil's expression hadn't improved since Alex had started talking.

Alex continued, "My gut tells me the guy who gave Evie this note had something to do with her disappearance. I didn't like the guys talking to her from the moment I saw them. Now I realize it wasn't just jealousy I'd been feeling. Plus, Caleb was the name of the guy who visited Evie's parents in Montana and questioned them about her."

The thought that I might not be out of reach seemed to spur Alex forward with a burst of energy. "So now we have a possible name, a description, and a phone number, though I doubt it still works. Do you know of any Daevos members named Caleb?" Alex's voice trailed off as Emil's face started to take on the distinct qualities of a corpse.

Emil nodded. "I heard rumors, but I didn't think there was any way they could be true."

A crease formed between Alex's brows. "Rumors about what?"

"About Caleb. About his Clan."

"He's the leader of a Clan?" Alex asked, surprised. "Are you sure we're thinking of the same Caleb? Because there's no way the guy who hit on Evie could manage his own Clan."

Emil seemed worried. He was gripping his car keys with a force that left his knuckles white. "I'm positive. I only know of one Caleb within the Daevos, and he fits your description. Plus, he's the only Daevos member capable of thwarting your abilities and taking Evie."

"How is that possible?" Alex asked. "The Daevos have limited powers compared to the Amaranthine."

Emil explained, "The Daevos's restricted powers make it difficult to fight the Amaranthine. Several years ago, there were rumblings throughout the Daevos community that a Clan leader named Caleb was trying to figure out a way to get more powers, either on his own, or with the help of the Daevos leaders. No Daevos member believed Caleb would be able to access the powers of the Goddesses; not while the Daevos were doing Callista's work and hurting people and taking souls.

"Almost all Daevos members ignored the rumor and thought that if Caleb was really trying to gain access to additional powers, he was wasting his time. That was the last I heard of it. Obviously Caleb figured something out, because Evie is gone, and we can't find her."

The situation was worse than I thought. I could tell by their morose expressions that Alex and Emil agreed with me. If the Daevos had access to more powers, it could threaten the entire Amaranthine Society and start a war between the two groups. "If Caleb has obtained other powers, how do I fight his Clan?" Alex asked. "I don't understand how their powers work, or even what powers they have."

Emil nodded in agreement. "I'll do some checking and try to get more information about this. Go back to your house; I'll come over as soon as I know something."

I could tell Alex didn't want to go home and wait, but Emil wouldn't get many answers if he was seen hanging out with a Protector. Alex seemed grateful that Emil was willing to risk himself to help me. "Come as soon as you can," Alex said.

Emil nodded. His determined expression was the last thing I saw as Alex and I drove away.

Emil showed up at Alex's house the next afternoon.

"What took you so long? Were you able to learn anything about Caleb?" Alex asked, sitting down.

Emil sat across from him. "Yes." The trepidation in his voice indicated Alex wouldn't like what he was about to hear. "I talked to one of the Clan members."

Alex went absolutely still. "You did what?" Alex fumed. "How did you find them? Did you see Evie? If you had one of them, why didn't you let me know?"

Emil put his arms out, palms up, and wrinkled his brow. "What was I supposed to do, hogtie the guy in the middle of the store aisle? That would have been a great way to earn his trust—and the trust of the rest of the Daevos."

Alex threw his hands in the air. "Dammit! I knew I should have been following you. If I'd been there, Evie would be home by now."

Emil sighed. "No, she wouldn't. If anything, she would be harder to find. Can you stop overreacting long enough for me to tell you what I learned?"

Alex took a few deep breaths to calm down. Emil started again, "I saw a Clan member's vowmark and followed him into a store. I showed him my mark so he agreed to talk to me. His name is Joshua, and he told me a little bit about what his Clan has been doing in Gunnison. Caleb was able to figure out how to get additional powers and has started using them—which is why you can't see him. He's also figured out how to make the bonds between Protectors / Trackers undetectable. I'm assuming he's the one who's been taking Trackers, but I don't know for sure. Right now, I think those are the only things Caleb has been able to master, but his Clan is trying to learn more, which, I assume, is why they took Evie."

Alex seemed confused for a minute, but the muscles in his face drooped as realization hit him. "They think they can get information from her because of the bonds we share."

"Exactly. I think they're using her to find out what you've told her, or what she might have gleaned in the process of dating you. They've been working on getting this information for a long time. We need to be aware that Caleb and his Clan could have powers even the Amaranthine Society and Daevos Resistance don't know exist."

Alex wore a determined expression. "Do you know where she is?"

Emil looked at his hands, intertwined like a basket. "Not exactly, but I have a pretty good idea. Joshua was getting supplies—coats, blankets, dry and non-perishable food—stuff you would take on a camping trip. I waited for him to leave and followed him as far as I dared. He stopped near Kneeling Camel Overlook at the north rim of Black Canyon."

"So they must be within walking distance of the Overlook."

"Joshua also mentioned Deadhorse Trail, which is near there." Emil shrugged. "It seems like a good place to start looking."

Alex jumped up from the couch. "I'll get the backpacks ready and meet you out front."

Alex rushed to the garage, pulling the fully-stocked hiking bags off a shelf. He scanned the cars in the stalls and grabbed the keys for a red Jeep Wrangler. Emil was waiting around front as Alex pulled up.

The Jeep's leather seats, state of the art sound system, and chrome accessories didn't go unnoticed as Emil got in. "How many cars do you have?"

"A few. I needed one Caleb's Clan hasn't seen me in. Plus a Jeep won't stick out in the parking area if the Clan sees it."

The guys were quiet as Alex drove, but Emil seemed to have something on his mind. After a few minutes he said, "Can I ask you something?"

Alex was guarded but replied, "You can ask, but that doesn't mean I'll answer."

"After all these years, what made you decide to try and have a relationship with Evie?"

I doubted that this conversation was going to be pleasant.

Alex took a deep breath. "I've been patient for a long time. I couldn't wait anymore. I *know* she's my soul mate, and I couldn't stop myself." He slid his glance to Emil. "The truth is, I was hoping she was done needing a Protector. I want to be with her—like we always *should* have been."

The muscles in Emil's neck strained. "You do realize that her soulmark still recognizes both of us, right?"

Alex tightened his grip on the steering wheel. "It's been two hundred and fifty years. I thought she might finally be ready to make a choice."

Emil raised an eyebrow. "That's quite a gamble. Are you really that confident she'll choose you?"

"Based on past history, absolutely."

Emil cocked his head to the side and gave a sly smile. "If you're basing it on the past, you *really* shouldn't be so cocky," he said. "She made a choice then too, Night. At least you've been able to spend time with her as her Protector."

Alex held his lips tight. "Eventually I *will* be more than that. It's not like you didn't have your chance with her." Emil frowned and opened his mouth to defend himself. Alex cut him off. "And since we're playing twenty questions, there are some things I've wanted to know for years." Emil didn't respond so Alex pressed on. "What synapses weren't firing when you decided you wanted Evie to be part of your Clan? You lied to her, put her life at risk, and used her! Now you have the audacity to tell me you're still in love with her? I don't think you love her now, and I doubt you ever did."

Emil's normally calm demeanor was replaced with quiet rage. "You have no idea what happened. Don't assume you do."

"So tell me," Alex challenged, "what did I get wrong?"

Emil's whole body tensed. "I knew from the moment I saw Evie that she was *my* soul mate. I wanted to spend forever with her. Becoming a Daevos member wasn't my decision. I couldn't leave her, so instead I brought her with me—even though I knew it was self-ish. When she left, I thought I would die. The only thing that kept me going was that I knew she would be safe with the Amaranthine Society and someday, I'd have the chance to be with her again. Although if I'd known *you* would end up her Protector, I might have reconsidered."

Alex exhaled in disgust. "I've always had her best interests at heart. That's more than you can say."

Emil locked his jaw until the muscles in his cheeks pulsed. Alex asked, "What do you mean being part of the Daevos wasn't your choice?"

Emil's face hardened at the memory. "I was brought in against my will right after my father died. I knew who the Daevos were and hated what they did. I didn't want to be a part of the Resistance and told my father I never would. Unfortunately, he made sure I wasn't the only one who knew his last request."

Alex's mouth fell open slightly. Emil noticed and smirked. "Not what you thought, is it?"

Alex held the steering wheel a little tighter. "No, it's not," Alex admitted. "I guess we both have a lot to learn about each other."

Silence hung in the air until Emil asked, "Did you tell Evie about my past relationship with her?"

Alex pursed his lips. "Not completely."

Emil considered that. "Did you tell her about yours?"

Alex shook his head. "I spent most of my time trying to get her to believe the Amaranthine and Daevos basics. She threatened to have me committed at least twice. Explaining our past relationship wasn't a top priority."

Emil didn't reply. As Alex pulled up to Kneeling Camel Overlook, Emil pointed out the car of the Clan member he had followed earlier. They got out of the car, grabbed their packs, and Emil started off toward a trail. Alex followed him.

About fifteen minutes into the hike, Emil veered sharply from the trail. "You want to tell me where we're going?" Alex asked.

"I think they went this way," Emil answered.

Alex raised an eyebrow. "You think?"

"I only followed them to the Overlook," Emil said. "I have a feeling they went this way though."

Alex ran his tongue along his teeth, debating the merits of trusting Emil's feelings, but ultimately Alex decided to follow him. They walked for another hour, backtracking frequently each time Emil felt like they needed to change directions. When they got to a large outcropping of rocks, Emil came to a standstill. The rock was part of a larger mountain peak that extended for what seemed to be miles into the sky.

"Is there a reason we stopped?" Alex asked, glancing around for signs that they were being followed.

"Joshua mentioned this area when I was talking to him. I think she's in there." He pointed to the rock, which, from what I could tell, didn't have an opening—like most rocks.

"In the mountain?" Alex asked.

Emil nodded.

Alex clicked his tongue against the top of his mouth as he thought. "How do you propose we get inside?"

Emil looked around. "I doubt all of Caleb's Clan members have the ability to disappear and reappear yet. I'm sure there's a physical entrance, we just have to find it. You take the right, I'll take the left."

Alex nodded, and Emil set off in the other direction, both of them following the perimeter of the mountain. Alex had been searching for ten minutes when Emil came toward him. "I found it. The entry is obscured by trees, but it's there," Emil affirmed.

Alex followed him to what seemed to be the opening of a cave. The dark entryway was about seven feet tall and three feet wide. "It's pretty brave of them to leave this area unguarded, don't you think?" Alex asked.

"Maybe," Emil assessed the area with a trained eye. "Or maybe they were hoping for visitors."

Emil's words seemed to make Alex more determined. "Then we shouldn't disappoint them," Alex said. He started into the cave, but Emil grabbed his shoulder and pulled him back.

"You can't go charging in there," Emil said. "We need to think this through."

Alex held his hands out, palms facing each other and widened his eyes. "What's there to think about? If they're hiding in here, Evie is with them. Let's go get her back."

Emil shook his head. "It's not that simple. If they set this up with the hope that you'd come looking for them, it won't be easy to find Evie. They have powers we don't know about or understand. Not only that, but they can sense you better than you can sense them right now; I'm sure they'll be prepared for a fight."

"Fine with me," Alex shrugged.

Emil held up his hands in a gesture of defeat. "If you want to get yourself killed, you're just making my life easier. If you're dead, I don't have to worry about who Evie will decide to be with." He stepped back and leaned against the side of the rock wall, crossing his arms.

"Fine," Alex said, conceding that Emil had a good point. "What should we do?"

Emil seemed to have a plan. "You need to follow me. Stay far enough back that you'll be hidden from view, but you can still see me. If I run into one of Caleb's Clan members, I'll tell them I met Joshua at the store and that I'm part of another Clan in Greece."

Alex thought about it, nodding his head once in agreement. "I'll be behind you. Let's go."

Emil started walking and Alex stayed back as far as he could. They were only about thirty feet into the cave when darkness enveloped them like a black hole. I saw a small light ahead and noticed it was moving. I wondered if someone was coming toward Emil and Alex, but the light disappeared like it was being blocked, and I realized it was Emil's light. He must have grabbed a flashlight from his hiking pack.

Alex turned his head each time he heard movement. He paid close attention to the crevices and alcoves in the cave walls in case someone was hiding from them. He also searched the walls for things out of the ordinary—a passageway, a cavern or room, someplace that I might be held captive—but he found nothing.

As they continued farther into the heart of the mountain, water dripped from the walls. In the blackness, they had to carefully dodge an array of stalactites on the ceiling and their companion stalagmites below. I wondered what other surprises the mountain contained.

As Alex and Emil rounded a corner, I heard a noise from ahead. It sounded like the muffled footsteps of people moving quickly through the cave. Alex crept forward, watching Emil, but Emil's flashlight abruptly stopped moving. Alex leaned back into the wall of the cave, searching silently until he found a slight crevice he could conceal himself in. At the same moment, I heard a voice.

Evangeline.

I glanced around, but couldn't see anyone. I turned back to Alex. He took a few deep breaths, pressing his hands to his head like he had a headache.

Evangeline. Wake up.

The voice had a soft, wispy quality to it, but still, I couldn't find the person talking to me.

Evangeline! You need to help him.

I could feel myself being pulled from the scene I'd been watching, like my mind was letting go of the connection to Alex. Things were becoming fuzzy again. I glanced back at Alex in time to see his face tugged tight with agony as he fell to the ground. The last thing I saw was Alex writhing in pain as my head began to throb . . . and then the light went out.

Chapter 20

Evangeline.
Evangeline. Wake up.
Evangeline! You need to help him.

I woke with a start, gasping for breath. My head pounded and my clothes were wet from a puddle on the ground. My mind was muddled like I'd been dreaming. I sat up slowly, taking in the cave that had been my prison. I didn't even know how long I'd been here. The candle on the table in the corner still burned, but how many times had it been replaced? I brought my knees to my chest and rested my head, trying to calm down and make the pain go away. I thought about what I'd seen while I'd been under Caleb's spell. I remembered bits and pieces, but not a lot of detail. I'd been watching Alex and Emil. I knew they were coming to find me, but I didn't know if they were in the right place. I put my hands on my head and rubbed the tender spots, hoping the throbbing would subside. Why had I woken up? Was Caleb done with me?

I got an answer, but it wasn't the one I was looking for.

Find your soul mate, Evangeline.

The voice was feminine and melodic. I quickly scanned the room looking for the source of the voice. No one was there. I snorted. Since I was hearing things, I might as well reply. "I'm stuck in this room, so I'm pretty sure my soul mate will have to find me." When the voice didn't answer back, I asked, "Who are you?"

A friend.

The voice paused.

Help him, Evangeline.

I lifted my hands rubbing my temples as I mumbled, "I don't know how."

As I said it, I felt something hit my back like I'd been punched, only the sensation was energizing and the pain in my head instantly subsided. My soulmark pulsed as I watched two ropes extend in front of me: one silver, the other blue. The ropes slithered across the floor, and out the door.

The door! It was open! I jumped up and ran toward it to make sure it wasn't a mirage. The heavy steel was pushed wide enough for me to slip my head through and look around. Candles flickered, but I couldn't see anyone on the path. I looked both ways trying to decide where to go. Surely, Caleb would know I was no longer synced with Alex and would try to figure out the problem. I didn't want to run into Caleb and his Clan if they came looking for me. The door opened onto a small pathway. I could go left or right. I wasn't sure which way to turn.

Follow the bonds.

As the voice said it, my soulmark pulsed and the ropes stretched to my left, vibrating with light. I checked once more for Clan members waiting to ambush me, then I crept into the hall. Light flickered from candles placed in crevices of the wall every ten to fifteen feet. I followed the path up: a maze of switchbacks balanced precariously next to a steep drop that would have put the Mines of Moria to shame. I huddled close to the rock wall, gripping it for balance as I kept walking, guided by the lighted ropes.

It took about ten minutes to reach the top of the switchbacks. There, the path branched off in three directions. I assumed the two ropes represented the bonds I had with Alex and Emil. I was relieved to see that both ropes turned in the same direction: right. The path was wider now and I didn't have to worry about the drop as much. But I still kept my step light, staying in the shadow of the cave wall so I'd have a place to hide in case someone came looking for me.

It wasn't long before I heard the sound of muffled voices. I slowed my step as my eyes darted in every direction, trying to sense where the voices were coming from. The ropes continued to guide me until the silver rope made a sharp left, enveloped by a bright light. The blue rope continued forward. I wasn't sure what was around the corner, but the light made me think I'd find people there. I scooted in close to the wall, hidden as much as possible as I tried to decide which rope to follow—then I heard a familiar voice coming from the lighted area. I crept closer, peering around the edge of rock into a cavern-like room where the voice had come from and almost jumped for joy when I saw Emil standing next to some other men.

I took a moment to consider whether to stay here and watch Emil, or continue on to find Alex by myself. I decided to wait and see what happened with Emil. There was strength in numbers and hopefully he'd be able to help me find Alex. Even in the shadows, I felt too exposed standing there, watching.

I shifted my eyes, noticing a ledge about four feet above me that offered a perfect vantage point of the room, yet still concealed my presence. I assessed the side of the rock, trying to figure out the best climbing path. I reached up, gripped the first hand hold, and started to climb. Trying to make the climb quietly was difficult, and took longer than I expected, but I made it to the top. I sat as far back as I could. I pulled my knees into my chest, trying to make myself as small as possible. Then I watched as I listened to the conversation, and waited.

Emil stood next to two men. He didn't seem nervous and wasn't being held against his will. I had the fleeting thought that maybe Alex had been right and Emil really was dangerous. What if he was working with Caleb's Clan? I let the thought roll through my mind, but it didn't feel right. I decided to see what else happened before I passed judgment.

Aside from the two men and Emil, I could see three other men in the room but didn't know how many others might be in different areas of the cave, or obscured from my sight. Emil greeted everyone, grinning when he got to the last man.

"Hello again, Joshua." Emil said, lifting his hand and giving the other guy a firm handshake.

"Emil. I didn't think you'd take me up on my offer, especially not so quickly," Joshua said. I wondered what offer he was talking about.

"You said you'd be camping near Deadhorse Trail. It's been a while since I've seen any other Daevos so I was glad when I ran in to you."

Someone else came into the room wearing a long black coat that fell to the middle of his calves, and a yellow dress shirt with black slacks. When he turned, I immediately recognized him. I had to hold myself back from jumping off the ledge and beating the crap out of him for what he'd done to me.

"Emil. It's nice to meet you. I am Caleb," he extended his hand. Emil shook it in response. "Joshua told me he met another Daevos in town. I thought he must have been kidding—it would be such an *odd* coincidence, especially since no other Clan is assigned to this area. But here you are, proving me wrong."

"I had some business to attend to in Gunnison," Emil explained. "The rest of my Clan is still in Greece."

"It must be *very* important business. Most people wouldn't have a difficult time making the choice between Gunnison and Greece," Caleb mused. His tone and actions seemed so much more mature and calculated than when I first met him.

"I hadn't planned on an extended stay," Emil said.

"Ah, well it is a nice location. The proximity to a college full of love-struck young adults is a perfect hunting ground."

Emil raised his eyebrows. "I imagine."

Caleb paced around the room, focusing on Emil and asked, "What about you? Have you ever found your soul mate?"

Emil smiled. "That would be a little difficult considering what we believe."

Caleb chuckled. "Yes, you would think so, wouldn't you?" He stilled for a moment. "And what about the visitor you brought with you? Do you think *he* has found *his* soul mate?"

Emil tensed, giving a slight glance into the darkness outside the room. "What visitor?" he asked, trying to sound innocuous. My heart beat faster with the knowledge that they knew about Alex.

Caleb was both irked and amused. "It's not kind

of you to barge in without notice, but to bring a guest, especially one of your enemies, is highly unlike a Daevos. I wonder how truly loyal you are to the Resistance?" Caleb seemed to mull that over while Emil tried to decide his next move. "Maybe we need a test." Caleb suggested.

Emil was cautious as he asked, "What do you mean?"

Caleb put his hands in front of his chin creating a steeple effect with his fingers. "Well, if you captured the Protector who followed you here, the same Protector who is in love with the woman you're in love with—the woman we happen to be holding captive—not only would you get Evie, but you would prove your allegiance to the Daevos."

My mouth fell open in horror. If Emil really wanted me—for whatever reason—Caleb's offer would be difficult to pass up. Instead, Emil's response was diplomatic. "You know that's not possible, Caleb. We can't capture Protectors. Daevos members don't have that kind of power."

Caleb smiled wickedly. "Ah, that is what most Daevos believe, but I have found a . . . loophole."

Emil's brow furrowed at the same time as mine. "How did you do that?" he wondered, a doubtful tone laced his question.

"Centuries of study," Caleb explained.

"Study of what?" Emil asked, bewildered. I listened, trying to learn as much information as possible.

Caleb nodded to Joshua and he walked out of the room. "We have been conducting research on the Daevos and Amaranthine for quite some time. We've had some people help us willingly. As for the others," at this point Joshua came back into the room, carrying a large brown leather-bound book, "we've taken the information we need."

As Emil's mouth dropped open, Joshua placed the book on the table. Caleb flipped through the pages. "This book holds secrets of the Amaranthine Society, the Goddesses, and information about Trackers."

Emil seemed as confused as I was. "But . . . how is that possible?"

Caleb gave Emil a patronizing smile. "Torture, murder, abductions—they're all rather effective. Plus, not all Amaranthine Protectors are happy with the life they've chosen, just like some Daevos members are more devoted than others." He looked pointedly at Emil.

"What do you mean?" Emil asked.

"I mean that in the course of our research, there have been some Amaranthine members who were more than willing to help my Clan in our quest for more power. Some assisted us by choice; others needed . . . convincing, but they eventually helped us find Amaranthine members and Trackers. Over the last few months, one Protector gave us much of the information we needed to enhance our powers. He wasn't even aware that he was doing it. The bond he shares with his client is impressive to say the least, and made it easy to get into his head."

I leaned back hard against the rock, taking a deep breath. I felt like I'd been punched in the stomach. I knew Caleb was talking about me and Alex.

I heard Caleb continue speaking, "We owe him a great deal of thanks. In fact, Alexander, why don't you come out here so we can express our . . . gratitude."

From the darkness, I saw Alex walk into the room held by his arms, one man on each side of him. His clothes were ripped. He looked exhausted, but determination settled on his face. Caleb's smile was sinister, predatory. "It's good to see you again, Alex," he said with a smug tone.

Alex looked him straight in the eye, confident.

"The first time we met, we weren't properly introduced."

"Yes," Caleb agreed, "and the other times, we were more interested in gathering information than dealing with pleasantries."

Alex cocked his head, as if considering the other instances he'd been around Caleb's Clan. "I've been watching your Clan members ever since I saw one of them in the park. Evie had some encounters with Clan members too."

"Those weren't the only times we saw you . . . or Evie," Caleb smiled.

A shiver ran down my spine, but a realization seemed to hit Alex. "You were the one responsible for scaring Evie outside her kitchen window." At the mention of the figure I'd seen, surprise flashed across Caleb's face. "If you wanted me, why didn't you take me?" Alex sneered.

Caleb's mouth formed a sinister curve. "You have a lot to learn about me and my Clan. There are a number of reasons we didn't capture you; the most obvious is that since your Protector mind shield prevents us from getting into your head, we needed to find another option. We realized we could get information from you by accessing your mind through Evie."

His words sent hot rage through me, heat burning in my eyes. Alex's expression echoed my own. The change of countenance was not lost on Caleb as he motioned to his Clan members to hold Alex tighter. Alex laughed, mocking Caleb with his tone. "Do you honestly think they can stop me?"

"No," Caleb admitted, "but since I have Evie, and her life is in my hands, I trust you won't do anything stupid—though maybe stupidity is part of your personality. After all, your carelessness is how we found out some of the Amaranthine secrets. You have no idea how much you let your guard down around her, do you? It was fantastic when you decided to have a relationship with her. And the night the two of you kissed the first time! We never guessed you would be that reckless. It made your bond stronger and easier to access." Caleb put his index finger to his smiling lips and for a moment, seemed lost in thought.

"You were able to find out how to enhance your powers simply because I had a relationship with Evie?" Alex asked.

"In all the years of Daevos existence, no one has ever succeeded in penetrating the Amaranthine Society defenses. We had been working on it with our allies and captives when we heard about you and your history with Evie. Gaining access to additional powers wasn't really something anyone believed was possible, on your side as well, I'm sure. Then again," Caleb said, tilting his head, "no one had ever seen a connection like the one you and Evie share." Emil and Alex both cringed, for different reasons.

"It wasn't a coincidence we were in the mountains the day you appeared to her. We knew of Emil's Clan and their obsession with Evie. We also knew about the history you, Evie, and Emil all share. One of our Amaranthine allies was able to find out that Evie was the soul you've been protecting for two hundred and fifty years. We knew she was moving to Gunnison, so we followed her. We had planned to abduct her as a way to draw you out. Your reunion made that unnecessary. The bond between the two of you was so strong when you reunited that we decided to see what would happen once you had an emotional and perhaps, physical relationship. We were glad we waited."

I saw the muscles in Alex's body tense all at once. Through his teeth he said, "If you hurt her, I will kill you.

Torture will seem like a vacation when I'm done with you."

Caleb gave a short laugh, waving Alex off. "That kind of emotional response won't help you. Rest assured though, Evie is fine."

Alex measured Caleb, his expression shrewd. "Why couldn't I see you when you took Evie? And why can't I find my bond with her?"

Caleb's eyes danced. I could tell he enjoyed having information that Alex didn't know. "Because I made sure you couldn't."

I had been so focused on the conversation between Caleb and Alex that I hadn't been paying much attention to Emil. Caleb was about to start speaking again when I heard a crash and a loud thud. Emil had turned on Joshua, smashing his head into a desk. Joshua was stunned. Emil grabbed him, putting his hands on the sides of Joshua's head and locking eyes with him. A dark red smoke immediately swirled around Joshua. Images from Joshua's past started flashing in rapid succession through the smoke. As each image formed, it floated into the air and disappeared.

I watched in stunned silence until Caleb's voice broke me from my trance. "Grab Emil, kill him if you have to!" he barked.

Caleb's minions rushed toward Emil. In the chaos, Alex broke free of the two men holding him. He punched one of them in the neck, collapsing his airway. The man gasped for breath as he fell to the floor. If he was anything like Emil, it wouldn't take long for him to recuperate. Alex kicked the other guy in the kneecap and punched him in the stomach. Alex didn't give the guy time to recover. Alex grabbed him and placed his hands on the side of the guy's head, locking eyes with him. The images started to swirl and rise in orange colored smoke, but Alex suddenly let out a grunt of pain and his eyes rolled back into his head. His hands dropped as he fell to the ground with the man whose soul he'd been taking, both of them unconscious. I gasped and heard Caleb cackle. Then the voice came again.

Help them.

Another punch hit my back. I jerked forward, the energy flowing through me. I moved quickly from the ledge, unnoticed in the chaos, and jumped down. I stayed to the shadows as I surveyed the scene. Joshua was sprawled on the ground, his soul gone. The two men Alex had been trying to kill were still on the ground with him, but they were stirring. That left Caleb and two more clan members as an immediate threat. We'd have to deal with the other guys as soon as they were healed enough to get up. And I still didn't know what had happened to Alex.

Emil stood stock still, staring at Caleb. The two other men moved in front of Caleb forming a barricade for Emil to get through. "It seems we've discovered where your true loyalties lie," Caleb said to Emil.

No one had noticed me yet, so I hung back, trying to figure out the best way to help the situation. "What did you do to Alex?" Emil asked.

Caleb curled his lip into a sinister grin. "The souls of my Clan members are spelled. Any Amaranthine member who tries to take our souls will be hit in the stomach with a lightning-like pain so intense that they become unconscious." He frowned. "We didn't anticipate a threat from other Daevos members, but I imagine traitors like you are in the minority. My preference would have been for the Amaranthine member to die when they attempted to take one of my Clan's souls, but our Trackers don't have that kind of power yet."

Emil blinked. "So you really are the one who's been

taking Trackers?"

Caleb looked at him like he was an idiot. "People have underestimated the powers of Trackers for years. They can do so much more than find silly bonds. With enough of them, we could rule the heavens. Even the Goddesses would have to bow to our whims."

Emil gave a dry laugh. "You're insane. It will never work."

Caleb laughed and gestured to Alex on the floor. "It already has." He looked back at Emil. "And now, we'll take care of you." The two men in front of Caleb stalked toward Emil. Emil grabbed a broken leg from the desk where he'd thrown Joshua as the two clan members circled him. Emil was surrounded. One man motioned to the other, and they both attacked at once. Emil used the leg of the desk to smack one of them in the side of the head while he flipped around and kicked the other. Emil pushed the splintered side of the desk leg into the neck of the first guy. He fell to the ground, blood flowing from his carotid artery.

It was then that I noticed the Clan members who had attacked Alex start to rise from the floor. I knew I couldn't kill them, but they could be hurt. I'd taken a self-defense class in high school and ran through the basics in my head, hoping my beginner skills would be enough to slow them down—and keep me, Emil, and Alex alive.

The guy Alex had punched in the neck seemed to be moving the slowest, so I targeted him first. His back to me, I rushed him and wrapped my arms around his neck, cutting off the air supply to his already fragile wind pipe. He gasped for breath, drawing the attention of the other Clan members and Caleb. I heard Caleb bellow, "Who let her out?" I wrapped my arms tighter, knowing I'd soon have Caleb and another clan member to contend with. Before either of them could reach me, the guy I was holding around the neck went limp in my arms. I let him go and he dropped to the floor in time for me to be jerked into the arms of the other man. He embraced me tightly. His arms wrapped around my body holding me below my elbows so I couldn't lift my forearms and break free.

I glanced at Emil. He'd also been subdued. Caleb walked toward me, fury radiating from his body with every step. "How did you get out?"

I blew hair out of my eyes and answered, "Your security system could use some work."

Caleb's face was pulled back in a snarl as he came closer. He stopped inches from me, running his hand down my cheek, lifting my chin to meet his eyes. "That. Was a mistake. Now that I know you're going to be a problem, I'll make sure your life isn't as easy as I'd planned for it to be."

He nodded to the guy behind me. "You know where to take her." He turned to the man holding Emil. "Kill him," Caleb said.

As soon as I heard the words, I felt another punch and the pulsing energy from my soulmark started again. I wasn't sure how, but I knew I had the power to defeat Caleb and all of his Clan. Instinctively, I closed my eyes, concentrating on the lily on my back. The power increased rapidly, a hum emanating from my body. My skin started to tingle and I felt like I was vibrating. I opened my eyes and concentrated my energy toward the guy holding me and thought, *release*. Instantly, he loosened his grip. I looked at Emil, focusing my energy behind him. The guy holding him let go, and Emil quickly stepped away.

Caleb's mouth fell open in shock as I lifted my hands. To be honest, I was pretty surprised myself, but I didn't have time to think about what was happening. The only thing that mattered was that it worked. I needed a way to immobilize the men. I shifted my gaze to each Clan member and as I did, I thought, *freeze*. As soon as the thought entered my head, each man stopped as if paralyzed in place.

When I got to Caleb, the urge to command him to *die* was overwhelming, but I knew death wouldn't be enough, and since he was a Daevos member, I wouldn't be able to kill him anyway. Caleb's soul needed to be taken, and I didn't have that ability. I made Caleb freeze in place as well. Emil gazed at me with wonder.

"Evie, are you all right?" he asked.

I nodded. "I don't know how long I can hold them like this. I need you to take their souls."

Emil put his hands on the head of the man closest to him and locked eyes with him. The memories started to circle and rise in a haze of green smoke. Emil worked his way around the room as I held the Clan members in place with my mind. It wasn't long until Caleb was the only Clan member left.

I wanted to ask Caleb questions, but I also didn't want him free. Instead I released the muscles from his neck up, allowing him to speak. His face was red and he seemed angry, but there was a sly undertone in his expression—like he had a secret he wasn't going to tell. He directed his comments toward Emil. "I knew you couldn't be trusted. You are a traitor and a fool. You will be caught, other Clans will be told about this," Caleb said in an authoritative, calm voice that was more menacing than a scream.

I was furious at what Caleb had done to me and Alex and Emil, not to mention the Trackers he said he'd been abducting. Anger radiated from me as I continued my hold on Caleb and watched Emil stalk over to him. Emil grabbed him by the arm and Caleb didn't even flinch. "Five of your Clan members are dead, Caleb, and you don't have a shred of remorse. *No one* will find out what happened here today."

Caleb chuckled. To me he said, "If you trust Emil to keep his word and continue to help you, you are even more of a fool than he is."

Emil wrapped his arm around Caleb's neck. "Tell me where you're keeping the other Trackers." His voice was threatening as he held Caleb in a head lock.

Caleb was livid, but couldn't move to struggle against Emil's hold. "You have nothing to bargain with, thus I have no reason to tell you."

"You're right," Emil admitted, "I will kill you regardless, but the method of your death is up to you. Tell me where they are, and it will be much less painful than it could be."

Caleb's lips curled into an ominous smile. "They're around."

Still holding his neck, Emil grabbed Caleb's right arm. He started to pull the arm backward as Caleb yelled. It seemed the paralyzing I'd done didn't numb a person's pain—good to know. Emil pulled Caleb's arm until his shoulder popped out of its socket. Caleb screamed. "Where?" Emil asked through his teeth.

Caleb took a few deep breaths. He forced another smile through his pain. "You'll never find them."

Emil let him go. His arm hung limply at an unnatural angle. Emil glowered fiercely, leaning over him only an inch from his face. Emil took Caleb's left arm in his hand, fracturing it below the elbow. He waited for Caleb's screams to stop and said, "I don't know what you're capable of and I won't take chances with Evie's life. Tell me now, or die forever."

Caleb's lips formed a hard, determined line. "Forever is such a subjective word. Trust me when I say I'm not afraid of you."

Emil gave Caleb a disgusted look, but his gaze

softened as he glanced at me. "The Amaranthine might be able to make him talk. I can try to get them here. Do you think you can hold him frozen?"

I was shaking with power, but I wasn't used to the new force inside me. I knew I couldn't stay at this level much longer. "I don't know," I answered, but even as I said it, I could feel my energy becoming more unstable.

Caleb watched and started to laugh. "She weakens even now. When I escape you, her death will be my motivation. Remember that. I will not give you, or anyone else the answers you seek."

Emil fumed, rolling his hands into tight fists. The anger compounded with each passing second. "Then you've made your choice." Emil moved over him and grabbed the sides of his head, locking eyes with him. A jet black smoke, darker than anything I'd ever seen, started billowing out of Caleb's mind, filling the room. An eerie smile formed at the corners of his mouth. Through the darkness, I could barely make out the images from Caleb's memories as they rapidly floated into the air. Like his Clan members, the pictures simply disappeared. Soon, Caleb's soul was gone, but the evil smile stayed on his face even after Emil removed his hands and stumbled away.

Emil bent at the waist, taking several deep breaths. Then he stood, met my eyes, and held my gaze as he reached me in three long strides. He swept me into his arms, holding me tight. I pressed into him, molding myself to his body, thawing my soul with his warmth. Emil let go of me enough to put his hands on my cheeks and search my eyes. I stared back, the shock of everything that had happened eclipsed by the man standing in front of me and the feelings raging inside me. I wanted to kiss him, feel his body wrapped around mine, enveloped in his essence. I leaned up, my eyes still locked with his.

He moved his arms around my waist as he slowly inched his mouth closer to mine. My eyes fluttered shut, Emil's breath sweeping a hot path over my lips—

"I don't mean to interrupt, but I could use some help."

I jerked my head around and saw Alex sitting up, a frown set firmly on his mouth. Emil released our embrace as he whispered a husky, "Later," in my ear. I glanced at him and hurried to check on Alex. I knelt down, taking Alex's hand, but he pulled back. I should have expected that after what he'd seen between Emil and I. Emil came over and we both helped Alex stand.

"Are you okay?" I asked.

Alex seemed weak, but stood firm. "I think so." He turned to Emil. "I saw you take Joshua's soul. Did the memories of the other Clan members vanish as well?"

Emil nodded, concern lining his face. "I've never seen anything like it," My confusion must have been obvious because Emil continued, clarifying. "Usually when a soul is taken, the images from their memories float into the air and burst into a fine dust the same color as the soul's smoke, completely destroyed. That didn't happen today. Instead, the memories disappeared."

Emil shifted his eyes to Alex and they seemed to share a silent conversation. "What happened after I passed out?" Alex asked.

Emil and I explained what Caleb had done to Alex. We guessed that when Caleb's soul was taken, the spell keeping Alex unconscious was released. I told him about the mind sync and what Caleb had done to get access to Alex's memories. I said Caleb had admitted to abducting the Trackers. We also told him about fighting the other clan members, and my sudden powers that had helped me find Alex and Emil, and helped us defeat Caleb's Clan.

Alex pressed his lips together and closed his eyes. He took a deep breath. "I can feel our bond again. I don't know where the powers came from that helped you defeat them, or how you used them. Your Tracker abilities haven't been activated, if they had, we would feel it. What happened before you felt the power?"

I explained what I'd experienced and the voice I'd heard in my mind. Emil and Alex exchanged a glance that seemed to be a combination of curiosity and concern. Alex scrubbed a hand over his face. "I need to talk to the Amaranthine leaders about all of this." He gestured to the bodies of the six Clan members scattered around the room. "Maybe the other Protector / Tracker bonds will be working again too. If that's the case, the Amaranthine should be able to find the missing Trackers."

Alex looked at Emil as he reached in his pocket. He pulled out his car keys and tossed them. Emil caught them with one hand. "Will you take Evie home and watch over her until I get back?"

Emil nodded.

"How long will you be gone?" I asked.

Alex's face took on a worried expression. "I don't know." He lifted his hand and pressed his thumb against his ring. He rubbed the ring in three counter-clockwise circles as a golden light flashed, enveloping him—then he vanished.

Chapter 21

*E*mil helped me on the hike back to Alex's Jeep. I didn't say much as we drove back to my house. Emil seemed to understand my need to take it all in. Maybe I was in shock, or maybe my mind was just trying to muddle through it. Alex said my Tracker abilities hadn't been activated, but something had happened to me. I wasn't sure what it was, but I felt different. In the past, I'd only noticed my soulmark when I'd touched Alex or Emil. Now I only had to think about them for the heat to be present. I hoped Alex would be able to get some answers from the Amaranthine about what had happened in the cave, and to me.

My house was empty when we got there. Emil opened the front door. He followed me inside, checking the house while I went upstairs to take a shower. I turned on the water, peeled off my grimy clothes, and took the longest, hottest shower I've ever had.

I didn't think about the two men in my life, or the information I had learned about both of them. Instead, I concentrated on getting things back to normal, at least as normal as they could be now. I was excited to see Jasmine and Zach and hang out with them again. I thought of my classes, my job, and homework that needed to be done. I remembered my Mustang still in the Western State parking lot and couldn't wait to take it out for a drive. I focused on the rituals in my life that were ordinary—the things I could control—because Alex and Emil were anything but normal and they both threw my life completely out of balance.

When the hot water began to turn cold, I finished my shower and put on my favorite cotton pajama pants and T-shirt.

Emil was sitting on the couch when I went downstairs. "How was your shower?" he asked, his eyes tracking over me, making sure I was okay. "Do you feel better?"

"Yeah, a lot better. Thanks." The familiar scent of cheese and tomato sauce hit me and my stomach rumbled. A large pizza was sitting on the table. I was overwhelmingly grateful Emil had the forethought to get food. I realized I hadn't eaten since I was taken by Caleb three days ago.

Emil stood. "Do you need anything? Are you hungry? Are you tired?"

"I'm fine," I said, as I maneuvered toward the table where I grabbed a couple pieces of pizza and a can of Pepsi. "I just want to relax and watch TV or something."

I ate my food and settled into the couch. Emil moved closer, putting his arm around me. I drifted off to sleep, comforted by Emil's arms and the smells of home.

When I woke the next morning, I was still on the couch. I sat up, running my hands through my hair as the enticing aromas of bacon and syrup hit me. I made my way into the kitchen where Emil was cooking breakfast. He smiled. "Good morning, beautiful."

I smiled back, knowing beautiful was probably not a very accurate description this early in the morning. He pushed me toward the table and put a plate of French toast in front of me. "How did you sleep?" he asked.

I picked up a fork and started to eat. "Better than I have in a few days."

Emil grabbed the milk off the counter and poured me a glass. He put it in front of me and went back to the stove, flipping the last pieces of French toast. "Are you feeling all right?"

I nodded. "My head is clearer, but I still don't remember everything I saw while my mind was synced with Alex's. I have a feeling it will come to me over time though."

Emil watched me carefully. "You saw and heard everything Alex did?" he asked.

I nodded again while I finished chewing. "I felt drugged and not very responsive, but I could see the things that were going on. It was kind of like watching a movie on pain killers." I took another bite as I thought about what had happened. "How did you find me? How did you even know I was gone?"

Emil turned the stove off and sat across from me. "There are some things we should probably talk about, Evie; one of them has to do with how I knew you were gone."

I eyed him suspiciously. "Okay."

He took a breath, exhaling slowly. "Alex has a bond with you, but so do I. When your bond with Alex was severed, he passed out, but I didn't. I should have been able to find you, or at least sense our bond, but whatever Caleb did severed every connection to you—almost like you were in a bubble. As soon as you were gone, I started searching for you. Once Alex was conscious again we agreed to work together. Alex thought my Clan had something to do with your disappearance, but my Clan is nowhere near Gunnison, so I knew we were dealing with a bigger problem. I didn't know who had taken you, but I knew with Alex's help, we could defeat them and get you back."

I wrinkled my brow. "But you fought other Daevos members." I wondered how he would get away with what he had done.

"Yeah, I did." He pulled his lips down and his eyebrows came together forming a line. "Hopefully no one in the Daevos Resistance will find out."

"What will happen if they do?" I asked.

Emil turned away. "I betrayed them. They'll take my soul."

I gasped, my eyes growing wide. "Why would you take that risk?"

Emil looked at me like I was an idiot. He leaned across the table and in a low voice said, "Because I love you more than I love my life, my soul, or anything else— I always have."

My chin dropped as I stared, then pulled my eyes away, looking at the table. "Emil . . . I . . . I don't know what to say."

"You don't have to say anything. The fact that you know how I feel is enough. All I want is your consideration." Emil reached across the table, placing his hand lightly on my cheek. "I know it's a lot to take in with everything that's happened lately. Think about it, that's all I'm asking."

Though it was difficult to comprehend after what Emil had said and done, I knew from my recent personal experience that Daevos members were masters of manipulation. I didn't know how to tell him what I felt without offending him and decided to just say it. "Thinking about it isn't hard, but how do I know you aren't just telling me what I want to hear so you can gain my trust and take me yourself?"

I watched Emil's expression contort into confusion. "What? Why would I want to abduct you? I risked my soul helping to save you."

I searched his eyes and found only sincerity. I answered his question with the information Alex had told me, "Because you pretended to be in love with me two hundred and fifty years ago to try and get me to join your Clan. How do I know you're not doing that again?"

Emil pursed his lips. "Alex needs to get his facts straight before he opens his mouth." The grinding of Emil's teeth was a clear indication of his irritation. "I didn't pretend two hundred and fifty years ago. I wanted to be with you because I loved you, and you loved me back. I knew our relationship could put you in danger, but finally, I got sick of fighting my feelings." Emil took my hand, looking directly into my eyes. "Evie, I loved, still love, you more than I have ever loved any soul." His eyes burned into mine and I couldn't look away. "You were the reason I never left my Clan—I was trying to keep them away from you."

I didn't know whether to believe him. Alex seemed to think Emil was rather untrustworthy, even if he *had* helped to save my life and told me he loved me.

"You don't believe me," Emil said, though it wasn't a question. "I stayed with my Clan because I decided it would be easier to protect you if I was with them and knew what they were doing."

"That's a pretty convenient excuse," I said, still hesitant.

"Did Alex tell you what happens to Clan members

once they leave a Clan?"

Actually, he hadn't. "No," I said, "but if it were important, I'm sure Alex would've said something."

Emil laughed. "Right, making me sound like less of a monster would have been his first priority. You can't leave the Daevos. If you want out of the Resistance, you have to escape. Even if you're able to get away, your Daevos Clan immediately starts hunting you. Once you're no longer part of the Daevos power source, you lose the benefits of the Resistance: the money, cars, houses, and people you've known for hundreds, sometimes even thousands of years. You also start to age again, only it happens rapidly.

"If I had abandoned the Clan when I wanted to two hundred and fifty years ago, I would have been dead within a few years. It was better to stay with them, watch you from afar, make sure you were safe, and try to keep them off your trail." He straightened his spine and rubbed his hands down his thighs. "I fell in love with you as soon as I met you and I couldn't let you go. Bringing you into my Clan and subjecting you to the Resistance was a mistake—one I've been trying to amend for centuries, but at the same time, I'm not sorry for the time we had together." I narrowed my eyes in confusion. He caught my expression and said, "Evie, you weren't just some girl I chose to try and tempt. You were my other half. I knew it then as much as I know it now." He took my hand and held my eyes with his. "Evie, your name used to be Cassandra . . . and we were married."

I dropped my fork on the table and my chin followed as my breath grew shallow. I was completely speechless.

Emil continued, "A year after we were married, you overheard some of the members of my Clan talking about a soul death. You asked me what was going on. I told you everything. I had tried to shield you from the Daevos, but it was becoming more and more difficult. You hadn't taken the Daevos vows so I knew you'd be safe with the Amaranthine Society. I told you that you had to leave me." He leaned back in his chair in thought. "You didn't want to go, but finally you agreed. Knowing I had to let you leave was the hardest thing I've ever done, but I knew it was the only way to protect you from my Clan. I'll never forget the last conversation we had. You said leaving would be harder than staying and I told you it would only be difficult until you forgot. You asked me if I would ever forget you—"

"And you said, 'no, never," I answered, staring at him, astonished. Emil had described what I'd seen the first time we touched. I'd been right, it wasn't a dream or a vision—it was a memory. That meant the scene I'd watched when I first touched Alex was probably a memory as well.

Emil quickly shifted his eyes to me in surprise.

"How did you know that?" he asked, bringing me out of my thoughts.

I glanced down at my hand in his. "The first time we touched, I saw what I thought was a vision or dream. It was of a girl in a dark blue dress with long chestnut ringlets. She was talking to a man I couldn't see and they had the conversation you just recounted."

Emil looked stunned. "I don't know how you were able to see those events," he said, "but you're describing things that happened to you in your past. Has this happened any other time?" he asked.

I nodded. "Only one other time. The first time I touched Alex."

Emil rubbed his chin with his thumb and index finger. "Sometimes people have memories that are strong and carry with them into another life. I imagine that by touching me and Alex, your soul recognized those memories for some reason and brought them to your attention."

I crossed my legs in the chair, still holding Emil's hand as we both sat in silence, thinking. After a few minutes I said, "I can't believe you did all that for me. You basically gave up your life to make sure I was safe. You've protected me as much as Alex has."

He lifted his shoulders. "I was the one who got you into the situation, it's the least I could do," he said. "It killed me to not be with you. I didn't appear to you in your other lives because I had to establish myself as a loyal member of the Daevos. Plus, Alex would have thrown a fit and probably tried to take my soul before I had a chance to explain. This time though, he needed my help—whether he wanted to believe it or not."

I wrinkled my brow. "How did you keep finding me in all of my lives?"

He looked up and gazed into my eyes. "I was your husband for a year and despite what Alex might have told you, we were completely in love." Emil paused, thinking about our past. "Our love stayed strong even after you left. You were gone, but the soul mate bond between us was still the same. After our marriage and your escape from my Clan, you eventually died. When that happened, I was able to track your soul through our bond, just like Alex does."

"Didn't your Clan find out?" I asked.

"No, I never told them. I wanted to keep them away from you. No other member of my Clan has ever been in love with someone as deeply as I loved, and still love, you. So no one knows about the bond. I've been able to keep my connection to you a secret. Before you left me, I told you I'd make sure they wouldn't find you. I meant it."

I watched him, stunned, as the words came stumbling out of my mouth, "I had . . . no idea."

Emil stood, taking the plates from the table. "No one did. I'm glad I've been able to help keep you safe." He started cleaning up. "You should go; you'll be late for class."

Despite the fact that I'd lived through a paranormal event, I still had classes to attend. Truthfully, I was happy to lose myself in the normal college-life routine instead of marinating over the details of Caleb, soul mates, and what exactly these new powers I had would mean. Luckily, I'd only missed one day of classes during the abduction. I spent the next few days at work, hanging out with my friends, and explaining to Jasmine where I'd been. I told her Emil had taken me to Denver for the weekend. Jasmine was easily distracted by talk about my relationships with Alex and Emil. She wanted to know what was going on, if I was dating both of them, and who I liked more. I wished I could answer that question myself. Emil joined me sometimes for a game of pool or lunch, but he gave me my space; though with Alex gone, I had a feeling Emil was never very far away.

I came home from class at the end of the week and as I unlocked the door and stepped inside the house, I was relieved to see Alex on the couch. Emil was sitting in the overstuffed chair. They both seemed to be talking, not in an unpleasant way, but they weren't about to become blood brothers either. They both stood when I walked into the living room.

I smiled. "Nice to have you back, Alex."

He returned my smile, a mischievous glint in his

eyes. "I'm glad to be here."

I glanced at Emil and he seemed to be taking the conversation in stride. "I didn't expect you to be gone for a week," he said to Alex.

Alex leaned back on the couch as I put my bag down and sat in the loveseat across from him. "There was a lot to sort through. There still is. I had to give them my account, as well as what you and Evie told me happened after I went unconscious. The Amaranthine leaders are concerned, to say the least. Now there's a push to find the Trackers still missing, but for some reason, their Protector / Tracker bonds weren't re-established like mine and Evie's was. Some of the Amaranthine are worried the threat isn't over."

"Why?" I asked. "Caleb admitted to abducting them and now he's gone."

"Since the other Trackers are still missing, the Amaranthine leaders are concerned someone else has taken up Caleb's cause. The Amaranthine leaders think all Trackers might still be in danger." Alex met my eyes. "There's also some question about your abilities and how you subdued Caleb's clan. The Amaranthine have never heard of a Tracker able to do something like that. They're very interested in you."

Emil and Alex both looked at me, worried. I was a little disconcerted myself. I had hoped the Amaranthine would be able to tell me how to handle my new abilities.

I drew in a breath. "So I'm not out of the woods yet?"

"Far from it," Alex answered.

"I guess this means you'll be sticking around as my Protector."

He nodded and glanced at Emil as he said, "I imagine we both will."

Emil shifted his attention to me and gave a slight

nod.

I raised my eyebrows. "Will you two be able to handle that?"

Emil answered, "We'll manage."

Alex's gaze slid to Emil's and there seemed to be some silent communication between them. Emil stood. "I have some things I need to do. I'll see you tomorrow, Evie."

"I'll walk you out," I said, standing up. Alex stayed on the couch as I followed Emil. On the way out the door, I noticed a vase with a dozen sterling roses—like the ones Emil had given me the first day we met—sitting on the table. Emil plucked one blooming rose out of the vase on his way by. I gave him a curious glance and followed him outside.

We walked to the middle of the lawn. Emil pulled a small knife from his pocket. He lifted the blade, concentrating on his task. "I'm assuming the roses are from you?" I asked, watching him cut the stem of the flower so only a few inches remained. He shaved off the thorns and reached for my hand as he nodded.

"Sterling roses used to be your favorite. Every few days I'd go to our garden and cut some for you so you always had fresh flowers. I thought it would be nice to continue the tradition."

Emil seemed like he wanted to say more, but couldn't find the words. I spoke instead. "Emil . . . I can't thank you enough for everything you've done."

His eyes were warm as he gazed at me. "I would do anything for you, don't ever forget that." Emil moved closer, gently tucking the rose behind my ear. The floral scent perfumed every breath I took as Emil brushed his thumb lightly over my lips. "Evie, I lost you once, I won't lose you again. Even if it takes a thousand years to earn your trust and win you back, I'll do it. You're the only person in my life who matters. You're the only person who ever has. I love you." He put his arms around my waist and leaned in to me. His kiss was deep, and full of the passion he said he felt for me. Immediately, I felt the heat from my soulmark letting me know Emil might be my soul mate. This man loved me truly, completely—and I couldn't help but feel like I loved him too. When the kiss ended, Emil held me close and I was breathless.

The warmth radiating from the lily on my back made me think of the Daevos using Trackers to find our soul mate bond—a bond that becomes stronger with kissing. I looked up at Emil and through staggered breaths, I asked, "How do you keep Daevos Clans from finding our bond when you kiss me like that?"

Emil looked surprised at first, then amused. "I have a feeling you'll remember the answer to that question on your own, but if you don't, I promise I'll tell you—eventually."

I stared at him in amazement. "I've hardly remembered anything yet, what makes you think I'll figure this out?"

He shrugged, his mouth quirking into a half smile. "Just a feeling."

"You won't even give me a hint?"

Emil cocked his head, thinking. "I'll tell you this much: our bond can't be Tracked by anyone other than the two of us. In time, you'll remember why," he said. He grinned as his hand slid over my waist, under my shirt, and up my back. "Because of that, I obviously don't have the same," he paused, "limitations that Alex does." His hand lingered on the spot where my soulmark was raging with heat. Emil ran his tongue over his top lip and it was all I could do not to reach up and kiss him again. He looked at me with a playful glint in his eyes. "Speaking of soulmarks, I bet yours is on fire." He winked as he slowly pulled away from me.

I wished I could come up with a witty response, but I was speechless.

"I'll see you tomorrow," he said as he lightly kissed my forehead.

I nodded, still stunned, and watched Emil walk away.

When I went back into the house, Alex was slouched against the back couch cushions, his hands resting behind his head and legs stretched out in front of him. He seemed relaxed—something I wasn't used to from him lately. I made my way to the couch, wondering if he'd been watching Emil and me outside.

"Did Emil leave?" he asked.

I looked at him deliberately as I sat down on the other end of the couch, crossing my legs. "You know he did."

He smiled and my stomach fluttered. "Good. I finally have you to myself." I smiled back and had a moment of guilt for thinking about Alex when I had just kissed Emil, but I had feelings for both of them and wasn't sure how to choose between them. It wasn't fair, but it was true.

I leaned back against the pillow resting on the arm of the couch. "What is it about you and Emil?" I asked. "Why is there so much hostility between you two?"

"Because we have a history," Alex answered flatly.

"No kidding," I said. "But I get the feeling it goes deeper than the Amaranthine and Daevos, and you being upset he brought me into his Clan. What happened between the two of you in the past?"

His face tensed and I could see the muscles in his neck pulse. "You," he said, meeting my gaze and holding it. "You happened, Evie."

I sat up. "What do you mean?"

He stretched his neck, breathing out a heavy sigh. "This isn't the first time you've had to decide between me and Emil. The last time you told me you were choosing him, I kissed you and asked if you were sure because I knew it was the wrong decision. You told me you loved him and he was the man you wanted to be with. We were at a party at the time. Once you had made your choice, I left you in the middle of the estate's gardens and immediately joined the Amaranthine Society so I would be able to protect you from what Emil was."

I stared at him in shocked silence, listening as he recounted the memory I'd been thrown into when I first touched him. I hadn't had the chance to think about the memory revelation much, or what it had meant, but hearing Alex's story made me realize both memories I'd seen involved my decision to leave Alex, and then Emil. I was about to tell Alex about the memories when he continued, saying, "We've fought over you in the past, and I'm sure it will happen again. Given what the Amaranthine said, I think Emil and I are both going to be around for a long time."

I answered without thinking, "That will be uncomfortable."

Alex's expression was bewildered. "Why?"

"Because, regardless of who I choose to be with, you'll both still be in my life. Plus, the fact that you can't touch me kind of impedes the progression of our relationship."

Alex pressed his lips together. "Speaking of that, I have something for you." Alex stood and took a square, sapphire blue box out of his pocket. He opened it and I saw the glint of silver as he pulled the jewelry from its case. "I've been working on a solution to that problem since the first time I left. Now it's finally ready."

He reached over and wrapped a shining silver bracelet around my right wrist. As the metal seemed to meld to my skin, a tingling feeling spread over me, making me feel lighter somehow. I traced the bracelet with the fingers of my left hand. The metal was smooth on each side; at its center, a faceted pink orchid glittered with white accents. I gazed at the jeweled flower, stunned. The petals sparkled like hundreds of pink and white diamonds.

The only thing that could pull my eyes away from the stunning gift was the feel of Alex's hand on my cheek, lifting my head. He held my gaze while he slowly ran his fingers through my hair. I stared at him in amazement. He took my hands and pulled me up, close enough to embrace me. His eyes burned as he leaned in until I could feel his mouth melt into mine and merge with my lips like we'd each found our missing puzzle piece. My soulmark flamed to life as our lips parted and the kiss became more urgent. I breathed in his cedar scent, the smell overtaking me. I ran my fingers over his hard chest while Alex's hands explored my back. I lost track of time until Alex stepped back, his hands on my hips. He didn't move his eyes from mine. "I can't spend any more time without you, and I'll be damned if you choose to be with Stone just because he can touch you."

My mind was muddled with the first kiss I'd had from Alex in months, but I managed to stammer out one word, "How?"

Alex smiled, moving his hand to my wrist and brushing his thumb lightly over my bracelet. "I had some help."

I stared at the meticulously crafted bracelet while

the rose petals flirted with my hair.
And my soulmark burned.

Author's Note

When I chose locations for *Eternal Starling*, there were a few things I took creative license with. The Western State College Campus is beautiful, but it doesn't have botanical gardens. Also, those of you familiar with Black Canyon of Gunnison National Park will know there are no caves in the area.

Acknowledgments

First, I want to send a huge thank you to my publisher, Kamilla Quast, who "got" my vision for this book and championed it in every way. Credit and major thanks for my gorgeous cover goes to photographer, Lani Woodland; designer, Alma Tait; hair-stylist, Lindsey Evans; and stunning cover model and make-up artist, Adrie Buchanan.

To my cheerleaders, critique partners, and beta-readers: Ashley, Angee, Autumn, Dan, Natalie, Craig, Amanda, Melanie, LaRue, Auri, Shelly, Brendalee. Thank you for your encouragement and support. Thank you to Dr. Ashley Argyle, Emily W. Jensen, Kamilla Quast, and Nancy Campbell Allen for your superior editing skills. Thanks to my fabulous author friends who answered a plethora of questions, gave me invaluable advice, and kept me from making many mistakes: Aprilynne Pike, Jennifer Murgia, Lani Woodland, and Shelly Fredman.

Dan—I don't know how to begin to thank the inspiration for a love that transcends time. How did I get so lucky? Thank you for putting up with constant conversations about my characters, bringing me treats during every crisis of confidence, and for telling everyone from the florist to the hairstylist about your wife the author. Without you, your love, your encouragement…I never would have taken the chance to tell this story. You are truly my soul mate and I love you.

Ashley—You're an amazing professor, literary and editing goddess, and most importantly, my best friend. Though, I've often cursed you for your high expectations, there aren't enough words to thank you for everything you've taught me. I live in terror that one day you'll stop answering my phone calls, returning my emails, and giving me advice. I imagine I owe you my own soul for all of your help.

Mom and Dad, you've been so supportive of this dream. Seriously, I won the parent lottery. Mom, thank you for believing in my writing long before I did, and for being so enthusiastic—hopefully the kissing scenes are adequate. Dad, thank you for teaching me to fall in love with reading before I could even ride a bike, and for showing me where the air filter was after I got out of that lake. To my brother, Colten, and sister, Natasha, thank you for your optimism and for teaching me long ago that absolutely nothing is impossible.

Special thanks to Angee for being my first fan and now my wonderful friend. Finally, a huge thank you to the most amazing fans in the world. Some of you I've known for years, others I've just met, but your constant support and excitement for Eternal Starling is the reason it's available today.